The Mind Readers

Book 1

Copyright 2010 Lori Brighton

Published by Lori Brighton

www.LoriBrighton.com

The Mind Readers Series:

The Mind Readers, book 1

The Mind Thieves, book 2

The Mind Games, book 3

The Mind Keepers, a novella

The Mind Readers
Book 1

By

Lori Brighton

Chapter 1

The man sitting across from me at the café was thinking about murdering his wife.

He imagined stabbing her and pretending like it was a robbery. Or perhaps, he thought, he'd take her hiking, push her off a cliff and say it was an accident; that she'd slipped. I wanted to tell him it wouldn't work, that in those CSI shows on T.V. they always suspected the husband first.

Instead, I huddled deep within my down jacket, the diner booth pressing uncomfortably hard against my back. I didn't dare move for fear of drawing attention to myself. I didn't want to know his thoughts. I wished he'd keep them to himself. But I suppose he couldn't help it. The thoughts seeped from his mind like the fog currently drifting in from the harbor.

Slowly, I slid him a glance out of the corner of my eye. With his thinning brown hair combed neatly into place, and his blue button-up shirt free of wrinkles, he looked like a normal suburban dad. But if there was one thing I'd learned early on in life it was that normalcy, as we thought of it, didn't exist. It was amazing and frightening what humans were capable of.

His pale blue eyes met mine. My heart slammed frantically against my ribcage. I dropped my gaze, my long, dark hair falling around my face like a curtain. He'd noticed me looking at him. He was wondering if I was a virgin. He hoped I was. *Pervert*. Bile crawled up my throat. I wrapped my hands around my cup of Chai tea, hoping the heat would warm my insides. It didn't.

But the guy sitting at the table next to me who'd been imagining killing his wife and was now imagining seducing me wasn't the problem. No, it was the guy sitting across from me, the man with his bright orange hunting cap pulled low over his eyes, the guy waiting for the right moment to rob the café… he was the one who worried me.

For a second I thought about alerting the owner. Common sense and years of warning got the better of me and I remained stubbornly silent. With a trembling hand, I latched onto the strap of my bag, gripped my cup and slid from the booth.

My conscience screamed at me to return, to help, say *something*. But those years of warning overtook any soft feelings. Shifting my bag strap to my shoulder, I rushed from the café before guilt got the better of me. Outside the air was crisp, cool. So normal. It was early fall and the bees were swarming an overflowing trashcan. Dumping my cup, careful to avoid the stinging insects, I pulled my hood atop my head and stuffed my hands into the soft, fleece-lined pockets on my jacket, trying to get warm…always trying.

A black truck zoomed by, sending fall colored leaves of orange, red and yellow into the air. For one brief moment, as the leaves settled around me, I felt like I was in the safety of a snow globe. But safety was an illusion. We were never safe. Not the people in the café. Not the few pedestrians strolling down the sidewalks. And certainly not me.

A deep shout resounded from inside the café, a muffled demand. I shouldn't have been surprised, still my heart made a mad leap for my throat. People screamed, the sound noticeable even through the thick glass windows. I wouldn't turn back.

I stepped off the curb, glanced left, then right and darted across the street. I had five minutes to make it home in time and couldn't be late…*again* or Grandma would worry. I focused on the long road that led to our small Cape Cod style cottage, focused on the crunch of brittle leaves under my sneakers, focused on breathing. I would not react to the scene around me. I couldn't. As Grandma repeatedly warned, my very life depended on silence.

Boom!

A sudden blast rang through the air, vibrating the glass windows. A flock of black starlings burst from the maples lining the road. I flinched, sucking in a sharp breath of cold air and resisted the urge to drop to the cracked sidewalk. Surprise faded quickly and guilt churned deep within my gut. A sickening shame that was almost unbearable. So much regret. Angry at myself, I shoved the feeling aside. Emotions would only weaken me.

A woman with gray hair who was walking her poodle next to me froze, her gaze pinned to the café. "My God, I think they're being robbed!"

I didn't respond but continued down the sidewalk, forced my feet forward as she fumbled with her cell phone.

Taking in a deep breath, I slipped the ear buds of my iPod into my ears. Home. I had to make it home before I was late, before nerves got the better of me and I was sick all over the sidewalk. Or worse, before I turned and raced back to the scene.

But even as I attempted to ignore the guilt thrumming in time with the music, anxiety clawed its way into my lungs, making it hard to breathe. I knew, deep down, I could have stopped it. If only I wasn't a coward. If only....

Sometimes it really sucked to be able to read minds.

Chapter 2

"Café was robbed, one person shot. They just announced it on the news." Grandma lifted her remote and turned the volume down on the T.V. nestled in the far corner of the counter. She was settled behind the round table where we ate all of our meals. A table that, according to her, had come across the ocean with her English grandparents over one-hundred years ago. I was pretty sure I remembered her buying it at a garage sale when I was a kid. Still, it was one of the few things that continued to travel with us as we moved from state to state, and its familiarity was welcome.

Hello to you too, Grandma.

I dropped my backpack on the kitchen table and headed straight for the refrigerator, my sneakers squeaking in protest over the pea green 1970's linoleum. I shouldn't have been annoyed by Grandma's blatant attempt to pry. I'd been living with her since I was five and my ability had surfaced. Grandma hadn't said so, but it was obvious Mom pretty much thought I was a freak and had shoved me into Grandma's capable arms, the one person who understood. Another freak.

I barely remembered Mom. But overall, my childhood hadn't been horrible. Lonely, as we'd moved a lot; a little complicated as Grandma had to explain away my uncanny ability to know what others were thinking. But I couldn't complain. I had a roof over my head and plenty to eat. Most importantly, she protected me as well as she could.

Grandma didn't look like your typical old lady. Yeah, she was in her fifties, but she colored her dark hair and refused to cover her trim body with something as hideous as a housecoat. I got my hair and eye color from her, but my smaller features from my mom's side of the family. Grandma was blunt and a little cold and it showed in her narrow face. But she'd taken care of me when no one else would, and for that I was reluctantly thankful.

"Anyone die?" I asked, pretending a nonchalance I certainly didn't feel.

"Nope." She said the word with ease. Her lack of empathy had always bothered me, but I guess years of running for your life would do that to a person. She snapped her cookbook shut and peered up at me through her wire-rimmed glasses. I tried to ignore her hazel eyes, but it was impossible. I swear Grandma's beady gaze could not only read a person's mind, but a person's soul. It was why I'd never lied to her. What was the point when she'd know the truth?

I wrapped my fingers around the handle of the refrigerator and couldn't deny the relief that released sweetly from my gut. No one had died. Just injured. No death. No guilt. At least not this time. But it was there, always in the back of my mind. Shame was the worst of it, knowing I could help if I'd just open my mouth. But as Grandma had taught me early on, there were worse things than feeling guilty, like feeling dead. I hadn't realized a person could "feel" dead, but knew it was pointless to argue with Grandma.

"Cameron, isn't that the café you visit?"

I pulled the refrigerator door wide, the burst of cold air adding to my unease. As if she didn't know where I went. As if she didn't know every tiny thing I did. "Yeah."

"Were you there?"

I pulled out a can of cherry coke, letting the chill aluminum numb my fingers, hoping that numbness would move to my heart, my gut, my brain. No such luck. "Yeah. I was there"

There was a short pause. I knew what she would ask next. Not that I could read her mind. I'd never been able to read Grandma's thoughts like I could others. Grandma had learned, over the years, how to keep her thoughts to herself. An ability she refused to share with me and I knew why…then she wouldn't be able to spy on me. Her power would be gone. And at times like this, I resented the hell out of her.

"Did you know?" she asked, her own voice casual.

Did I know the man was going to rob the café? Did I know he had a gun? Did I know someone might die and I could stop it? I swiped my hands on my jeans, wiping away the condensation. Slowly, I nodded.

"You didn't say anything?"

Annoyed, I released a puff of air through pursed lips. Why did she even bother asking? She knew the answer. "No," I grumbled.

"Good girl."

Why did I suddenly feel like a loyal dog? She pushed her chair away from the table, the legs screeching across the linoleum, and stood. "You'd only be courting questions and trouble. You remember what happened in Michigan. Always remember that when you want to warn someone. I'm going to the garden."

Michigan. There it was again. As if I could ever forget the incident. The time I'd blabbed and we'd almost been caught. The time I'd realized I couldn't trust anyone with my secret.

I watched her move to the door, my bitterness growing with each step she took. Whenever she praised me for keeping quiet, it felt so patronizing. Like inside she was smirking. Good little girl had done what she'd been told once again because she was too afraid to rebel.

The screen door banged against the frame and she disappeared into the back garden. Truth was, Grandma controlled me; she knew every one of my dark secrets, and I couldn't do a damn thing about it. At times I felt beaten down, exposed, exhausted. Imprisoned like an animal at the zoo, constantly watched. One of these days she'd find me pacing my room…back…forth.

At other times I felt ready to explode, like a giant piñata full of secrets. I'd imagine myself standing on top of a table in the cafeteria and proclaiming to all that I could read minds…that for the past year I'd read every single one of their ridiculous thoughts. The idea left me grinning.

But in less than one year I'd be free of Grandma. She had to know I was eager to attend college, yet she never said anything. She had to know that when I went away, I could do whatever I wanted. She had to know I had plans to visit her as little as possible. Part of me worried that she had some nefarious plan to keep me by her side forever. I shuddered at the thought.

Slowly, as if pulled by some invisible string, I made my way to the screen door. Grandma stood in the middle of our small, overgrown yard, just stood there, looking at her stupid lilac bush.

She worked on that thing night and day and still it didn't bloom. Why, I wanted to know, would she waste her time? But she never could give me a proper answer. She'd lost her son, she'd lost her daughter-in-law and maybe she knew she was losing me. Was the lilac some desperate attempt to hold onto something?

A horn blared out front, pulling me from my morose thoughts. For a brief moment, I paused, feeling bad about leaving her here alone. She didn't have friends, she didn't have family but for me. Her entire life revolved around some desperate attempt to keep us safe from unknown enemies. I knew, deep down, she was only trying to protect me, but it didn't make me feel any less caged. The horn blared again. If I stayed here, I'd become alone and bitter. I'd become her, and I couldn't let that happen.

I set my pop on the counter and moved to the front door. Emily was parked alongside the curb, her new red convertible shiny, free of dents and scratches. I knew that wouldn't last long, the girl had almost flunked Driver's Ed. I hadn't said how ridiculous it was to get a convertible when you lived in Maine. Icy roads and convertibles didn't mesh. But Emily loved the car and Emily got what she wanted, everything but attention from her parents.

Blonde and blue eyed, she was everyone's idea of perfection and she was my best friend. I couldn't hate my abilities, no, because if I couldn't read minds, I would never be friends with Emily. I would never get the grades I got, and I wouldn't be as good at soccer as I was. I knew answers, I knew game plays, I knew what people were thinking practically before they did.

"Come on!" She waved me over, large Chanel sunglasses covering half her face. Fall in Maine was far from warm, but she liked to pretend she was some incarnate version of Audrey Hepburn. If anything, with my petite features and dark hair, I looked more like the old movie actress. But if Emily wanted to be Audrey, Emily got to be Audrey.

I rushed down the brick steps, eager to escape if only for the evening. Some days were harder to get through than others. Today was one of those days. At times I felt like I was acting; no one knew the real me. My smile wavered and I swallowed over the sudden lump in my throat. They only knew the person they wanted me to be. It was exhausting. But today I didn't care. I wouldn't care. Today no one had died at the café and I was going driving with my best friend. And most importantly, after today I'd no longer have to take the bus to school.

"It's gorgeous," I said the one thing she was waiting for me to say, the thing she wanted to hear. She could have gotten a car months ago, but had waited for them to ship this one specially from Germany or some other car-loving country. "You're so lucky."

Because we were constantly moving, it made it hard for me to get a job and buy my own car. Heck, I'd be happy to have my Grandma's rusty Toyota.

Emily shrugged, but I knew she was thrilled I was envious. Emily's desire was to be worshipped and envied by all. Not that she was a horrible person. No, she wasn't. At least not deep down. I was the only one who knew she cried herself to sleep most nights. Both doctors, her parents were often gone and Emily looked for attention where she could get it. Of course she'd never admit that dark secret, but she didn't need to. I pulled open the passenger door and settled onto the soft, black leather seat.

I held no illusions. I knew Emily and I wouldn't be friends if it wasn't for my ability. I knew exactly what Emily wanted me to do, think, say, and because of that, I was her perfect B.F. We sure as heck wouldn't be friends if I told her what I was really thinking, but today that didn't matter because the sky was clear and the air somewhat warm for October.

I smoothed my fingers over the armrest as Emily took off. I didn't bother leaving Grandma a note. She knew where I was going. At least, she would until I got out of range. At some point, and I still wasn't sure where, she wasn't able to read my thoughts. It was a realization I'd stumbled upon three years ago when I'd gone off with a friend without telling Grandma, only to return and find her frantic with worry. The only time she'd shown she cared.

It was a thrilling feeling of escape that coursed through my body as we drove out of town toward the coast. Emily whipped around a curve and I fell into the door, laughing. Excitement followed Emily wherever she went. It was part of the reason why I had liked her immediately; she could make me forget that I was a freak. The world was a movie, and she was the star. At the moment she was pretending she was some hot spy and being chased by an equally hot guy. Of course she'd never admit how many times she invented movies in her head and she'd probably kill herself if she realized I knew.

Still, the days with my shallow friend were growing more difficult. There was only so much a person could take. I brushed aside the depressing thought.

"Where should we go?" I asked, a secret smile playing on my lips.

"Lakeside!" she said.

Lakeside was a diner near the ocean. Half the teens worked there after school, the other half hung out. There wasn't a lot to do in our small town, but years ago the students had quickly taken over the restaurant as their own.

"So get this, Trevor suddenly has to study Saturday night." Emily glanced briefly at me, interested in catching my reaction. The wind was blowing her hair around her perfect face. But while my hair was getting stuck in my mouth, whipping me in the eyes and wrapping around my neck in a chokehold, she somehow managed to look like a model in a print ad. Ugh, so not fair!

"What do you think?" she asked.

I thought, no, I knew Trevor was seeing someone else from another school. But I also knew how Emily wanted me to answer. I shrugged, not quite meeting her gaze. "Maybe his parents are on him about his grades." Emily didn't want to know he was cheating. Most people didn't really want to know the truth.

"Yeah," she seemed relieved. "That's what I figured."

Emily couldn't stand the idea that someone would dump her. No, Emily dumped boys, boys didn't dump her. Hurt them before they hurt her. She was worried that was exactly what was happening with Trevor. I was no psychologist, but I'd seen enough episodes of Oprah to wonder if her need to be adored had something to do with the fact that her parents were never around.

"Still, if he keeps this up, I just might dump his ass. God, what does he expect? Doesn't he know how many people would go out with me?"

She was arrogant, but she was right. I'd read plenty of horny teenage minds to know that 99% of the school's male population wanted Emily. The other one percent were gay.

She followed the curvy road that ran along the coast, lurching this way and that. Thank God I didn't get motion sickness. The ocean was rough, the winds and weather making the waves crest into white peaks that looked like snow. It was a volatile life we led here on the coast, and more than one fisherman drowned every year under the unrelenting power of the ocean. Despite the danger, I loved the feeling, the energy that surged from the waves...that secrecy of not knowing what was there underneath the water.

"I swear Kevin was checking me out the other day."

For a moment I thought I'd heard her wrong. That the roar of the ocean had made me hear something she hadn't really said. But no such luck, her thoughts were as clear as my own. My heart squeezed, even as I forced my smile to remain in place.

She was looking at the road, but she was wondering what I was thinking. "If Trevor doesn't get his shit together, maybe I'll go out with Kevin."

My heart thundered painfully in my chest, my palms growing damp. The urge to shout out *No!* bounced around my skull. But I didn't move, didn't dare move for fear she'd read something in my gestures. *Never show weakness. Never show weakness...*

She slid me a sly glance. "You don't still have a crush on him, do you?"

Yes. "No," I somehow managed to get out, although my voice sounded strangled.

"I didn't think so."

Just like that my good mood fled. Time to face facts. I'd known she was changing, but most of us were. Half the senior class was nervous at the thought of graduating and being alone, the other half were eager to taste freedom. It was an odd year, full of odd emotions and I'd wanted to ignore the signs that Emily had finally taken a step fully into the dark side. Mostly, I had ignored her attitude because I didn't want to look for new friends this late in the year, and her attacks had never been personal.

Morose, I rested my elbow on the window and gazed at the passing scenery. Less than half a year and I'd be gone. Another year and another new school. I'd been through so many educational systems, never staying long enough to make true friends, that I'd been desperate when we'd moved here a year ago.

When Emily had taken an interest, I admit my self-esteem had savored the attention of the most popular girl in school.

I'd had a plan, enjoy senior year as best I could and try to go out on top. For the last two months I'd noticed her changing, but had hoped I could stick it out until graduation. But I couldn't ignore her bitterness anymore. It was only one issue in a long list with reading minds… you knew a person's true self. The self that was so dark and desperate, they'd do anything to keep it hidden.

She wanted me to feel horrible, less than her, she loved it. Knowing she could get any guy she wanted, and knowing I couldn't, made her feel special. And so we used each other. Believe me, the irony wasn't lost. But how much longer could I take her cattiness? Suddenly, graduating with friends didn't seem so important.

The gray clapboard sided diner came into view, perched there on the edge of the sea, looking ready to tumble down at the first sign of a storm. Emily pulled into the parking lot, gravel crunching like boney victims under the wheels of her perfect car.

Although school had only been out an hour, the lot was already half full. And there was Kevin's black SUV. A guy I hadn't even had a chance to start a relationship with because I'd already lost him to Emily. And that's how it was; I was friends with girls who were popular because I knew what they wanted from me. I knew exactly what to say, when to say it. But while they got the boys and got to be prom queen, I stood cheering on the sidelines.

I barely listened to her happy chatter as we made our way up the rickety steps to the front porch. Emily was so caught up in her own conversation, she didn't even notice the rat scurry across the steps. Every time we came to the diner, I was amazed it was still open. I'd expected the Health Department to shut the place down long ago. But if they shut it down, we'd have no place to go and that's why the city left it alone.

"Hey! Cameron, I need to talk to you." Annabeth came rushing across the deck where she'd been serving drinks to students brave enough to sit outside in the wind. She stuffed a couple dollars into the apron tied around her waist. Her pink sweater clashed with her red hair, and she'd never exactly been called gorgeous. Still, she was friendly and had soft brown eyes and a wide smile that always made me want to smile back. I liked her the moment we'd met. I'd been a new student and she'd been the first to talk to me. For that, I'd always be grateful.

"I'll wait for you over there." Emily hated Annabeth, not because she didn't think Anne was popular or pretty enough. Nope, Emily was jealous because she didn't like the fact that I spent time with someone other than her. She was also jealous that Annabeth was a genius at math and science while Emily could barely pass. I'd tried to explain this to Anne, but she couldn't possibly believe the most popular girl in school would be jealous of her. Of course I couldn't tell her that I knew it for a fact.

"What's up, Anne?" I asked.

We leaned against the railing; I huddled deep within my jacket. The sun was setting, sending brilliant reds and oranges shimmering across the waves. When the sun set, the temperature dropped fast, but I wasn't eager to go inside.

"I've met someone."

I snapped my gaze toward her, more than surprised. As far as I knew, Annabeth had never dated anyone. "Who?"

George Miller she thought right before she said the words. "George Miller." A man popped into her mind, an image she'd conjured. Tall and thin, with dark hair, brown eyes...actually kind of cute, but older than her. Definitely older and she was nervous that he was older. She didn't want anyone to know.

"How old," I blurted out before I thought better.

Her round face grew red and I knew she was wondering why I'd brought up the topic. Frantically, she tried to decide what to tell me, I could almost taste her nervousness.

Twenty-five. "Twenty," she squeaked.

You'd be surprised how many people lie and how often. It was common, but still, it annoyed me because we were friends. I nodded slowly, wondering if I should call her out on her lie. Even a person without my abilities could tell she was fibbing. But I could sense Emily's impatience from across the porch. She was about ready to interrupt and that would hurt Anne's feelings.

"That's cool," I said.

She grinned, relieved I didn't say anything more. "Yeah, gotta work, but do you want to meet him? He's inside."

No! I nodded. *Not really.* What creepy twenty-five year old would go out with someone who wasn't even seventeen yet? "Yeah, sure. In a bit."

She briefly clasped my hands, her fingers cold. "Okay great! See you in a minute."

"Can't wait," I lied.

I watched her as she walked inside. Anne was only sixteen and looked even younger. Her mom would freak if she knew her daughter was dating someone nine years older. What would a man twenty-five years old want with Anne? Something was off and I couldn't help but feel like everything was changing, and not for the good.

"What'd she want?" Emily muttered bitterly as she came to stand next to me.

"Nothing." I sure as heck wasn't going to tell Emily so she could mock Annabeth.

"Hey, ladies, what's up?" Trevor strolled out the door, that arrogant smirk on his face that only the captain of the Basketball team could get away with. He leaned over to kiss Emily. What an idiot, he actually thought he could juggle two women and they wouldn't find out. Okay, so maybe my opinion of Trevor was influenced by the fact that he thought my breasts were too small for his liking. Although I'm happy to report he'd still "do me," as he'd thought the other day. As if he'd ever have the chance.

With a huff, Emily turned her head to the side. She was playing hard to get. She wanted him to beg and plead. I rolled my eyes. This could get nauseating real fast.

"What did I do now?" he asked with a sigh.

She snapped her head toward him. "Where were you last night?" She placed her hands on her hips; she meant business. "I called you, I text'd."

He averted his gaze and rubbed the back of his neck. "With the guys."

Allow me to translate. *With his other girlfriend.*

"Playing video games in the basement."

Making out.

He smiled his charming smile, those blue eyes twinkling. "You know I don't get reception down there."

He'd turned off his phone.

With a sigh, I spun around, giving them the privacy they didn't seem to care about since they were arguing in the middle of the front porch. I didn't have to read minds to know this wasn't going to end well and then I'd have to pick up the pieces until Emily got a new boyfriend, which shouldn't be long. A boyfriend who would most likely be Kevin. I felt sick.

Taking in a deep breath of chilly air, I gazed out over the ocean, attempting to calm my racing heart. You'd think a person who could read minds would be able to get a boyfriend. It's not like I was totally disgusting, but I knew some people thought I was weird; quiet, standoffish and I knew a little too much. It was the same no matter where I'd lived. Still, being friends with Emily had helped keep the whispers at bay. No one would dare talk bad about the most popular girl's best friend. What would they say about me when I finally had enough and dumped Emily?

"What do you mean you don't believe me?" Trevor demanded, his voice rising with anger and panic.

I rolled my eyes. They'd had the same fight at least once a week for the past three months. I seriously didn't understand why some people dated and honestly I didn't think they really understood either. Afraid to be alone, I guess. I didn't blame them. I'd been alone much of my life and frankly it sucked. I wanted that normalcy of living in the same town for more than two years. Of having life-long friendships, an actual boyfriend. Hopefully someday.

"Of course I don't…." She paused for one long moment. "What's that?" Emily was looking toward the shore where a piece of drift wood lay upon the gritty sand.

"Just driftwood," I said.

She moved toward the steps, only to hesitate. "No, there's something else…"

I narrowed my eyes and leaned over the railing, trying to get a better view. She was right, there was something there just behind the drift wood. I stepped closer to her. Near the shore lay a bundle. Something…I couldn't quite see in the fading light. I moved off the steps, Emily following.

"Em," Trevor whined, he wasn't used to people just walking away from him.

I resisted the urge to tell him to shut up. It was most likely garbage, but I'd do anything to get out of listening to their fight. If Emily thought it was something great, like buried treasure, I'd follow along.

"Oh my God, Cameron, what is it?" Her fingers bit into my upper arm.

I shrugged off her tight grip. Emily was way too dramatic. Usually it was amusing but right now annoying. "It's nothing. Probably…"

What was it? Something pale and narrow. The closer we got, the more our footsteps slowed. An odd sense of foreboding tingled through my body, yet I couldn't seem to stop moving. Closer… closer. *Turn back!* My instincts screamed, but I couldn't stop my feet from crunching through the sand. Something was sticking out of a bundle…something pale, narrow…a leg.

The fine hairs on my arms stood on end. My heart denied what my mind knew was true.

A gray leg covered in dirt with brown seaweed wrapped around the calf. Sickening dread sank into the pit of my belly. I knew what it was, I knew what lay there, what horrors life was capable of.

Numb, I barely felt my body as I moved around the driftwood; was barely aware of Emily clutching my arm once again. It was like I wasn't even there, but watching a television show. A green woolen blanket covered the body. But from that blanket her head was visible; long blonde hair matted with seaweed and sand. I froze, Emily pausing beside me. My body started trembling… shocking, violent trembles I couldn't control.

Her pale eyes were wide open, staring unblinkingly at me. A familiar face. Now a ghastly face that would give me nightmares for the rest of my life.

I was aware of Emily screaming, but the high-pitched noise barely registered.

Savannah.

A girl who had moved to our town only a month ago. A sweet, southern girl, although I didn't know her well. Now, a dead girl.

I staggered back into Emily's warm, living body. My stomach roiled, the scenery before me going blurry. The scent of ocean and fish was too much. Acid rose to my throat and I knew I was going to be sick.

I was vaguely aware of people rushing from the diner, the panic of their jumbled thoughts mixed and clambered around in my head. Too much, too many thoughts. My brain ached; my skull felt as if it would burst open. I pressed my hands to my temples and stumbled back.

"What is it?" Trevor asked.

Someone pushed me aside and I spun around. A blur of people rushed by, blocking Savannah from view. Still, I merely stood there, jostled back and forth by curious students. I couldn't think. I could barely remember to breathe.

"Oh my God," I heard Emily cry, "is she dead?"

I killed her.

The foreign voice whispered through my head. A voice I didn't recognize. I jerked my gaze upright. No one was looking at me… ten, fifteen faces pale in horror, focused on that body. But someone had said the words. I hadn't imagined them, had I?

I killed her.

My heart jumped into my throat, my hands growing clammy. With a muffled cry, I spun around, studying the faces behind me. No one was smiling with accomplishment. No one looked guilty. More people were spilling from the diner, at least five kids were on their cell phones talking desperately to the police.

"Excuse me." I pushed my way between the horrified group of gawking people.

I killed her.

I froze in the middle of the crush, a shiver- hot and cold-skimming my body. A male voice. Who? I turned, jerking my head this way and that. I had to find him. I must! I knew them all, some better than others, but this voice was unfamiliar. Who, here, would be capable of murder? The girl in front of me shifted, trying to get a better look. Behind her, near the parking lot, stood a stranger.

For one moment the entire world stilled. Nothing existed but that guy.

My heart thumped madly, almost painfully, against my rib cage. Dark hair, but I couldn't see his eye color. Tall, average build, around my age. Dressed in jeans and a black jacket. As if sensing my attention, he turned his head ever so slightly and his gaze met mine.

I sucked in a sharp breath and stepped behind Trevor like the coward I was. The world came roaring back into focus. My breath came out in rapid pants, and fear was bitter on my tongue. Unable to resist, I peeked around Trevor.

The boy was gone.

Chapter 3

"You don't have to go in."

Grandma's voice was barely audible over the antique she called a car. I'd been on the faux leather seat for five minutes, waiting for the courage to go into school. I knew, when I entered that brick building, everything would be overwhelming. The emotions, the thoughts, my own and from others, would kill me. Savannah wouldn't be there. There would probably be some stupid memorial around her locker, placed there by students who hadn't even talked to her while she'd been alive.

"Cameron, you don't have to go today."

So tempting to head back home. I turned toward her, preparing to agree, but then I saw her gaze. Sure, her face looked passive, full of grandmotherly concern. But in her eyes I saw the truth. The same look she got right before we moved. How many times had I come home from school to see our bags packed, no explanation other than it was time to leave? Panic flared through me.

"No!" I yelled, louder than I'd intended.

She frowned. "Fine, go to school. Most kids would love a day off."

I shook my head. She was trying to twist the truth like she always did. "No, that's not it. I know what you're thinking and we're not moving."

She looked out the window toward the kids streaming reluctantly into the school. Almost every two years now we'd moved. I was exhausted with it. I'd finally started to settle, I'd finally made friends. Less than six months and I'd graduate.

"I wasn't saying that," she said.

My fingers clenched the door handle. I wanted to escape, at the same time I needed to make sure she understood. "You were, and I'm not leaving, not when I have less than a year left." The thought sickened me. I would not start over in another school, not senior year. "I want to graduate with people I actually know."

Her sigh annoyed me, as if I was being some irrational kid. "Cameron, you can't deny something odd is happening here. The violence, first at the café and now the murder, isn't exactly normal for this area."

The first bell rang, the yard out front clearing of students, but I didn't dare leave now. "That's not true! The news broadcast said it was totally normal to see a surge in violence with a bad economy, and that it would usually leave as soon as it arrived."

"And if it doesn't? If it is something more?"

I shrugged, pretending an ease I didn't feel. "Like what? Like something to do with us and what we can do?"

"Who knows. Maybe they've found us."

"They." I released a wry laugh. I didn't believe her for a second. If they had found us, they'd come after us, not Savannah. This was just another excuse. "And who is they? The government? The cops? Who?"

She frowned, her fingers growing white as her grip tightened on the steering wheel. I should have known something was wrong when she'd offered to drive me to school. Usually she went to work early and made me walk.

I swallowed my anger and tried to speak rationally. "I can't protect myself unless I know who I'm protecting myself from."

"We've been over this, Cameron—"

"Right, you'll protect me. Do you realize how ridiculous that sounds? You can't protect me forever!"

"If you would homeschool—"

"And have no friends?" Exactly what she wanted.

I could leave her. Believe me, I'd thought about running away plenty of times.

"And where would you go?" she asked softly, reading my mind. "Who would you stay with? You have no money."

She was right. I had no true friends. She'd made sure of that.

She was silent for a moment, the rumble of the car the only noise. Her face had grown tight and I knew she was fighting to regain control. "I've lost everyone, I will not lose you too."

She'd said the words before and they sank into my body like a weight, anchoring me to her side. Tears stung my eyes. She was afraid. I got that. But I was so tired of being scared. So tired of living a lie. So tired of having the life only she deemed appropriate.

I sniffed, biting my lower lip to keep the tears from actually falling. I wouldn't go into school with red-rimmed eyes.

She released a breath of air, her shoulder sinking. "I'm doing this for you and for your father because I promised him before he died that I would take care of you no matter what."

Yeah, but dad probably had no idea how obsessive she'd become. My skin felt itchy, I felt trapped, like I couldn't breathe at times. She knew this. She knew it all, but she still didn't back off. "Dad wasn't killed by some nefarious group out to get us, it was an accident." She didn't respond. She was oddly quiet as she stared out the window. My suspicion flared. "It was an accident, right?"

"Of course it was."

I swallowed my relief. At the same time, I realized her reaction made no sense. Why was she so paranoid about being caught? "I'm going to college," I warned her.

She was quiet for one long moment. I wondered what she was thinking, but didn't dare look her in the eyes.

Finally, she glanced at me. "You'll be late. Go on."

Without another word, I grabbed my backpack and pushed open the car door. The air was chill, bitterly cold as it sliced through my sweatshirt and jeans. I didn't even nod a greeting to the few people who remained on the front lawn, daring to be late.

Her body was so gross...

Dead...

Wonder who the murderer is...

As I'd figured, Savannah's death was on everyone's mind, their thoughts bombarding me the moment I stepped from Grandma's car. I was more interested in the sound of the old Toyota rumbling away. I'd rather be here, now, with a thousand thoughts hitting me, than with Grandma. Don't get me wrong, I felt bad for her. Truly I did. I had no idea what had happened to her

parents or her husband, but I knew all were dead. My dad's death
had apparently pushed her over the edge of sanity.

I knew she cared about me, but there were times when I
wondered if she didn't want to so much protect me, as win this war
she'd had waging to keep me safe from these unknown foes. When
I asked her who was responsible for the death of our kind, she
merely said anyone. As if even now, my math teacher, Mrs.
Williams could be out to get me as she rushed by, mumbling
something about being late.

Maybe Grandma was insane. Maybe there really weren't any
enemies after us. Sadly, I wouldn't be surprised. I weaved my way
through the crowded halls as announcements were being read over
the intercom. The football team had won last week's game. Who
cared? Apparently the football team as they cheered and did chest
bumps in the hall. I rolled my eyes and turned the corner, heading
to my locker. Emily stood there chatting with a small group of
cheerleaders. She barely even nodded an acknowledgement as I
opened my locker door. She had an audience already, this early.

"It was horrifying," Emily said, her lower lip quivering for
extra emphasis. I didn't understand why she made fun of the drama
club when she could out act them all. Really, the girl could be in
movies. "I actually found her body."

"Totally disgusting," Sarah whispered, resting her arm around
Emily's shoulder in a show of compassion…for the wrong person.
"I can't imagine how you must have felt."

I couldn't believe I had to stand there and listen to this. I let
Emily get away with a lot because deep down, I knew she was
insecure and like most people, she felt unloved. But this was too
much. I'd had too little sleep and too many odd things happening
lately to take her crap.

Annoyed, I slammed my locker door shut, but they barely
noticed, Emily too intent on being the center of attention. As if she
didn't have enough already, she had to take it from a dead girl.
This was too far. Someone had died. Been murdered. How dare she
use Savannah's death for her own gain. Without waiting for her
like I usually did, I started down the hall.

Savannah's face had been haunting me since that night. Could
I, somehow, have prevented it? Grandma was right, violence in our

town wasn't normal. Did no one else see that something odd was happening here?

"Cam," Emily snapped, annoyed I wasn't hanging on her every word, nodding my agreement with her half-truths.

There was some sick psycho out there who had killed Savannah and, once again, Emily was acting like everything revolved around her. I had barely slept all weekend, but Emily looked like she'd just had a visit to the spa.

There were days when humanity seemed like a lost cause. Today was one of those days.

"Cam, wait up." Her high heels clicked against the linoleum. This was Maine, for God's sake, not Beverly Hills 90210. People didn't wear heels to school, but Emily did. She was panting as she reached my side. "What's your problem?"

Problem? I had so many I wasn't sure which to focus on. Might as well be her. "I just think it's sick that everyone's discussing what happened like it's the weekly gossip." And by everyone, I meant her.

"We're scared, Cam. It could have been anyone of us." Her gaze darted around the hallway and she shuddered dramatically. "It could have been me."

I rubbed my temples, my headache growing. Of course, and we were back to her.

The bell rang, warning that first period would soon start. Ignoring Emily, I walked into homeroom and continued toward the back of the class. We didn't dare sit in the front because apparently when you're popular, you never sit at the front of the class. So many ridiculous rules. They'd never bothered me before, but today I was worried and tired; today everything was annoying. Emily sat on one side while Kevin sat on the other. I'd always thought it was the perfect spot, between the two of them.

Even now I couldn't help but watch Kevin make his way toward me, those blue-green eyes smiling, that blond hair fashionably messy. He was gorgeous, and I was totally in love with him even though the guy spent 95% of his time thinking about his abs and biceps. Seriously, I didn't know a single girl who worried about her body more than Kevin worried about his. But he was athletic, funny and nice. Which was so uncommon within our group that I couldn't help but like him. Add that to the fact that he thought I was pretty and he was nearly perfect.

Still, the thought of spending the rest of my life listening to him worry about his abs and biceps had me second guessing marriage. But then again, most people's thoughts were annoying. Insecurities, depressing anxiety…thoughts of turmoil. Sometimes they drove me insane with their constant self-involved mind-chatter.

I rested my elbows on my desk and my head in my hands. Rumor was that Savannah had been taking drugs. I didn't buy that for a second. But the rumor made my mom come to mind. I hadn't thought about her in months. I could barely remember what she looked like and for some reason that realization made me panic.

"I mean seriously, it's weird you don't want to talk about it," Emily said. She was angry with me because I'd made her feel stupid and guilty. Well, she should feel guilty, but it wouldn't last. Like always, she was trying to place the blame on me and usually I'd silently accepted it. Not today. How badly I wanted to tell her to go screw herself.

"I mean, what is your problem anyway?" she snapped. "Does this have to do with Kevin?"

"Shhh!" I hissed, and jerked my head upright. Too much. She'd crossed a line by trying to embarrass me and I knew that's what she was attempting to do. She'd said the one thing she knew would get a response.

I slid Kevin a glance. Thank God he was talking to someone else and hadn't noticed our conversation.

"If you're jealous, I won't go out with him." She was silent for one long moment, wondering if I'd get mad if she asked to switch seats with me. She didn't have to say it, I already knew…Kevin had asked her out and she'd already said yes.

Unbelievable! Her father was having a long-running affair with his coworker. A secret Emily knew, if not Emily's mom. If anyone should have understood that it was wrong to steal a boy from another girl, it should have been Emily, my supposed best friend.

"Whatever," I said softly, resting my face in my hands and staring at the faux wood of my desktop. Nothing mattered anymore. Nothing mattered because my mom wasn't here to ease my fears. Nothing mattered because there was a murderer nearby and Savannah was dead. Dead.

Emily huffed and turned her back to me, talking to Sarah, who sat beside her. I didn't care. At the moment, I didn't care if Emily and I were no longer friends and my status would plummet to that of the girls who were friends with the teachers. I didn't care if no one asked me to prom. I didn't even care if Kevin and Emily got married and had five freaking kids. What did it matter when there was a murderer stalking the town?

Yeah, most people had some pretty horrifying and scary thoughts at times, but hardly anyone ever acted those out. Violence was pretty uncommon in our town. The police were trying to connect the murder with the shooting at the café, but I knew better. Something was wrong. Something was off. It was as if the very air vibrated with unease.

"Good morning children," Mr. Banks swept into the room, his briefcase in hand, his cat on his mind. Fluffy hadn't been eating. "Open your books to page fifty-five."

Only last week Savannah had told me she was going to try out for the soccer team. I'd encouraged her to. She was nervous, but I said I'd help her practice. According to the news report she was going to her friend's for the weekend. But she'd lied and probably met up with some guy. The guy who'd killed her. The guy whose voice I'd heard.

The stranger from the parking lot flashed to mind. That brown hair had an ever so slight curl, tousled by the ocean breeze. His face had been tense, those dark brows drawn together like he was worried. Worried he'd be caught? Was he the murderer? Was he the man whose voice I'd heard?

I shivered, hunkering down into the Yale sweatshirt that had belonged to my dad. If it wasn't the stranger, then it could be anyone. I wasn't used to not knowing. I couldn't stand the suspense. Irritated, I flipped open my book, pretending interest in the Civil War. Most people were whispering to each other about Savannah's death. People who'd barely paid attention to her before.

The useless chatter sometimes got to me. But I tried to have patience; people talked to either ease their worries or get to know each other. I rarely asked questions and not because I was shy like most people thought, but because I didn't need to learn. I already knew every little secret about everyone. Some secrets I wished to God I didn't know…things that would make you gag, things that would make you cry.

We'd had to move a lot when I was younger, before I'd learned to keep my mouth shut. I'd say something inappropriate and people would become suspicious. Grandma would pack the car and we'd move to another state, another city. Since I so badly wanted a home and friends, I'd learned quickly to keep all thoughts to myself for my own sake. But Grandma had another reason why she'd wanted me to keep silent. When I was old enough, Grandma had told me the truth. People like us didn't last long, they had the habit of disappearing.

But it didn't mean those thoughts I heard were ignored. I could ignore them as much as I could ignore my own thoughts. Sitting there in the classroom it was like I was the center of a bike wheel. Every spoke led to a student; their thoughts vibrating along that wire to me. Usually I could focus on each thought individually and pinpoint the person. Unless the thoughts were too fast and emotional, as they'd been at the beach the evening we'd found Savannah. If only I'd tried harder to focus.

There was a sudden shift in awareness that caught my flagging attention; almost a collective sigh from the female population. For a brief moment surprise washed over the room, and then curiosity invaded. I looked up. Some guy with brown hair stood next to Mr. Banks, his back to the class. A nice, broad back that filled out his blue polo shirt.

"Who is that?" I whispered to Emily, forgetting for a moment she was mad at me.

She narrowed her eyes into an unattractive glare. "How should I know?"

I brushed off her cattiness, and eager to think about something other than Savannah, I focused on the new student. We'd seen students come and go often. People moving to the north, then realizing how cold it got and after the first winter, moving back to wherever they'd come from. This guy probably wouldn't last.

He wore jeans that fit him well…really well. I could tell by the quality of his clothing that his family had money. I shifted my attention from his butt upward, focusing on his thoughts.

The odd thing wasn't that he was here, but that I couldn't read anything coming from him. I frowned and focused harder on the guy, even closing my eyes to concentrate. Nothing but silence.

Oh my God, he's cute.

Emily's thought slipped into my mind. Curious, I opened my eyes. A clear blue gaze met mine. For a brief moment I noticed nothing but those eyes. My heart jumped, heat rushing through my body. He was staring directly at me. Me. Why me?

Why her? I heard Emily wonder. She wasn't the only one. Just about every girl in class was wondering why this gorgeous guy was staring at me, wondering if we knew each other. But I didn't care. I didn't care in the least because my brain had finally started working again and I recognized his face. I froze in shock.

I didn't want him to stare at me. I didn't want him to stare because he was the guy from the parking lot...the guy who had killed Savannah.

****

Those mental spokes vibrated, thoughts pouring into my mind from every chair, but for one. His chair. For thirty minutes now he'd sat two chairs behind me, for thirty minutes I could feel his gaze burning into my back. For thirty minutes I'd had to listen to all the girls wondering why he was staring at me. But there was one thought I hadn't heard. *His.*

The bell rang. I bolted from my chair and scurried toward the exit. Emily and Sarah stood by the door, whispering about the new guy and preventing my escape.

"Excuse me," I snapped, almost panicked.

They turned and glared as one. Well, it hadn't taken Emily long to turn Sarah against me. Just freaking great. All those months of hard work and my status was sinking faster than the Titanic.

"Cameron," Mr. Banks called out.

Crap. I resisted the urge to ignore his voice and bolt out the door. Instead, like the good girl I was, I glanced back. The new guy leaned against Mr. Banks' desk, watching me. A shiver of unease whispered across my skin. This couldn't be good. "Yeah?"

"This is Lewis, he's new."

Obviously.

Lewis was staring at me, an odd gleam to his blue eyes. Really blue, like the bay in summer. Square jaw, straight nose and those lips…

For a murderer, he was cute. He looked away briefly, breaking our connection and I wondered if I'd imagined the amusement in his gaze.

Mr. Banks was barely paying attention to us, eager to get to the teacher lounge before all the cookies were gone. "Show Lewis around, take him to his next class, will you?"

No! "Sure." Wild panic sent my heart racing.

Lewis smiled, a smile that produced a dimple in his left cheek. For a moment, my panic was forgotten. Oh God, how could I be attracted to a murderer? I was sick.

"Ready?" he asked, his voice deep and smooth.

I nodded dumbly and led the way into the hall. I was safe. I mean, I was in the middle of the school, in a hall crowded with people. What could he do? Still, it didn't stop my heart from racing.

"Hello, Cameron," he said, stepping closer to me. So close, I could smell his soap and aftershave. He smelled… wonderful. "It's nice to meet you."

I nodded, not even bothering to look at him as I tried to think of a way out of this mess. Why the heck couldn't I read his thoughts? Was he a droid? A robot? Or maybe psychos didn't have thoughts. I rarely dealt with them, so who knew what they were capable of. But no, that didn't make sense. I'd heard the murderer's thoughts.

"Where's your locker?" I dared to look at him. I was eager to dump him off at his next class and be done with the whole charade.

He was smiling, although why, I wasn't sure. He didn't seem in a hurry. In fact, he seemed quite relaxed, his stroll slow and unhurried, as if he had something he wanted to say. Instantly, my suspicion grew.

"I've never known anyone in such a hurry to get to class."

"Yeah, well, I take school very seriously." Why did I have to sound like such a loser? Of course the moment that thought popped into my head, I wondered why I cared what he believed.

"Here." He tapped Savannah's old locker. The locker next to mine.

I froze, slightly horrified. "What?"

He frowned. "My locker. It's here. You all right?"

"Yeah, sure. Just…" I tried to judge his expression, to understand what he was feeling, if anything. It had been so long since I'd had to read someone based on their body language alone that I found it impossible to know. He looked normal, which was the problem. He didn't look guilty. Then again, maybe he wasn't. I'd heard the killer's thoughts, yet couldn't hear Lewis.

His dark brows raised in question. "Just?"

"Your locker. The girl who died, Savannah, it was her locker." I could barely get the words out, my voice sounded hollow and muffled. There were too many emotions swirling through my body.

He nodded slowly. "I see."

But I didn't see. I didn't see how he could be so calm, act like he cared…unless he hadn't killed Savannah. "Where are you from?"

"North."

Vague answer. Mysterious or shy? Completely confused, I opened my locker and shoved my books inside, trying to focus on his thoughts yet again. It was like hitting a brick wall. Surely if he had killed her he'd be thinking about it right now, wouldn't he?

"Did you know her well?" he asked, his voice soft and kind.

I wasn't sure how to respond to that compassion. "Well enough that I didn't want her murdered." My voice came out harsher than I'd intended. I was angry, angry that I was attracted to a guy who could be a possible murderer, angry that I couldn't read his thoughts, angry that everyone in this school was more worried about their own pathetic problems than the fact that a girl, a living, breathing girl, had died. I didn't know what I thought anymore.

"Where do you go next?" I murmured, contrite. After all, I didn't know Lewis. Maybe he was just a normal guy.

"English."

I frowned, finding it odd that we were going to the same place. It didn't matter, we had assigned seats. I'd drop him off at the door and hopefully avoid him for the rest of the day. We were silent as we walked slowly to class. My thoughts were in turmoil, rushing this way and that in full panic mode. I practically oozed nervousness. But I had a feeling he was completely in control of his own mind.

"I'm sorry about your friend," he said and it seemed like he meant it, but did he?

"It's all right, you didn't know." The bell rang and the halls emptied. We were alone. Completely alone. The school grew quiet, the only sound the soft murmur of Teacher's voices and the buzz of the fluorescent lights above.

"Do they have any suspects?" he asked, his deep, smooth voice oddly calming.

"No," I said, wondering why he asked. But wondering more where he came from, why he was here and why the heck I couldn't read his thoughts.

He paused near some benches and sat, looking thoughtful as he stared at nothing in particular. I glanced nervously down the hall at the classroom door. I'd always been a good girl, never skipped class, always did my homework, didn't smoke or drink…it felt odd knowing I'd be late, as if I was on a path to ruination.

"What's sad," he started, breaking into my thoughts. "Is that someone knows something."

I shrugged, feeling slightly sick. "Yeah, the murderer. I'm sure he knows a lot."

He crossed his arms over his chest, his biceps bulging. He was lean, but fit. "How do you know it's a he?"

Shoot. Heat shot straight to my cheeks. *Because the voice in my head had been male.* "Most likely."

He nodded slowly, his gaze on me the entire time. I found myself shifting under the intensity of his scrutiny. Did he believe me? "We really should get to class; the principal likes to roam the halls." It was a lie, but he didn't need to know that.

He grinned. "You don't lie well."

I stiffened, startled by his blunt comment. "I'm not, I'm…"

He arched a dark brow.

I took a few steps back. My brain felt muddled, my body buzzing with some unidentifiable emotion. "Fine, I want to go to class, so sue me. Are you coming or not?"

He didn't respond for a few moments, his gaze on the wall behind me, as if lost in thought. "Yes, of course the murderer knows what happened."

I sighed. Was he going back to that now? Why was he so interested in Savannah's death? I pressed my fingers to my throbbing temples and took a step back, intending to leave him then and there. I had a feeling he was playing some odd game with me, and I'd never liked games.

"But what I meant," he stood, looming over me. "Was that usually there is someone else who knows what happened. Someone too afraid to tell the truth. And because of that, a murderer kills again, might even go free."

He didn't look at me as he said the words, but started down the hall. So why then, did I suddenly feel totally guilty?

He turned, walking a few steps backward. "It's too bad we can't, say, read minds." He flashed a brilliant smile as my heart slammed erratically against my chest. He hadn't just said those words. "Then perhaps we'd know the killer's identity."

My insides froze; the world around me fading and all I could do was focus on him…the source of my trauma. He turned around and made his way into the classroom, leaving me alone with my paranoid thoughts.

He knew. Oh God, he knew.

My stomach twisted and I pressed my hands to my belly. I would swear on my life he knew. But how much? Surely he didn't know about my powers. He couldn't know. I'd never told anyone here. Unless Grandma had. Was this some sort of test from her? I wouldn't put it past the old bat. But that didn't explain why I couldn't read his mind. I swallowed hard and on trembling legs, I made my way toward class.

There was only one other person whose mind I couldn't read… Grandma's. And that was because she had learned to control her thoughts. What if…what if this Lewis…

No.

I froze outside the door and studied the classroom through the small window. Lewis sat near the back, his gaze focused on the front of the room.

Could Lewis read minds too?

He turned his head and looked directly at me, answering my question.

Chapter 4

"You sure they won't mind that I'm coming with you?" Annabeth was so nervous it was making *my* stomach roll. I really, really wished she'd keep her emotions to herself. I hadn't been this nervous since we'd moved here.

"They're not going to kick you out," I said, slipping my arm through hers as we made our way up Emily's sidewalk. That was exactly what Anne was thinking they'd do. As if they'd scream she wasn't popular enough and toss her from the house. I almost laughed at the idea, but didn't want to hurt her feelings.

Heck, I wasn't even sure if Emily still wanted me to come to her party as she'd barely talked to me the past week. It was also the last time I'd talked to Lewis, even though, oddly, we had every class together. Emily had been on him like a freaking tick on a deer. She was jealous I'd gotten to hang out with the hot new guy.

I hadn't had a chance to question him about his odd comment, and honestly, I wasn't even sure I wanted to. All I wanted to do tonight was get lost in a rush of teenage hormones. I was determined to make my last year of school as normal as possible. Yet, as much as I tried to stop thinking about him, Lewis was never far from my mind.

"It's too bad we can't, say, read minds. Then perhaps we'd know the killer's identity."

I'd caught him looking at me a few times during the week, but other than a passing glance he'd seemed to have forgotten my existence. And it irked. For one moment I'd thought I wasn't alone, that someone finally understood me. The moment had passed and I began to wonder if I'd imagined his odd comments and attention.

The front door burst open and Trevor stumbled outside. His hair was mussed, his blue t-shirt half untucked from his jeans; already wasted even though the party had just started. "Hey," he muttered, then leaned over and threw up in the bush, producing a wrenching sound that made me want to gag in kind.

Annabeth gasped like a mother who'd just heard her kid curse for the first time. Well, she'd wanted to go to these parties; she should get used to it. I shook my head, laughing. "Every party starts the same way. I swear I don't understand why anyone wants to go to these."

I was getting bored with them to be honest, but I couldn't stand to be home tonight with only my thoughts keeping me company.

Anne shrugged, flushing. "It's just nice to be included."

I brushed off my guilt. Sometimes I forgot that Anne wasn't as popular as the rest of my *friends*. She was hoping that would change tonight, I wanted to tell her not to hold her breath. Not because Anne didn't deserve to be popular, but because my friends were…to be blunt…kind of asses.

As we made our way into the huge foyer of Emily's home, or should I say mansion, Anne gasped again. "Oh my God."

"I know," I said with a sigh. And I did. I didn't need to read minds to know exactly what she was feeling because I'd felt it the first time I'd gone to Emily's too. A loser…who didn't belong here, unless I was serving food. From the marble floors to the crystal chandelier hanging above, Emily's home reeked of money.

"Hey, you think they'll care if George comes by? I told him to pick me up at ten."

I resisted the urge to roll my eyes. A twenty-five year old hanging out at a high school party? What was his deal? "Yeah, sure, its fine." But I knew better. Emily would have a fit. It was one thing to bring quiet and unassuming Annabeth, but her loser boyfriend wouldn't exactly be welcomed with open arms.

We made our way through the throng of dancing kids in the living room, their cups of illegal beer splashing onto the floor as they jumped and spun in a mock imitation of dancing. They looked like ducklings trying to fly.

Emily held this party every year when her parents went to Boston for some conference. Usually the next day I'd help her

clean. Correction, I'd clean. Instinctively, I searched for her
familiar blonde hair. I admit I did kind of miss her, or her company
anyway, now that the excitement of Savannah's death had faded.
Over a week and still not one suspect. People were nervous, but
had started to assume the murderer had been merely traveling
through town. I wasn't sure what to believe. For the most part, it
was back to homework, sports and flirting.

"There's Emily," Anne yelled over the pounding music.

I glanced toward the French doors that led to the back patio.
I'd been in this house so many times I knew it as well as Emily
did. Her parents had practically adopted me. Even though I knew
they thought of me as a charity case, I didn't care. Emily's family
was the closest I'd come to a real life.

She was easily noticeable standing near the doors. Only Emily
could get away with wearing a super mini skirt and tight white t-
shirt that did little to cover her red bra. I felt Anne's envy tickle the
back of my neck. I understood it well for I'd had the same feeling
often enough, but I'd learned how to deal with my emotions. Plus,
I knew the truth. Emily's life wasn't all roses and kittens. Emily
tossed her hair back and laughed as she leaned in, pressing her
huge boobs to some pathetic guy with dark hair. I started to snort
in disgust when something about the set of his shoulders, and the
curl of his hair sent warning bells through my head.

I stiffened as realization hit.

Lewis.

My heart stopped for a brief moment. I couldn't seem to
move, couldn't stop staring as anger washed through me in a
sickening wave that left me shaking. Her hands fisted in his
vintage New York t-shirt. Bunching the material, she pulled him
closer. Bile rose in my throat. She was going to kiss him and he
was going to let her. I realized, in that panicked moment, I didn't
want them to kiss. She could have Trevor, she could even have
Kevin, but she couldn't have Lewis too.

Lewis turned his head and met my gaze. I should've been
startled by his sudden attention, but I was only relieved that he had
finally noticed me. Emily was saying something, trying to regain
his attention, but he didn't break eye contact with me. In fact, he
moved away from her and started toward us, those broad shoulders
easily pushing aside everyone else. He was tall and lean, like a

swimmer. I couldn't help but be attracted to him. My heart thundered madly in my chest. I could barely hear Anne's chatter. The music faded, the people around me faded. There was only me and Lewis.

"I…I need some air," I think I said.

Before Anne could follow I darted toward the open doors and into the backyard, leaving Lewis and Emily behind. I was abandoning Anne and I'd feel bad about it later, but at the moment I needed to worry about my own survival.

Truth was, I didn't really believe Lewis had murdered Savannah. The person who had murdered Savannah couldn't hide his thoughts. But that didn't mean I trusted Lewis. And I certainly didn't trust my feelings around him. I liked him, a lot. So did Emily, and Emily always won. I wasn't about to set myself up for humiliation…again. Besides, soon school would be over and I'd be off to college. What did it matter?

The evening air cooled my heated skin. Reality rushed back on the breeze and I could breathe again. A few students were outside, some making out in the shadows, others hanging around the pool. Sarah, the attention whore, had even jumped in with her clothes on and was currently screaming and splashing for help. I shook my head, disgusted with her antics. Even more disgusted with what my life had become. I was hiding in the shadows, for God's sake, becoming the very person my grandma wanted.

Not wanting to make conversation, I moved toward the perimeter of the yard where the trees thickened and the woods spread out into a forest so dense, you couldn't help but wonder what was lurking out there. How I loved coming here where no one could read my thoughts. If I didn't turn on the charm and win Emily back, I would lose her, my status, and any sense of normalcy I had. But did I care anymore?

"Hey."

Lewis' voice caught me off guard. I froze there, in the shadows of two maple trees that had lost their leaves days ago. Of course I was surprised that Lewis had followed me. Surprised and thrilled, although I knew Emily wouldn't be.

With my heart racing in my chest, slowly, I turned. "What do you want?"

I couldn't see his face in the darkness and I wanted so badly to read his features. "Sheesh, nice attitude when I'm just being friendly."

"Bull." I crossed my arms over my chest, a defensive action, as if that could keep him from reading my mind. I suddenly felt cold and warm at the same time, like I was getting sick. Wouldn't that just be the icing on the cake, if I puked all over his Adidas. "You want something, I just haven't figured out what yet."

He shrugged and leaned his palm on the tree. His hand was next to my head, close to me, too close. He smelled like soap and minty toothpaste and something else, something warm and lovely, something that made my insides twist. "Maybe I just want to be friends."

Maybe I would puke after all. Fun. He wanted to be friends. Story of my life where guys were concerned.

He looked away, his eyes sparkling with humor, as if hearing some unspoken joke.

I stiffened, realizing the joke could be me. *Crap!* Had he just read my mind? *Oh God, think boring thoughts…the tree.* I flattened my palms to the rough bark. *The tree. Yes, the tree was nice, the fall colors, the bark brown…*

"I think you need a friend."

I laughed a little hysterically, my attention slipping unwillingly back to him. "No, I don't."

He reached out and took a strand of my hair in his hands, twirling the lock around his finger. It was a romantic action, something a boyfriend would do. Not a friend.

"A good friend." He dropped the lock and looked directly into my eyes. I couldn't seem to breathe as I waited for his next words, as if they were the most important words I'd ever hear. "Someone who understands you and what you're going through."

"And you do?" I whispered, daring him to answer.

"More than you think."

He was admitting it. Practically admitting he could read minds, wasn't he? Confused, shocked, I wasn't sure how to respond. Was he playing with me?

He smiled, a slow smile. "I think I like you."

Such simple words, such silly words, so why did my heart stop beating and sigh with ridiculous longing? I wanted to push him away and run home to the safety of my small cottage. I wanted to pull him close and kiss him, taste his lips. What was it about this guy that had me so confused?

"I think…" He looked away briefly as if carefully weighing his next words. "I think we could be very good together."

Good together? A warm tingle spread across my back. Okay, I was no expert, but I was pretty sure that was boyfriend talk. "I thought you were interested in Emily."

He laughed, a deep chuckle. "No. How can I be? She doesn't understand."

"Understand what?" I latched onto the word and dared him once again to tell the truth; to stop beating around the bush.

He was silent for one long moment, his gaze drilling into mine, so intense that I had to stop myself from looking away.

"You know. Surely you know," he said softly.

Frantic to hear the truth, I gripped his shirt much like Emily had done earlier. The guy was going to be a wrinkled mess by the time he returned home. My mind spun with the possibility of knowing another like me. "Tell me, Lewis. Tell me the truth."

But he just stood there, merely staring at me, his face so close to mine his breath was warm across my lips. And I wanted him to tell me, and I wanted him to kiss me. Which I wanted more, I wasn't sure.

"Are you two coming back inside or what?" Emily's shrill voice echoed across the garden. I felt her anger like a slap, breaking through our haze of lust. The vile words she called me inside her thoughts sort of ruined the mood. The entire garden glanced our way and I could've killed her for drawing attention to us.

I stiffened, but Lewis didn't move away immediately. He didn't fear Emily and her retribution. But I did. Reading minds wouldn't help if she decided I was her mortal enemy. I shoved my hands into his hard chest and pushed him back. The girl was as vindictive as she was arrogant. He finally moved aside and I got my first look at Emily. She was furious all right, that perfect face flushed red.

"It's one thing to invite your pathetic friend to my party, but to have her loser boyfriend here as well?"

"What?" Lewis had made me stupid and I was confused for a moment, but quickly realized she was talking about Anne. George had arrived. I no longer cared about myself, but was more worried about Annabeth.

I pushed passed the few students on the patio and made my way into the house, Lewis forgotten. Anne stood near the fireplace, clinging to some tall guy. I paused, surprised that he was as good-looking in person as he'd been in Anne's mind. He leaned down toward a beaming Anne and gave her a quick kiss.

"Ughh," Emily sighed in disgust, pausing next to me.

She was pissed that even someone as frumpy as Anne had landed a decent guy and she had no one at the moment. She'd already moved on, growing bored with Kevin. What else did she want?

"We'll leave," I snapped.

She didn't want me to leave and for a moment I felt her panic. If I left, she wouldn't have anyone to torment, anyone to make her feel important. "What are you talking about?"

I had to resist the urge to smirk. "If you don't want Annabeth here, we'll leave."

She laughed a forced, desperate sound. "You're so dramatic."

Anne started toward me, her face beaming, her boyfriend reluctantly followed. My attention moved away from Anne and landed on George, focusing on his thoughts. He was nervous. He felt silly being around such a younger group. Good, he should feel silly. Still, I kind of felt sorry for him and I knew Emily would tear him down the moment she got the chance. I wasn't going to let that happen.

They stopped in front of us. "George, this is Cameron."

He smiled at me and shook my hand. Dead giveaway that he was old. No one my age shook hands. His palm was damp too, showing his nerves. I had to resist the urge to swipe my hand on my jeans.

"Hey, nice to meet you." He had soft brown eyes. Nice eyes, I supposed.

"You too," I said, giving him a friendly smile. Although I still had my misgivings about him, I'd been brought up to be polite. I just hoped we could escape before Emily had her fun.

"Lewis." Lewis brushed by me, introducing himself and shaking George's hand.

I stiffened, surprised to see him. Usually I was warned by a person's thoughts when they appeared. But not Lewis, no, of course not. My mind went back to our conversation. He was going to admit he could read thoughts. I knew it. Damn Emily for interrupting.

"George and I are going to Lakeside. Wanna come?" Anne whispered, apparently hoping Emily wouldn't overhear.

"They reopened?" Emily asked, a sneer to her voice.

Anne blushed, the color clashing with her red hair. "Yeah, yesterday."

Emily crossed her arms over her chest and looked away, as if we weren't good enough to stare directly at. "Gross, I could never eat there after what happened."

"She wasn't killed inside the restaurant," Anne muttered, showing some backbone.

"It's still insensitive." Emily brushed her hair back and sashayed away, fully expecting me to follow. As if her gossiping about the body wasn't insensitive. She was hoping I'd turn Anne down flat and scurry after her. She was contemplating forgiving me if I did. She obviously didn't know me that well.

"Don't listen to her," I said.

"You want to come?" Anne asked, her large brown eyes pleading. She wanted George to think she had a lot of friends, that she wasn't some loser like Emily obviously thought.

"Sure we will," Lewis answered for me like he had the right.

I jerked my head toward him. What was he doing? How dare he. Besides, I had no desire to hang out with Anne and George. I wanted to go home, where I could be alone with my thoughts, and only my thoughts. He glanced down at me and smiled. A knowing smile, as if he realized exactly what I was thinking.

"Oh, great." Anne grabbed George's hand, the two of them more than ready to leave.

"Just a minute." I latched onto Lewis' arm and pulled him a few feet away, where the music would cover our conversation. "What are you doing?"

He shrugged. "She wanted us to go with, obviously."

"So, why do you care? You don't even know her."

"Just because I don't know someone doesn't mean I can't care. Haven't you ever helped someone you didn't know?"

I looked away, ashamed. Not really. I played it safe, as Grandma had taught me. And yes, it made me feel guilty as hell. Anne obviously was floundering for some support and I wasn't willing to give it to her. Here was Lewis, some new guy, helping out my friend when I hadn't.

"What will it hurt?" He rested his hand on my arm. His touch was warm, comforting in a way I didn't want to admit or really understand. "We—"

I killed her.

I stiffened and jerked my head toward the dancing couples. Teenagers were writhing and squirming around the living room, laughing, kissing, talking in a big blur of movement and thought.

God, it felt good.

I shoved my hand into Lewis' chest, pushing him back. My heart pounded frantically against my ribcage. The killer was here. I rushed into the throng of people. Music pulsed around me, beating heavily against my body, taunting me almost.

The urge is too strong. I have to find another.

I spun around, fear and panic bitterly cold. Damn it! Who was it? I wouldn't let the guy escape again.

So many to pick from.

The words whispered through my mind, barely distinguishable from the other thoughts in my head. But he was close, so close he was practically beside me. A tremble raked my body. Slowly, I turned.

"Ready?" Anne asked eagerly.

I lifted my attention from her excited gaze and focused on her boyfriend. George was smiling down at me, those soft brown eyes suddenly hard.

Maybe I'll pick her next.

Chapter 5

"Keep calm," Lewis whispered near my ear, his warm breath offering little comfort.

Keep calm? How could I keep calm? My entire body was trembling and I knew I'd lost any color from my face. I felt cold, sick. The entire room faded, my world becoming a tiny fraction of what it had been...merely Lewis' warm body next to mine, keeping me grounded in reality. Anne looked worriedly at me and then George...George lurking there in the background like some nightmare ready to pounce.

"Cam? You okay?" Anne's voice sounded hollow.

Oh God, Anne. Anne was dating a murderer.

Reality rushed back on a roar of protest that only I could hear. My stomach roiled. Lewis' hand rested on my lower back, as if he knew I was close to losing it. The room began to waver and I leaned back against his solid body, needing his support.

"We'll follow you," I was vaguely aware of Lewis' voice, but could only seem to focus on keeping my knees locked.

"Oh, okay." Anne looked worried, but thinking I was in Lewis' capable hands, she made her way toward the door with George. I was relieved, until rationality invaded. Oh God, George.

"No," I muttered, pushing Lewis away and going after them. I had to save Anne.

"Cam, stop." Lewis grabbed my hand and jerked me into his embrace. He wrapped his arms around my waist and held me close, so close that to anyone else it would look like we were hugging. And in another time, another moment, I might have enjoyed his arms around me. But, he was trying to keep me from saving Annabeth.

"Let me go!" I seethed, my hands fisting against his chest. "I have to stop her, you don't understand!"

"I do," he snapped, the hardness in his voice giving me pause. "Let her go, for now."

Warm tears slid from my eyes, tears of fear and frustration. "He'll kill her!"

"Shhh." He took my hand and pulled me toward the front door where Anne and George had disappeared. A few people were watching us curiously, noticing our odd behavior. They were wondering how I'd managed to steal the hot new guy away from Emily. Stupid, insignificant thoughts.

"He won't kill her. Not now. He's using her." Lewis pushed the front door wide and pulled me into the cool night air. The music and noise faded and the rustle of autumn leaves was the only sound as the night insects were long dead. He led me toward a small silver car and because I was numb, I let him.

"He's using her as his alibi. He wants to charm her, pretend he's a normal, law abiding citizen." He opened the passenger door for me.

But I didn't get in. Instead I spun around to face him. "And how would you know?"

"Get in," he demanded.

I slammed my fists against his chest. He didn't even flinch. "No! Not until you tell me the truth."

He merely stared at me with those knowing eyes. "Get in." He wasn't intimidated by Emily's social power, he wasn't intimidated by George. He sure as heck wasn't intimidated by me. What did scare him?

I realized I wasn't going to win, and I didn't have time to argue. With a frustrated groan, I pushed him away and sank onto the passenger seat. He moved around the front of the car, pulling open the driver's door. I tapped my foot impatiently, studying the road ahead for those taillights.

"Lewis! Cam!" Emily called out, waving to us from the front stoop.

He didn't even pause, merely settled behind the wheel and started the car. We took off, driving out of Emily's subdivision. Emily would make my life miserable for ignoring her and taking off with the very guy she'd laid claim to. Our relationship would be completely over, but I didn't care.

I curled my hands, my fingernails digging into my sensitive palms. "Can't you go faster?"

He slid me an annoyed glance. "I told you, she's fine."

"For now."

He didn't respond and the atmosphere remained tense as I struggled to keep from cursing.

We left the subdivision, the large mini mansions giving way to a stretch of coastal road. "Have you thought about what you'll say to her when you get there?"

I gazed out onto that inky ocean. Not even the moonlight highlighted the waves tonight. Unforgiving waves, how many lives had they taken? "Yeah, how about your boyfriend's a murderer."

He nodded slowly. "That might work, but how will you explain the fact that you know?"

He turned a corner and I slipped further down into my seat. Slumped over, I felt defeated, unsure. He was right. Anne wasn't three. I couldn't just tell her to stop dating George, and she'd trust me without argument. Besides, George would just move onto another victim. Could I let him go knowing what he'd do? I'd let people get away with crimes before.

How many people? How many times? I pressed my hands to my stomach and groaned, the guilt overwhelming and unbearable. I'd never dwelled on my shame, pushing it to the far corners of my mind. But I'd also never heard the thoughts of a serial killer. I felt dirty, gross, my skin tight and itchy, as if my body didn't belong to me.

"You don't have to feel this way." Lewis pulled into the parking lot. Lakeside was empty but for a few cars. The yellow police tape and Savannah's body were gone; no indication that she'd ever been there.

How could George do it? What kind of sick monster was he? I could see Anne through the window, laughing at something George had said. I felt sick. It didn't even bother him that he was sitting only feet from where his victim had washed ashore. To him it was a game he played.

How could I go in there and pretend like nothing was wrong? How could I make Annabeth understand without telling her the truth about what I could do?

"I have to say something," I insisted.

Lewis nodded. "I understand. But she won't believe you. They never do."

Was he right? I was silent, letting the intimacy of the moment comfort me. Even though he was a complete mystery, here with Lewis, I felt safe. "Tell me you understand," I whispered, afraid, even though we were alone, that someone would overhear me. I was about to admit something that I'd never admitted…something completely taboo.

He looked at me, his eyes shining softly under the glow of the parking lot light. "It's okay to talk about it, Cameron. As long as you talk to the right people."

"And how do I know who the right people are?" *How do I know if you're the right person?*

He leaned closer and cupped the side of my face with a warm, comforting hand. "I know you're scared. I know you're tired but you can trust me."

"How can I? I don't even know you."

"*I* know *you,* Cam. You don't have to be alone anymore."

His words were so tempting. I wanted to believe him, but he still hadn't said what I needed to hear. "Tell me the truth. Tell me exactly what I want to hear." *Tell me you can read my thoughts. Tell me you understand. Tell me…tell me you're not going to leave me here to deal with this alone.*

But he didn't respond. "Come on," he said, pulling back. "I know you want to tell her, so let's get it over with."

He pushed open his door and stepped outside, my thoughts left unanswered. If he could read my mind, why hadn't he responded?

Confused, I pushed open the car door and followed him. Lewis was already on the porch waiting for me. I paused next to him and looked through the window once more. Anne was leaning over the table, kissing George.

I looked away, bile rising in my throat. "How am I going to do this?"

Lewis opened the door, the hinges screeching.

I stepped inside the warm diner, but still felt chilled. I didn't pause, I couldn't or I'd let nerves overtake me. But as I started to move forward, Lewis latched onto my arm, stopping me in midstep. Confused I glanced back. He pulled me close, my back hitting his chest.

"Lewis, what—"

He leaned down, his lips on the shell of my ear. A shiver raised the fine hairs on my body.

"I understand, Cameron. I understand," he whispered. "And I'm not going anywhere."

****

I'm not going anywhere.

The words whispered over and over through my mind. They gave me strength when I wanted to run. When I wanted to reach over and punch George in his smiling face. When I wanted to vomit.

I leaned back against the cracked vinyl seat and sucked in a steadying breath. Lewis could read minds. I wasn't alone. I clung to that realization like a lifeline.

"So, how'd you two meet?" Lewis asked. His thigh was pressed to mine, his side to mine. He was warm, strong and comforting in a way only I could possibly understand. Finally, I had someone to trust.

"Oh, umm, George was hungry," Anne explained with a shrug. Her face was flushed. She was wondering if Lewis realized how old George really was. It bothered her, although she wouldn't admit it. She, too, wondered why George would date someone so much younger. I realized, with that thought, I might have an in.

"You in college?" Lewis pinned his hard gaze to George.

George gave us a half smile and rubbed his short crew cut. "Oh, no, had to take a break. My mother was in the hospital and I needed to take care of my little sister."

Crazy enough, he was telling the truth. Anne sighed and rested her hand atop of his. She was wearing a silver ring with a blue topaz. Had George given it to her? Please tell me it wasn't some sort of promise ring. "He's going back as soon as his mom gets better."

It would have been a nice story if George hadn't been a murderer. I slid Lewis a glance. He looked at me, understanding in his gaze. He knew George was a murderer. It was the first time I could share the truth with someone. My heart expanded and for a brief moment I finally felt warm on the inside and out. I was sitting across from a murderer, yet I was practically in tears because I wasn't alone anymore. I looked away, feeling off balance and at the same time, oddly alive.

"He's so sweet," Anne said.

I almost snorted, but caught myself just in time. As sweet as a serial killer could be. I'm sure his mother would be really proud if she knew what he did in his spare time. I forced the bile to remain firmly in my stomach. Anytime his gaze met mine, I wanted to puke. For thirty minutes we'd sat here, drinking pop like nothing out of the ordinary was happening. I kept waiting for Lewis to do something about George. Surely he had a plan. I sure as hell didn't, as this was all new to me. Yet as the clock ticked the moments by, I realized perhaps he was waiting for me to do something.

"Anne, go with me to the bathroom?" I blurted out, unable to stay silent any longer.

"Sure!" She kissed George on the cheek and moved from the booth. With a giggle, she slid her arm through mine. "Isn't he freaking cute?"

I smiled. Although it probably looked more like a snarl, she didn't seem to notice. Inside the small, one-stall bathroom, she opened her purse and pulled out lipstick. I'd never seen her wear makeup. "Since when are you dating Lewis?"

"What?" I washed my hands, looking at her in the silver framed mirror, trying to decide what to tell her and how.

"You're dating, right?" She looked confused. "I mean I saw you guys all cuddly and he drove you here." She put her lipstick away and leaned against the counter, smacking her now pink lips together.

"I don't know. I...I like him." It was more than like. We were connected in a way no one else could possibly understand. Vaguely I wondered how far away he could read minds. Could he hear my thoughts even now?

She grinned. "Emily's going to be pissed."

"I know."

She rested her hand on my arm. "Hey, you can't not date him because of her. Please, she can't get every guy. It's not fair." Anne felt like she could give dating advice since she now had a boyfriend. I wanted to roll my eyes at the thought. There were so many more important things to worry about than school crushes.

"I know," I repeated more forcefully, hoping she'd drop the subject.

"So don't let her stop you."

I nodded as I dried my hands on a paper towel. "That's a pretty shade of lipstick."

She grinned. "George likes it when I wear lipstick."

Gag, what else did George like? Besides killing innocent people? I so didn't want to know. "So you and George…"

She grinned, her excitement nauseating. "He's so cute, isn't he?"

I nodded numbly, inside my blood boiled. How could she not see that something was wrong? How did she not see the chill evilness in his eyes? Feel the anger in his touch? "He's older than you, does your mom know?" The words slipped from my mouth. It wasn't exactly the route I'd wanted to take, but couldn't help myself.

She frowned. "Not that much older."

"Nine years!"

She paled, silent for one long moment. "How'd you know?"

I blushed and looked away. Crap. We'd been in here less than five minutes and I'd already screwed up. "I could tell you were lying."

She sighed. "I'm sorry for lying, but you don't understand—"

I turned on her in a fury. "I do, I understand that it's weird."

"Excuse me?" Her face flushed, her body trembling. Okay, this was getting way out of hand. She knew it was weird, why couldn't she admit it? We were friends, weren't we?

I tried to calm down, taking in a deep breath, realizing I was going off track. Someone had to be in control. "Listen, I don't mean to be rude, but seriously, Anne, have you wondered why someone so old would be interested in a high school girl?"

"No," she snapped, lying. "Are you saying I'm not good enough?" Her lower lip quivered.

Oh God, this was so not going the way I wanted it to go and she was getting ready to bolt. I grasped her arm, begging her to understand. "Please, Annabeth, you're my friend. I'm worried, that's all."

The words seemed to have some effect and she sighed, her face softening. "You don't need to worry. He's great, he's—"

"Was he here? That night we found Savannah?" Had I actually said that? No! No, this was not going right. Somehow the words had just spewed from my mouth.

She frowned, her face growing hard again. "I don't…yeah, he was." She shook her head. "Why?"

Why couldn't she just get it? Why couldn't she sense the evilness in him? Why did I have to explain? "He said he just came back from college, right?"

She nodded and crossed her arms over her chest, a defensive action, one I did often enough to know.

"He comes back. No one has ever heard of him before. He was here the night Savannah was found." *Two and two together…*

"What are you saying?" her voice was high-pitched.

She was upset, she couldn't believe I was actually implying Savannah's death had something to do with her boyfriend. "Please, Anne, please, I think…*I know…*" I paused, realizing I couldn't come out and accuse him of murder without telling her about my ability. "I want you to break up with him."

She laughed, a harsh sound, her normally soft brown eyes had gone hard as obsidian. "You're jealous. Or…or Emily put you up to this."

"No! I would never do that to you!" The thought of being grouped with Emily repulsed me. But I supposed I deserved it, considering I'd been friends with the witch. I reached for Anne but she turned, spinning away from my touch.

"Don't! I can't believe you." She pushed the swinging door open and fled into the hall.

"That went well," I muttered. Tears of frustration burned my eyes, but I refused to cry. Lewis had been right all along. With a sigh, I pushed open the door and walked straight into a hard chest.

"Woa, you okay?" Firm fingers bit into my upper arms, holding me tight.

I jerked my gaze upward, staring into George's cold eyes. I couldn't respond, couldn't breathe. My heart slammed erratically against my chest. I told myself he couldn't do anything here, in a public place, but my body refused to believe what my mind said.

"Annabeth seemed upset. Is everything alright?"

"Yeah," I managed to get out.

He didn't reply, merely stared down at me. *God, I want her.* His evil thoughts whispered to me, unwanted thoughts that sent bile to my throat. Lucky me.

A cold sweat broke out between my shoulder blades. I couldn't look him in the eyes and dropped my gaze to the buttons on his shirt.

"Annabeth is lucky to have a friend like you." His fingers moved up my arms to my shoulders. Spiders crawling over my skin would have been more welcome. I bit my lower lip to keep from slamming my knee into his balls. Dare I tell him off? Dare I tell him that I knew the truth? Or would that put me in danger?

Lewis!

George's hands moved up my shoulders. "She really is luck—"

"Everything okay?" Lewis suddenly appeared at the end of the hall.

My terror fled and rationality rushed in on a heated wave. "Yeah." I nudged George aside, shoving my elbow into his gut and racing toward Lewis.

"Annabeth is asking for you," Lewis explained, slipping his arm around my waist and drawing me near. And I let him, because I was pathetic and scared and he knew it. Both of them knew it.

George's face flushed and he rubbed that short crew cut. "Oh, sure." Without a backward glance he hurried away.

For one moment we merely stood there, while I was wrapped in my shame and embarrassment. George had practically mauled me and I'd let him, too stunned and afraid to react. "Go ahead," I whispered, moving away from him. "Tell me I told you so."

Lewis watched me with a sympathetic, but knowing look upon his face. He'd either read our minds, or he knew from experience that telling Anne wouldn't work. "She's leaving."

Anne. I pushed past Lewis and stepped into the main room.

"Come on, George, we're leaving." Anne gripped her murdering boyfriend's hand and pulled him toward the front door.

He looked confused, worried. He should be worried. "Oh, okay. Is everything all right?"

She sniffed, as if offended. Anne was finally showing some backbone. Unfortunately, it was for the wrong reason. "Yeah, let's go."

"See ya," George said, turning and waving. "It was nice meeting you."

I didn't wave back. I couldn't stop shaking as I watched them leave together. Why wouldn't she listen to me? We'd been friends since I arrived in this stupid town. I rested my hand on the back of the booth, resisting the urge to go after her. I couldn't very well force her to stay. "Tell me he won't hurt her, at least tonight."

Lewis stood next to me, staring out the window. "He won't. She's his cover. His attempt at looking normal."

"She's not even seventeen, he's twenty-five. How normal can they look?"

"I didn't say it was a good plan."

We were silent, watching them as they drove away while Elvis sang about hound dogs in the background. "I tried to warn her. I said I didn't trust him. I said pretty much everything I could without admitting the truth."

"She didn't believe you."

I nodded, tears burning my eyes. "You said we could help."

"We can." He took my hand, his fingers warm and strong. "And we will."

I was shocked by his sudden touch, even more surprised when he leaned forward and pressed his lips to my forehead. Was it a brotherly kiss or something more? My heart slammed wildly in my chest as I prayed it was something more.

"I'll take care of it," he promised.

Maybe I was too afraid to deal with the situation fully, or perhaps I actually trusted him, but I knew Lewis would do as he said. The question was... how?

Chapter 6

Lewis said he'd take care of George. And I'd believed him. But with a forty-eight hour time period to gain perspective, my trust in a guy I barely knew was starting to waver. How would he take care of psycho George? What could he possibly do without admitting his own ability?

"Did you hear?" Emily paused next to my locker, a smirk on her perfect face. She wore a dress so short she'd make a hooker blush. Always comfort before fashion, I was dressed in my typical jeans and zip-up hoody, my dark hair in a ponytail.

I was surprised Emily was talking to me again and instantly suspicious. She had to be after something. It was way too early and I'd had too little sleep to play her guessing games. But I didn't have a choice. Her excitement rolled off her in waves, and with her excitement came her thoughts. Annabeth.

I heard her name whisper through Emily's mind. She wasn't the only one. I glanced down the crowded hall. Anne's name was bouncing against the walls, back and forth in the minds of everyone present. Thoughts so fast I could barely catch full sentences.

Crying...

Can't believe she didn't know...

Her own boyfriend...

Arrested...

I slammed my locker shut and spun around. "What happened?"

"What a freak," Emily said loudly enough to be overheard. Of course she loved the attention. But underneath her glee I realized there was something more... Emily's parents were getting a divorce. It had pushed her over the edge. She was looking for anything to focus on and Anne had become her target. I should have felt sorry for Emily, but I didn't.

"How could you not know your boyfriend was a murderer?" She shivered dramatically.

Oh God, Lewis had taken care of George! I wasn't sure if I should be thrilled or horrified.

"I knew he was a sicko the moment I met him. I can't believe she brought him to my house." Emily pressed her manicured hand to her heart. "He knows where I live! I could've been his next victim."

Surprise quickly gave way to irritation. Unbelievable. How had I been friends with Emily for so long without strangling her? Please, if George wanted to kill her, he was going to have to get in line. "Where's Anne?"

She slammed her locker shut with a flick of her hand. "Who knows and who cares. In my opinion, she's just as sick as him..."

I spun around and started down the hall, leaving Emily behind. She didn't need me anyway, she had her ego and the entire school to hang on her every word.

As I pushed past students hurrying to get to class, I couldn't help but notice people giving me sidelong glances, their whispers ringing through my mind. They all knew I was friends with Annabeth and they wondered if I had realized her boyfriend was a murderer. Wonderful, guilt by association. I pushed aside the hurtful feelings, determined not to care. I had to find Anne. I had to make sure she was okay. How could Lewis do something so dramatic and not tell me?

Tara was walking toward me, another girl who worked at Lakeside. "Tara," I latched onto her arm. "Have you seen Annabeth?"

She frowned, tucking a black curl behind her ear. "My God, Cam, did you hear?"

I nodded, wishing she'd skip the pleasantries and answer my question.

"Can you imagine what could have happened to Anne?"

Finally someone who actually cared about Annabeth. "Have you seen her?"

"She's in the bathroom, but—"

"Thanks."

I had five minutes before school started, but I'd be late if I had to. So much for that perfect attendance record. I pushed the door wide and burst into the girl's restroom, a white space smelling of lemons that had provided more than one student with solitude. The place was surprisingly empty, as if the female population could sense the depressing aura and was purposefully keeping away. "Annabeth?"

No response, but I heard her thoughts whispering from behind one of the closed stall doors.

Why is she here? It's her fault. God, I hate her. She did this on purpose...

I cringed, feeling her words like a knife to the gut. "Anne." I paused outside the middle stall, resting my hands on the cold steel door. "Come on, please, come out."

Why does she care? She wanted to humiliate me. She did it. I know she turned him in. She's just like Emily. I never should have trusted her. George told me not to.

"I'm not," I cried out. "I swear I'm not like Emily."

There was a stunned moment of silence and then, *Oh my God, how'd she know...*

I realized my mistake and at the same time, I didn't care. I was tired of hiding. Tired of being alone with my secrets. Meeting Lewis had taught me that I didn't have to live in fear. I felt more in control of my life than I'd ever felt before. Anne was a friend, she would understand.

"Anne? Please, come out."

The bolt screeched back and the door pulled inward. Her round face was splotchy, her eyes wide and bloodshot from crying. The dress she wore was a wrinkled mess. In our shallow school where fashion mattered, her state of disarray wouldn't help her cause.

"Did you turn him in?" she demanded.

"No, of course not." Resisting the urge to tell her the truth, I bit back Lewis' name.

Her brown eyes narrowed. "You're lying."

"I'm not! I didn't, I swear."

She looked reluctant to believe me. I wanted her to believe me, but at the same time, wondered why she cared. Shouldn't she be happier that her life had been saved? Or was it merely embarrassment that had her crying?

I grabbed some toilet paper and handed her the wad of tissue. "Anne, I'm just so relieved you're okay."

She ignored my offer. "He didn't do it." She moved to the sinks lining the wall and turned on the water. "I know everyone thinks he did, but he didn't."

She splashed water on her face. I stared at her, horrified, the toilet paper forgotten in my hand. Wonderful, she was going to be one of those women who stood by her man, even when he went to prison. She'd marry him and write to him every day, proclaiming his innocence on some talk show. I sank back against the wall, sick. They'd write a movie about her and it would be on *Lifetime*, that channel Grandma liked to watch. She didn't want to believe because if she believed, then she'd wonder if there was something wrong with her for falling for a guy like that.

"Anne, he did it."

She spun around, her face furious and red. "He didn't. They don't have any legitimate proof."

"I know he did it."

She snorted. "How? How can you possibly know?" She turned her back to me and grabbed a paper towel. *How dare she think she knows my boyfriend better than I do.*

"I do know him better."

She stiffened and I could see her face go pale in the mirror. *Oh my God. How'd she know what I was thinking?* There was a moment's silence. *What else does she know? Can she read my mind? What the heck's going on?*

It was my opportunity. Prime opportunity to tell her the truth. To finally tell someone the truth. My heart slammed wildly against my chest, knowing once I admitted it, I couldn't go back. I could leave, leave her here to deal with her problems alone. Go back to my old life. But I'd had a taste of freedom and I craved more. I wanted to tell the truth.

"Yes," I whispered and touched her gently on the shoulder. "I can read your mind."

She spun around and flattened herself against the edge of the sink, her eyes wide with terror…afraid of me. Startled, I pulled back. It wasn't the first time I'd seen that look. My heart sank.

"I've never told anyone. My grandma told me not to, but I don't care," I blurted out, hoping she'd understand, praying she wouldn't judge me. "We're friends. I have to tell you."

She shook her head. Obviously I hadn't gotten through to her. Perhaps she didn't understand. I started to reach for her, but thought better of it when she flinched. "Anne, I can read minds, I've pretty much always been able to."

"No." *She's crazy.*

I stiffened. The word hurt more than she could understand. Crazy. What Mom had most likely thought the day she'd dropped me off at Grandma's. God, I hated that word. Hot tears stung my eyes.

"I'm not crazy." I stepped closer to her. She shrank back. "I can read minds and I heard George's thoughts. He killed Savannah."

She shook her head. "You're crazy." She released a harsh laugh. "They say George is insane? And all this time I stood up for you when people whispered behind your back." She moved away from me, scurrying toward the door. Outside the bell rang.

"Anne, please! Wait!" I latched onto her arm before she could escape. If I didn't make her believe me…

She jerked away. The expression of disgust upon her face was like a punch to the gut. "Don't touch me. Don't talk to me, nothing." *She's a freak.*

Anne rushed out the door, into the empty hall.

I raced after her, no longer worried about making her understand, but worried about keeping her quiet. But she was already running toward her next class. Chasing after her would only cause a scene. How long before she told someone else? Oh God, what had I done?

"Stupid move, Cameron," Lewis said from behind me.

I spun around, furious. "Excuse me?"

His blue-eyed gaze had turned icy hard. He was angry. I'd never seen him angry. "You never tell your secret to people who aren't like us." He raked his hands through his hair; his fingers were trembling. "Shit, you have so much to learn."

Incompetence and sorrow dug deep into my body like a bur. I wrapped my arms around my waist as tears slipped from my eyes.

I'd told her my secret and she hadn't believed me. She was my friend, why hadn't she believed me? "This is your fault!"

"Are you serious?"

"How could you do this to her? She hates me now."

He released a harsh laugh. "I saved your friend's life."

I stomped my foot, the thump echoing down the empty hall. "You humiliated her!"

His jaw clenched and he took a step back, intending to leave me as well. I didn't want him to leave, at the same time I blamed him for this mess.

"Better humiliated," he said, "than dead."

****

I felt miserable. More than miserable. I felt like someone had drained me of all energy. I'd always been able to at least dim the thoughts coming from people by focusing on other things, but not today, not now. Every feeling, every thought burst into my brain like an explosion, leaving me weak, trembling. I knew why, too much had happened. My defenses were down. I needed to go home, be alone with my thoughts and no one else's. I needed sleep. Unfortunately, first I needed to get through French class.

Hefting my books in my hands, I left Biology and started down the crowded hall. Emily stood at her locker, which was near mine. I couldn't ask her if she'd happened to hear anything about me, oh, say, reading minds. I knew she was done with me even before she glanced over her shoulder, as if sensing my presence. She smirked and turned away. It was a direct cut and a lot of people saw it happen. I kept my face passive, not daring to show how crappy I felt, but my hands were visibly shaking.

"You think it's true?" someone whispered as I moved by.

"Oh please, no way," someone else responded.

God, what if she can read my mind?

I stumbled and glanced back. Tara leaned against the wall, watching me. She jerked her head down, focusing on the floor. *Does she know what I'm thinking?*

I froze there, in the middle of the hall, the scent of lemon cleaning product sharp and strong, making me want to gag. They all knew. The roar of conversation became a muffled murmur. No.

This was not happening. Frantic, I looked up and down the hall. More than one student was looking at me, whispering, some giggling as they moved by, careful not to get too close.

Can she read minds? Emily thinks she can.

Oh shit, what if she knows I cheated on that math test?

Will she tell Emily that I really hate her?

I wanted to throw my books to the floor and scream for them all to shut up. I didn't care about their stupid, insignificant problems.

Instead, I lowered my head and made my way toward class. This was horrible. Worse than horrible. Why had I trusted Anne?

"Excuse me," someone snapped.

I looked up. Anne stood in my way. She'd changed, no longer meek and shy, I could see that in the hardness of her gaze. Life had turned her. No one seemed to notice her wrinkled outfit anymore. Her hair had been combed back, and her face was its natural color. Throwing me under the bus had given her strength.

At least now they're talking about her and not me.

My heart stopped, for a brief moment as realization struck hard. She'd done this on purpose...spread the rumor that I could read minds. She'd wanted to hurt me because she still thought I'd been responsible for turning George in.

"You did this," I seethed.

"Did what?" She lifted a brow, daring me to respond.

I bit my tongue, refusing to give in. She had friends behind her. Friends who had previously been my friends as well. Friends who looked uneasy, unsure. They were wondering if they could trust me. Wondering if Anne was lying. Wondering if I could really read minds.

"You're in my way." She glared at me.

This morning Anne had been a pariah, but there were those few who felt bad for her and those few were supporting her now. This afternoon, I was the one with leprosy, but the difference was that I had no one to back me up. Alone. Everything I'd worked so hard for was gone. I realized, in that moment, I had no idea what to do.

"Anne!" Sarah came to a skidding halt beside us. "It was just on the news...they've found evidence, it's not looking good."

Anne's large brown eyes filled with tears. My heart actually clenched for her. She dropped her books with a loud thud and raced down the hall, disappearing around a corner. Her friends didn't follow. Some friends.

"Are you serious?" Toni asked.

"Yep." Sarah was more excited about being the first to know, than being worried about Anne's welfare. They darted a glance at me, but realizing they didn't know what to say, they wandered reluctantly away.

I sniffled, my nose burning from unshed tears. How I wished I could go home and cry. If I went home and gave into my tears, Grandma would immediately wonder what had happened. Not that she wouldn't read my mind tonight and know anyway. She would realize I'd told Anne about my ability and then there'd be hell to pay. Would she make us pack up and leave? Had I ruined everything once again, just as I had in Michigan?

The bell rang, indicating the start of last class period. The hall emptied but I still stood there. Confused. Lost. Alone. So much for wisdom with age.

The thud of footsteps sent my heart racing. *Lewis?* I spun around, but it wasn't Lewis. No. It was Trevor. Slowly, he looked me up and down, a smirk playing on his lips. No thoughts of me and my mind reading abilities flashed through his brain. Thank God. Same old Trevor, wondering if now that he and Emily had broken up, he could get some from me. He thought I'd be happy to take Emily's place because he was, well, Trevor. School star athletic. Of course I wanted him. *Not.*

"Hey, Cameron." He paused in front of me, too close. I really didn't have the time to deal with him right now.

"Hey," I muttered, brushing past him and heading toward French class.

"What's the hurry?" He latched onto my arm, pulling me to a stop.

"I've got class," I said, trying to shrug off his touch. "Don't you?"

She'd be easy, he thought. *Screw her and move on. She won't say anything, she'll be too worried about Emily finding out.*

I sighed and tried to jerk my arm away. "Listen, I gotta go or I'll be late."

"So," he shrugged, grinning that grin that made many a girl's hearts flutter. Fortunately, I was totally immune. He pulled me back. Off balance, I stumbled and fell against the wall.

"Aren't you ever bad?" He took the opportunity to step closer, his body pinning mine to the wall.

I was so stunned, I let him. The idiot didn't think he was doing anything wrong. He actually believed that I would be so grateful to have his attention, I wouldn't mind the fact that his hands were currently traveling down my waist and creeping dangerously close to my ass.

"You know I've always liked you."

"Bull," I snapped, using my French book as a barrier between us. I wish I could have explained his actions away because his parents didn't love him, or deep down he felt insecure. But nope, he was just an ass. "You've never liked me; you're just horny and have some delusional belief that I'm so desperate I'll let you use me."

I saw the surprise flash in his eyes, heard the mental curse come from his thoughts, but he recovered quickly. He was good, and if I couldn't read minds, I might have actually fallen for his crap.

"Cam, it's always been you I was interested in. I only dated Emily to be close to you."

"Wow," Lewis' voice suddenly reached out, a beacon of hope. "That is the worst pick up line I've ever heard."

He crossed his arms over his chest and leaned against the wall not ten feet from us.

Trevor looked unimpressed. "We're having a private conversation here, Newbie. Might want to make yourself scarce."

Lewis glanced at me, a quick glance, but I didn't miss the look. Something was there in his eyes. Something I'd never seen before. A hardness, a darkness that surprised me. He was angry at me, or maybe Trevor.

"Really? Because Cameron doesn't look like she's enjoying the subject of conversation."

"I think I know Cameron better than you." Trevor turned back to me. "As I was saying…"

Lewis gripped the man's shoulder and spun him away from me so fast I barely had time to register the movement. Before I could even blink, Trevor—big, tall, strong Trevor—was pinned against the wall.

"You touch her again, you'll regret it," Lewis said softy, yet the quietness of his voice only somehow added to the threat.

"Back off, man," Trevor said.

Was it my imagination or had his voice quivered? How the hell was Lewis, preppy Lewis, holding Trevor immobile? But then I noticed it, the hardness of Lewis' body, the muscles that bulged under his shirt, the way he held Trevor's arm pinned behind the idiot's back.

In that moment I realized two things: Lewis was much stronger than I'd first thought and Lewis knew some sort of martial arts. I was no Kung Fu expert, but I knew a trained person when I saw one.

"I'll back off when you swear never to touch her again." Lewis' voice was calm, as if he was in complete control. And he was. I wasn't sure whether I should find his protective nature sweet or ridiculous. Shocked, I just stood there like I was watching a movie.

"Fine," Trevor snapped, grimacing as he struggled in Lewis' hold.

Finally Lewis released the man and stepped back.

"Freak," Trevor whispered as he rushed down the hall, horrified and embarrassed. Silence lengthened between us, an odd, uneasy silence. The only sound was the soft murmur of teacher's voices behind closed doors. "You didn't have to do that."

"Maybe I wanted to."

"Oh." For one long moment we just stared at each other. My body felt odd, hot and trembling. My heart raced and in my mind was this desperate need to be closer to him. The one person who understood me. "Thanks."

He nodded, a short, curt nod.

"Annabeth told everyone," I blurted out, because he needed to know and because I wanted him to stay with me just a little longer.

"I know," he said, his blue eyes softening. "Emily's helping spread the rumor."

"To get back at me," I whispered. It was bad enough having Anne as an enemy, but Emily would be a million times worse. "Why is she doing this to me?"

"Self-preservation." Lewis leaned next to me, so close I could feel his warm breath. "Humans will always try to protect themselves; always throw another under the bus if it will save them. She's hurting, to her you're the cause of that hurt. Plus, if people are whispering about you then they aren't about her."

I clutched my French book tightly to my chest. "I don't believe that. People can't be that horrible."

"You've read their minds." He shrugged. "You know how dark their thoughts can be."

He was right; I'd heard things that would make people question the whole of society. Was it true, would people always think about themselves over others? Mom didn't care about me, she'd dumped me first chance she got. What kind of parent would do that? Grandma wasn't any better, keeping me under her constant control. Maybe Lewis was right.

"I am." He grinned.

I sniffed, finding no amusement in the fact that he could read my mind. It wasn't fair. In the span of a week my life had completely changed, and why? Because I'd tried to help someone. Grandma was right about one thing, it was best to keep your powers hidden. And Lewis was right…you couldn't trust anyone. I wasn't even sure I could trust him.

"Lewis, why can't I read your thoughts?"

"Cam," Lewis sighed and leaned closer to me. "It doesn't have to be like this. There's a way to be able to use your powers and at the same time feel safe and protected. There's a way to be around others like us."

Startled, I looked up at him. "How?"

"The café," he said, taking a few steps backward. "Where you go after school—"

"How'd you know about that place?"

He grinned. "I know a lot about you. You think my being here is just a coincidence?"

I started toward him, my heart racing. "You knew about me even before you arrived?"

He shrugged. The hall was empty so we didn't have to worry about being overheard. "Meet me after school at the café. We'll discuss things." He turned and started toward the exit, apparently skipping his last class.

"Lewis!"

"We'll talk later," he called over his shoulder.

And with that he was gone, leaving me in the hall frustrated and alone. But I knew one thing… for the first time in days I had something to keep me going. I had hope.

Chapter 7

I wasn't sure what to expect when I—wet, cold and nervous—entered the café. The place had been closed for a week after the shooting and they'd lost plenty of business. It wasn't nearly as crowded as it had been and I knew the owner was worried about money. Poor guy had a family to support.

I easily found Lewis sitting at a table by the windows. His hair was damp, the ends curled over the collar of his dark jacket. For one moment I stood just inside the doorway, watching him. He certainly must have felt my presence and if not, seen me walk up the sidewalk. But he kept his head bent, his gaze on the cup in his hands.

He was so cute it almost hurt. But it was more than his good looks that attracted me to him. Finally I had someone who understood me. Someone who didn't think I was a freak. Someone I admired. He'd given me hope when I had none left. He wasn't afraid to get involved. He'd called the cops, which had led to George's arrest over the weekend. He was a freaking hero, while I was…

He looked up and smiled at me.

Giddy warmth swept through my body. This was welcoming. This was someone I could trust. This was someone I could completely fall in love with. I moved across the room, eager to be closer to him.

"Chai tea with cinnamon." He pushed the cup toward me as I settled in the chair across from him.

I dropped my backpack on the floor. "How'd you…" But I didn't need to finish that sentence. I flushed. Of course he knew. "Thanks."

He gave me a sheepish grin. Outside, rain pelted the windows. It was a cold, dour afternoon, but I felt warm. I didn't have a clue what Lewis had to say, but knowing what I did about him, I prayed it was going to change my life for the better.

I sipped the spicy liquid, my insides heating for once. It felt good, so very good to be here, settled in a café on a cold autumn day with this guy who understood me like no other did.

"You want to know?" he laughed.

"Yeah," I admitted. I was used to Grandma being able to read my mind, but no one else. It was a bit disconcerting. He knew I was eager to learn the truth. He obviously knew I was attracted to him.

He leaned forward, his blue gaze intense. "Alright. The truth?"

I nodded, clasping my cup tightly and letting the warmth seep into my skin. He was going to pretend like he didn't know I had feelings for him, which was fine by me.

"I was sent to help you."

Stunned, for a moment I merely sat there with my mouth hanging open, my mind spinning. I wasn't sure how I felt about this revelation. Who the hell had sent him? And did this mean he was only here because he had to be? "Who sent you?"

He settled back in his chair, as if he was relieved to get the truth out once and for all. "His name is Aaron. For years he's taken mind readers under his wing."

"Where did he come from?"

Lewis laughed. "Same place you and I came from, our parents. The man is a genius. He's taught us everything he knows, he's empowered us."

Empowered. What I wouldn't do to feel that way. My excitement was almost unmanageable and I scooted my chair closer to the table. "Such as?"

"How to control your thoughts so other mind readers can't read them."

That would be really, really good…especially when I was around Lewis.

"How to focus on certain people's thoughts. How to block thoughts…anything you can imagine."

He'd already sold me and I wanted to ask him where to sign up but I managed to keep calm. I didn't really know who Lewis was or where he'd come from, but to me he was an angel.

"You guys doing all right?" A young waitress interrupted our session.

I jumped, startled. I'd been so mesmerized by Lewis, I hadn't even heard her or her thoughts approach.

He's cute, but too young, she thought, glancing at Lewis. I frowned, annoyed. How did she know Lewis and I weren't together? Rather rude, if you asked me.

Lewis grinned, obviously hearing her words in his own mind. "We're good, thanks."

She moved on, leaving us alone. I had so many questions it was hard to contain myself. "Mind readers. That's what we're called?"

He shrugged. "It's what we call ourselves."

"How many are there?"

"A few hundred, at least. Not a lot."

But so many more than what I'd known. I sank back into my chair, shocked to my very core. "And they all live with Aaron?"

"No, of course not. Just a few."

I stared out the window, watching raindrops chase each other down the glass. Overwhelmed, I wasn't sure what to say, to ask. My entire world had changed in a moment. Why hadn't she told me there were others? "All this time I thought Grandmother and I were alone."

Lewis' face grew serious. "You're not, and there's so much more you could do, if you were trained. So many things you're missing out on."

His words were tempting. He'd touched something deep within, a feeling of worthlessness that had taken root in my soul. I was different. I was wrong. But for once, I felt right.

"I want to show you something." Keeping his arm on the table, Lewis opened his hand, fingers spread wide. The clear salt shaker next to me rattled. Startled, I drew in a sharp breath. The shaker slid across the tabletop, stopping directly against his palm. Lewis closed his fingers around the shaker and he set it back in its rightful place.

"No freaking way," I whispered. "How'd you do that?"

"Telekinesis. Moving things with your mind." He grinned. "It's amazing what the mind can do if trained properly."

My heart leapt with excitement. "You're saying I can do that?"

He shrugged. "We don't know what you can do, unless you try. Unless you're trained."

I took my lower lip between my teeth and played with the cardboard sleeve on my cup. "But my Grandma…"

He sighed. "Your grandma is trying to control you."

True enough. How often had I thought the same thing? How often had I been so incredibly angry with her because of her controlling and demanding nature that I'd wanted to run away? Heck, I was counting down the days until I could leave for college. Still…

You're not alone, Cameron.

I jerked my head upright. "What?" I wasn't sure if he'd spoken the words aloud or implanted them in my mind.

Lewis smiled but didn't move his lips. *You're not alone.*

I looked around, afraid the other two patrons in the café would notice I was talking to myself. "You can talk to me…my mind?"

"Of course I can," he said aloud this time. "It's simple, a mere thought directed at you. And you can do the same to me." He leaned closer, temptation in his eyes. "Try it."

What to say? I looked around again to make sure no one was watching. I'm sure to the other customers we probably looked like two teenagers intensely attracted to each other, the way we were leaning in close, staring so intently. If they only knew what we were really up to.

I stared into his blue eyes. *All right. Here goes. What happens next, if I agree?*

He took a sip of his drink. *You come with me.*

I didn't respond immediately, too surprised. Leave? Leave this town? Leave Grandma? Leave the only life I'd ever known? *Where to?*

Aaron's home.

Suddenly a picture flashed through my mind. A mansion really, of red brick. Rolling green hills, fall colored trees, the blue ocean sparkling in the distance. A beautiful, peaceful looking place.

"Did you do that?" I demanded, blinking the picture from my mind and focusing on him.

The waitress looked our way, hearing the sound of my shrill voice and wondering if something was wrong. I sipped my tea and focused my thoughts on him. *Did you send me that picture?*

Yes.

But...but how?

It's easy, when you know the way to do it. We sense emotions, we can hear thoughts, worries, and we can see and send mental images as well.

So many things my Grandmother had never told me. I wasn't sure if I should be angry or confused. Why was she keeping me in the dark? *My God, that's amazing.*

He grinned.

"Why didn't she tell me? Why hasn't she helped me develop these abilities?"

His smile faded. "Some people are frightened of what they can do."

I laughed, a forced, hard sound. "My Grandma's not afraid of her abilities."

He looked at his cup, tracing the rim with his finger. "Your Grandma's different. She's never fully accepted what we can do."

I stiffened. "You say that like you know her."

He looked up at me. "I know of her." He sighed and leaned back in his chair. "Decades ago, Mind Readers stuck together. Almost like a family. They lived and worked as a group. Unfortunately, there was some falling out and they divided. Some went the way of your Grandmother, going into seclusion and hiding. Others went with Aaron, not hiding, but being proud of what they could do. I don't really know the details, but I do know your Grandmother wants to keep her powers to herself."

For some reason I felt the need to defend the old bat. "Maybe she has a reason for hiding. You saw how the school treated me, how it backfired."

He latched onto my hand, his grip strong and sure. "No. You saved countless lives today, Cameron, don't ever forget that."

He was right. I was being selfish by worrying about my social standing and not proud of the fact that I had helped put a murderer behind bars. "But how can we fit in?"

He shrugged, his gaze shining with excitement. "Why should we? We don't have to fit in. We don't need others. Humans don't understand us."

I pulled my hand from his. I couldn't think straight when he was touching me. For the longest time my goal had been to blend in, to be normal. Now, he was telling me I didn't need to. "You say humans like we aren't."

He glanced outside onto the wet streets, deep in thought. "Maybe we aren't. Who knows where our abilities come from."

What the heck was he saying? How could we not be human? We were quiet for one long moment, my mind spinning with confusing possibilities. "What do you know?"

He looked directly at me. *We know the ability to read minds is passed down in the family, although it can skip generations.*

I nodded. That certainly made sense. *My Grandma.*

Your dad.

I stiffened. No. If Dad could read minds, Grandma would have told me. But then I didn't know much about Dad, and Grandma didn't speak about him. I'd always assumed it would be too painful, having lost her only child. Confusion gave way to anger.

My dad could read minds?

He nodded. *Your father was great, Cam. One of the best. The things he could do...* He shook his head, a smile playing on his lips. *He's the stuff of legends.*

I wasn't sure whether to feel proud or confused. Honestly, I wasn't sure what to think about a man I hardly knew. "Why didn't Grandma tell me?"

The smile faded. "Your father was killed, murdered, and she doesn't want the same thing to happen to you."

"What do you mean?" I whispered.

"There are people out there who are afraid of our powers, people who want to use us and if they can't, destroy us. People we call S.P.I., Society for Paranormal Investigation. In the past, many Mind Readers worked with SPI. Until they turned on us, wanted to control us. The battles have died down, mostly because we've gone into hiding."

It was all too much. I'd gone from being thrilled, realizing there were more people like me, to terrified I'd be hunted down. "So then my Grandma was right to hide."

"No," his voice was hard, insistent. "There's power in numbers, Cam. Besides, by not being able to use your powers to your fullest ability, you're just a sitting duck, waiting for them to find you."

A shiver of unease raised the fine hairs on my arms. How could this War of the Worlds be happening without my knowledge? "We've been okay so far."

"Have you really?" When I didn't respond he sighed and raked his hand through his hair, the strands shifting and shimmering under the light of the cafe. "Why do you think your Grandmother keeps moving you so often? God, Cam, they're coming. Rumors are circulating that they're on the move again, searching for ones with the ability."

Fear settled in my gut. "Why?"

He shrugged. "The world is changing, my bet is the government wants to use us again."

"Would that be so bad? We'd be helping...right?"

He released a harsh laugh, shaking his head. "Yes, it would be bad. We can't trust them. Not after what they did to us in the past. You think you have no freedom now, wait and see if they get ahold of you. Your life will no longer be your own. And if you even think of rebelling they'll know and they'll make you regret it."

Regret it. That definitely sounded like a threat. Grandma had told me Dad was accidentally shot by the cops. That memory combined with my newfound knowledge made me suddenly sick to my stomach. "S.P.I. killed my father?"

Yes.

The word whispered softly through my mind and I wondered for a moment if I'd imagined it. But no, there was Lewis looking so serious that it must be true. My father. A man I knew nothing about...dead because of some abnormality he'd been born with. Something he'd passed to me. I wrapped my arms around my belly, my chest feeling suddenly hollow.

Lewis reached out, laying his hand on the table, an offering of comfort. I paused for only a moment, then settled my hand atop his. His grip was strong, sure, comforting. "Your father would want this, Cam. He'd want you to know how to use your abilities. He'd want you to be protected and to know how to protect yourself and your Grandmother."

I didn't know what to say, who to believe. Lewis, a boy I barely knew, wanted me to trust him, but I couldn't, not until I talked things over with Grandma. "No offense, but how do you know what my father would want?"

"Aaron knew your father."

My mouth dropped open. Over the years, I'd thought many times about my dad; what he was like, what he believed in. I'd never even seen his picture. Did I look like him? And here was Lewis, telling me this man named Aaron knew my dad.

"Cam, you're a sitting duck right now. Think what you could do, who you could help. There would be no one to judge you where we live. Come with me, Cam."

Leave Grandma? The thought was shocking. "Where would we go?"

"To see Aaron. He'll train you, he'll protect you."

The urge was strong. I was like a kid in front of a candy store full of temptation. It would be so easy to merely slip back into my old life. To pretend I was normal. I could laugh off Anne's rumor, say she was as insane as her boyfriend, somehow get back into Emily's good graces. Yet, how happy had I truly been pretending to be someone I wasn't? Emily was turning into the bitter bitch her mom had become.

"Think of the people you could help," he insisted, but I was still hurt about Anne's reaction.

"Maybe they don't want my help," I muttered, annoyed at the confusing thoughts rumbling through my mind. Too much had happened in the last few days. I needed time to think and he wasn't giving me time.

He was silent for one long moment. "I'm leaving tomorrow, Cam. I'm going back."

I felt his words like a slap to the face. He was leaving? Leaving me? I'd only just found him and already he was leaving. "But you can't!"

"I came here for you." His words excited and scared me. He looked out the window and so I looked too. The rain was tapering off, the sun breaking through the dark clouds, but I felt heavy, drained. A police car parked in front of the building, reminding me of my father's supposed death.

"What about school?" I whispered.

He smiled. "Cam, I'm eighteen. I graduated last year."

Shocked, I could merely sit there and stare at him. He'd lied to me? To the school? What else had he lied about?

His face grew serious and he reached out, taking my hand in his. "Tomorrow, I'll come by your house to pick you up. Eight in the morning. Come with me...please."

"What about my schooling?" I was frantically trying to find some reason to stay, fear of the unknown sharp and bitter. Yet even as I fought for an excuse, I realized I had nothing holding me here.

"You'll be home schooled, like I was. You've only got half the year left anyway."

His gaze slid across the café, landing on the waitress who was whispering something to a man seated at a table. She looked upset, he looked angry.

"Let me ask you something. Does that woman deserve to die?"

I jerked my head toward him. "What kind of question is that?"

"She has a child, a little girl who's five. It's only the two of them. She wants to go to college, but can't afford it. She's hoping if she keeps working, she can save enough. But she worries that while she's working, she's not spending time with her child. The worst thing she's done is get pregnant at seventeen. She wanted to keep the baby. Her parents didn't want her to and kicked her out of the house. It's only been those two since."

He looked at me, his gaze piercing and direct. "So, does she deserve to die?"

"No," I whispered, my voice harsh. "Why are you asking me that?"

"Because that man is her ex-boyfriend. He's jealous, ridiculously jealous. He's hit her and she broke up with him just last week because of his temper."

The words shocked and angered me. I knew he was going somewhere with this conversation and I wasn't sure I wanted to head in that direction with him. "And?" What wasn't he telling me?

"That man has a gun. He's going to wait until she gets off work tonight and he's going to kill her in her apartment."

My heart froze. For one brief moment I saw Savannah's pale, lifeless face.

"Her daughter will go to foster care, of course, because she'll have no one to take her in." He drank the rest of his coffee and then leaned back, letting the words sink in. "So tell me, Cameron, does she deserve to die?"

No! I yelled at him in my head, as tears stung my eyes.

"We can stop it from happening."

"How?" Dare I trust him? He'd told me that we could help Anne, and look how well that turned out. Sure, George was behind bars, but I wouldn't be surprised if the town showed up at my house with pitch forks and torches once word of my ability got out.

Lewis stood, threw a few dollars on the table. "Eight o'clock tomorrow morning."

He was leaving and as he made his way across the café, I let him go, too stunned to stop him. I watched him out the window as he strolled so confidently down the sidewalk. When he came face to face with the Police Officer, he paused, his lips moving. The officer glanced at the café and pulled out his walkie talkie.

Lewis looked into the window, directly at me. *Go, Cam, he's calling for backup.*

He'd told on the waitresses' ex-boyfriend. He'd saved yet another life, while I sat here like a scared little girl, doing nothing. I grabbed my backpack and calmly made my way out of the café, past the cop who was thrilled to have something interesting to do on this dreary day. They weren't taking any chances as they'd already had one shooting at the café.

I had to find Lewis. He couldn't leave me like this, with so many unanswered questions.

I rushed around the corner.

But Lewis was gone.

Chapter 8

I'd stayed out late, sitting in the park until eleven, knowing Grandma would be sleeping when I came home. Fortunately, she couldn't read my thoughts while she slept. For hours my mind had warred with my heart. I wanted to go; I wanted to know what I could be. And I was so damn angry at my Grandma for keeping all of this from me. But I was afraid. Afraid to leave what I knew.

I finally gave up and returned to our little cottage around midnight. But being home, out of the cold and dreary weather, offered no comfort. I paced my room, walking over the scuffed, wooden floorboards until the sky turned light and mysterious shadows morphed into furniture.

I'd done what I could with my small domain; painted the walls a Caribbean blue, dreaming of warmer climates. But the floorboards creaked and the window leaked cold air reminding me of where I truly lived.

I'd been content here and I couldn't help but fight the tears at the thought of leaving. And I was leaving. I suppose I'd known that even before Lewis had left me in the café. But it wasn't until three a.m., with the moon high, when I'd finally admitted the truth to myself; I couldn't stay here any longer.

As the moonlight began to fade, I flicked aside my white curtains to look out onto the quiet neighborhood where mostly old couples had retired. Gray dawn was giving way to yellow light. The sun just peeking over the horizon. The promise of a new day, a new beginning. Under the brilliant rays of the sun, the pavement sparkled with light, with hope. I'd showered and dressed, a suitcase packed since 4 a.m. Now, it was time to say goodbye to my life.

There was only one young couple on our block; a married couple with a five year old girl. I watched as the man made his way down their front drive to his car, headed to work. A perfect, happy family. We could have had a life like that if…if what? If my father hadn't been killed? If Mom hadn't been a druggie? I didn't even know where my father was buried. No one had bothered to tell me. The anger I'd been trying to keep at bay flared to life, giving me courage.

Grandma had made me think I was a freak, alone in this world. Someone who should be ashamed. She hadn't told me my father could read minds. Now I had the opportunity to learn more about my dad. Learn about who I was, but more importantly, who I could be. I knew if it were up to Grandma, I'd live here the rest of my life, hiding my true self. But I couldn't take that any longer. It was time to live.

The soft clatter of utensils against pans alerted me to Grandma's presence. She was awake, which meant she probably already knew what I was planning. My heart skipped a beat. She wasn't going to let me go without a fight.

Time to leave. I reached for the Swiss Army Knife on my bedside table and slipped it into my pocket. The piece was old and worn from age, but, besides my sweatshirt, it was the only thing I owned that had once belonged to my father. Steeling my nerves, I pulled my suitcase into the hall, leaving it there. Wearing her long, gray robe, the same robe she'd worn since I could remember, Grandma stood at the stove frying eggs. She had her routine to do and nothing would stop her, not even me.

She had to hear my thoughts; I couldn't keep them to myself. Yet, she didn't say a word when I settled at the kitchen table. Her silence made me nervous. She pushed the eggs onto a plate and placed them in front of me, avoiding my gaze. The same plates I'd used most of my life, beige with brown roses. How many meals had I had on these outdated dishes? My stomach revolted at the thought of eating. Instead, I took a glass of orange juice and drank deeply. But the acid only made it worse. I pushed the plate and glass away. What to tell her? How to explain? Then again, why even bother when she knew. And I could tell by her stiff movements that she knew.

"You're not leaving," she finally said.

I swallowed hard, my mind racing so fast I couldn't grasp hold of an argument, but one thought remained clear, Grandma could read my mind. She knew what I was planning to do. She knew even before I said it.

"And what if I want to see what they can offer?"

She slammed the pan onto the stove, making me jump. Rarely did she lose control. "Damn it, do you have any idea what you're getting involved with?"

I surged from my chair, anger propelling me into action. "No! I don't because you've never told me anything."

Still she didn't face me. "You've never asked."

She wasn't even going to deny these Mind Readers existed, wasn't going to pretend they were dangerous. Which meant everything Lewis had told me was probably true. I released a harsh laugh. I'd asked her plenty of times about my ability. Maybe not recently. But I had years ago, before I'd given up that she would respond. "When I was a child I—"

"You were too young then."

My fingers curled into the back of the chair. Her voice was calm again, as if she was in complete control and it made me furious. "Of course, you always have an excuse." The same words she'd used on me whenever I got in trouble.

Why didn't you tell me my father was murdered by S.P.I.? I was so angry, I couldn't say the words aloud.

She was quiet for a moment, quiet and still. But I knew she'd heard. I'd surprised her. We'd never chatted via our mental voices before. "You didn't need to know."

"He's my father!"

"He's dead." She spun around toward me. Her face was pale, her eyes wide and a bit wild looking. As scared as I was, I almost felt sorry for her. She was out of her element here. She sure as heck wasn't expecting me to talk back.

"He's dead, gone," she said in a softer voice. "There's no use in rehashing the past."

The words killed me. Like a knife to the chest, they were actually painful. "I need to know the truth, to understand what I am, what I'm capable of. I'm tired of feeling like there's something wrong with me."

She closed her eyes, showing her first signs of sympathy. "I've never said there's something wrong with you."

"No, you just made me hide my ability, made me feel like I was a freak."

She opened her eyes, her gaze pleading. "Because of other people, not because of you!"

I released a harsh laugh and paced across the small kitchen. My skin felt too tight, my heart racing to go somewhere…anywhere. "Yeah, explain that to a five year old who has been abandoned by her mother."

"Your mom was addicted to drugs, Cameron, you know that had nothing to do with you."

I paused. The truth hurt.

So Grandma had no problem dishing the dirt on Mom, telling me her every dark secret and repeatedly reminding me, but wouldn't even tell me where Dad was buried. "What about when I was little and you made us move away from Michigan?"

"I was protecting you."

"I'd only told one person—"

"And she told five others, including the cops who showed up—"

"And you made me feel horrible! Like I couldn't be trusted! We could have lied to them, brushed it off. They would have believed us."

"Like they believed my parents?"

Wait, what? I froze, confused.

"Everything I've done is because of what I've experienced. They tested me, Cameron, when the government found out what I could do, they took me away from my parents and kept me locked away. They tested me until I finally realized that if I pretended I couldn't read minds, they'd release me. But it was too late, my parents were already dead. Killed in some freak accident."

"I'm sorry," I whispered, stunned she was finally telling me the truth. "But you can't keep me locked away because of what happened to you."

We fell silent, both of us fighting our anger. She had the stubborn look to her gaze once more. I wanted to scream in frustration. Why couldn't she understand? She'd made me feel like

I was a freak. She'd kept the truth from me. She wouldn't keep this from me too.

She snorted, a sarcastic laugh. "So, what will you do? Rush out and help people like some damn superhero?"

"What's wrong with that?"

"That's what got your father killed!"

She'd stunned me into silence. Was she lying in some pathetic attempt to make me afraid? If so, it had the opposite effect. Lewis had been right, my father was a hero. He wasn't a coward, like me. "And so I'm supposed to stay here, never say a word, let innocent people die?"

"Better them than you."

I shook my head, ashamed of her. I didn't want to feel guilty; I didn't want to grow up afraid, like her. "I can't stand by anymore and let horrible things happen to people I care about. Maybe you can, but I can't."

She pressed her hands to her temples, her entire body trembling. She looked weak and pale under the brilliant light of the rising sun coming in through the small window above the sink. "You're not some superhero, Cameron. A bullet can kill you as well as anyone."

"I know," I said, softening my voice. "But I'm leaving, for me. Please understand that. You could come with."

She slammed her fists onto the tabletop. "You will not leave this house! Until you're eighteen, I control you!"

"Not anymore." She wouldn't understand. Not now, maybe never. "I have to, they're coming for us."

The fury seemed to drain from her face along with any color. "What are you talking about?" Before I could answer, she turned toward the stove, obviously intent on ignoring me.

"Lewis told me about S.P.I., whoever they are, using people like us."

She turned and pointed her spatula at me. "As long as we stay out of trouble, they'll leave us alone."

I moved around the table. Everything felt oddly off balance. The tides had turned and Grandma wasn't in control. She seemed to know less about S.P.I. than I did. "Will they? Are you sure about that?"

"Of course." She tossed a plate of bacon onto the table.

"What if you're wrong?"

She looked directly at me, her hazel gaze hard. "We are safe, Cameron. Aaron is only causing trouble where there is none!"

"You know Aaron?"

"Of course I do. He talked your father into using his abilities when he shouldn't have. They were going to save the world," she said, her voice bitter.

My determination wavered. Could I trust her? I should, shouldn't I? She was my grandma after all. But she'd also kept the truth from me about my father and about what I could do. "Tell me you'll teach me how to block my thoughts, how to…how to show people mental images. Tell me you'll teach me everything you know."

"You don't need to learn," she insisted. "Nothing is going to happen to you."

"Is that what you told my dad?"

She went pale and I knew I'd gone too far. I hadn't meant to say the words, I hadn't meant to be so cruel.

"How dare you," she hissed.

It was too late. I couldn't take the words back. Unless I apologized, our tumultuous relationship would be over. My pride wouldn't let me apologize because deep down, I did blame her for everything that had happened. I turned and on shaking legs made my way to the hall where I'd left my suitcase. And I told myself, as I moved through the kitchen, that I was doing this not only for me, but for her.

"You are not leaving!" she screamed.

My heart lurched. I didn't dare look her in the eyes. I refused to respond because I knew I couldn't. I was afraid she'd scare me into staying. It was five minutes until eight. If I was going to do it, I needed to leave now. I moved around her and made my way to the front door, my suitcase wheels whizzing over the hardwood floors.

"I'm sorry, Grandma." My voice caught as I fought the tears. "But I'm done hiding."

I pushed the front door wide, the hinges screeching, and stepped onto the stoop. I fully expected her to stop me. She didn't. The cool morning air eased the sweat gathering between my shoulder blades.

"You don't think it's insane to leave with a guy you barely know?"

I paused for a moment as my grandmother's words hit me. She was right, I knew that, but couldn't seem to care. Lewis's silver car was parked directly in front of our home; Lewis leaning against the door. He called to me, not mentally or verbally, but something pulled me toward him. The dark blue sweater he wore stretched across his broad shoulders. He'd come for me. My heart leapt with joy. He pushed away from the car, and when our gazes met, a wide smile spread across his handsome face. I rushed down the steps, my suitcase thumping after me. I didn't stop until I was only a foot from him. Fisting my hands, I resisted the urge to throw my arms around his neck.

"You're coming," he stated the obvious.

"Yes."

Don't go, Cameron, please. Grandma's voice whispered through my mind. It was the first time she'd asked me for anything and for a moment I paused, her plea stinging.

Indecision held me captive. Could I really leave and take the guilt? Could I stay? I'd die here, maybe not physically, but mentally and emotionally I'd die. Grandma had had her chance.

"Cameron, are you ready?" Lewis asked, taking my bag.

"Yes," I whispered. Without looking back, I slid my hand into his.

****

For the two hour drive to the harbor we sat in relative silence. Lewis let me stew in my thoughts and emotions and I was glad for it. I wasn't ready to talk. I felt guilty as hell. I was doing what was best for me and for Grandma. Someone had to learn how to protect us.

Grandma had practically admitted that S.P.I. existed and I knew the reason she'd made me hide my powers was because she didn't want to bring attention to us. She was afraid. I could understand that, but I was my own person and I couldn't accept that for myself. And as the minutes ticked by and the distance between me and my old life grew, my guilt faded. When we were on the ferry that would take us to Haddock Island where Aaron lived, Lewis finally spoke.

He nudged me with his shoulder, a playful push. "You okay?" He didn't move away, but kept close, his body warm next to mine as we leaned against the railing watching the main land become smaller and smaller. I wanted to go. I was doing the right thing. So why, as the land became a blur, did I feel the stirrings of panic?

"Cameron?"

"Yeah, sure. I'm fine," I said a little too quickly.

The wind tossed his hair and gave a flush to his cheeks. My body practically tingled when he was near. He was cute. Gorgeous. Realizing he had probably just read that thought, heat shot to my cheeks and I looked away. "I can't do this."

I felt his body stiffen. "Cam, you're doing the right thing, what your father would have wanted."

"No, not that." My embarrassment grew. We'd never discussed any feelings between us, if there were any. Heck, maybe I was the only one thinking of romance. But surely he'd read my thoughts and knew how I felt. Wouldn't he have shot me down by now? Unless he got some perverse pleasure out of seeing me lust after him. "No," I said softly. "I mean I can't stand here while you read my thoughts."

He laughed, those gorgeous blue eyes turning into half-moons as he looked out at the waves. I frowned and shoved him in the shoulder. "Not funny and it's not fair." I hated this, but I certainly knew how Anne must have felt. "It's…embarrassing."

He looked at me, his eyes sparkling. As much as I wanted to be angry at him, all I could think about was how pure his gaze was, blue like the ocean churning below.

"Cam, I turned off my abilities."

"Turned off?"

He shrugged, wrapping his hands around the wood railing. His blue windbreaker rustled in the breeze. "Well, only with you."

"I don't understand."

He leaned super close, his breath warm on my cheek. "I'm not reading your thoughts."

I wasn't sure if I believed him, but with him so close, I didn't really care. "But, how? I've been able to dim people's thoughts by focusing on other things, but they still seep in."

He turned, leaning his back against the railing. "Just one of the many things you'll soon learn."

I gazed out at the water, silent as I wondered if what he said was true. There really wasn't a reason for him to lie. "Why?" I finally asked.

He glanced at me. "Hmm?"

"Why'd you stop reading my mind?"

He looked thoughtful for a moment, and then shrugged. "It didn't feel…right." He turned toward the railing again and clasped his hands together. There was a flush to his cheeks, as if he was embarrassed to be talking about his emotions. Such a stereotypical guy.

The horn on the boat released a deep bellow, indicating the shore was drawing near. My excitement flared, sending my stomach into a nervous fit. I hadn't wanted to sit inside on the lower deck as I'd needed to keep my mind clear of the other passenger's thoughts. But that meant I was chilled to the bone and eager to get on dry land.

"There it is," he said, pointing toward the shore.

I leaned closer to the railing, the wind pulling my hair from its ponytail and tugging at my jacket. There, on a sloping green hill that was apparently the highest point of the island, stood a massive brick mansion, even more ornate and intimidating than it had been in my mind. Only a few trees dotted the landscape, but the lack of foliage didn't take away from the savage beauty of the place.

"Wow," I whispered, in awe.

Any unease about leaving Grandma was gone. I felt my very life changing as that boat docked and the small village came into view. Clapboard homes lined the streets and boats of various colors and sizes docked along the shore. It was a tourist town in the summer, Lewis had told me, a place where people vacationed to go whale watching, fishing and shopping.

Today the island was quiet. Most of the residents had left their summer homes boarded up and empty. The few residents who remained were safely ensconced, bundled up against the chill afternoon wind. But for the few squawking gulls, it was quiet. So incredibly, blessedly quiet of thoughts!

Lewis took hold of my suitcase and started for the dock. I followed, weaving my way around the small group of tourists who had braved the autumn winds. The scent of saltwater and fish was a comfortable and familiar scent. Everything seemed clean, fresh, full of possibilities.

I stepped off the dock and onto solid land and my heart surged with hope. The visitors rushed off to their destinations, leaving Lewis and me alone, just as I liked it.

"Come on," he said, taking my hand in his warm grip. I don't think he realized it, but his touch was becoming almost normal now. Instinctively I reached for his hand, when I shouldn't have. When his fingers wrapped around mine, it felt so wonderful.

His excitement was contagious. He was coming home. He loved it here, and I knew I would too. My suitcase thumped, rolling across cobbled stone. The place was picture perfect, like something from a holiday card. I could imagine that in winter, with snow falling, it would look even better. Down the main street, historic stone and clapboard buildings lined the sidewalks. Grandma would love this place. I squashed that thought just as quickly as it had arrived.

"There he is." Lewis nodded toward a sleek black car where a man stood, leaning against the hood. His arms were crossed over a slate grey button up shirt. His blond hair was short and trimmed neatly.

Seeing us, he pulled the black sunglasses from his eyes and smiled a brilliant smile that showed perfectly white, perfectly straight teeth. I almost paused, not expecting a man obviously wealthy. So refined, so well-dressed. I wasn't sure what I'd thought he'd look like, maybe an old, wise-looking Dumbledore complete with a beard and robe.

"That's Aaron?" I asked, the disbelief apparent in my voice.

Lewis nodded.

I felt suddenly nervous. This man had known my father, known him well, when I hadn't even known his middle name. This man was going to teach me how to use my powers. This man was going to change my life.

Aaron's blue gaze went to me and his smile widened. "Cameron." He didn't pause until he was in front of us. He took both my hands in his strong grip, his palms warm and comforting in some odd way. "It's so wonderful to finally meet you." He was silent for a moment, his gaze studying mine until I blushed.

"My God, you look like your father," he said.

I took the words as a compliment. Even though he was dead, I felt closer to my dad than I ever had. Nervously, I tucked a lock of hair behind my ear. "Thank you. I...I've never even seen a picture of him."

He frowned, his light blue eyes narrowing. "Well, we'll have to remedy that. I have plenty of pictures." He took the handle of my luggage and started toward the back of the car. "Come, I'm sure you'd like to rest."

I'd had little sleep in the past twenty-four hours and was physically exhausted. But inside, I was as giddy as a kid on Christmas Eve. I sank into the passenger seat, marveling over the smooth, soft leather seats as Aaron threw my suitcase into the trunk.

Lewis settled in the backseat. "You excited?"

"You could say that," I beamed.

Lewis leaned forward, resting his hand on my shoulder. "You won't regret coming here, Cameron, I promise you."

I didn't have time to respond. Aaron sat behind the wheel and maneuvered the car down the main road. "I'm so thrilled you decided to join us."

I certainly was too. As we drove through town I knew I'd done the right thing. Call it instinct, but I was meant to be here, on the cobbled streets with the clapboard and Victorian homes. Here, where I would learn to thrive, instead of hiding.

"There are so many things I want to show you," Aaron continued.

The town ended and we started up the hill that would lead toward the mansion Lewis had pointed out on the ferry. "So many things you'll be capable of, I just know it. If you're anything like your dad."

Just like that, my excitement faded. I shifted, feeling uneasy for the first time today. What if I wasn't as powerful as my dad? What if I failed them? But now wasn't the time to worry. I pushed aside depressing thoughts and focused on the scenery. There were only a few oak trees that lined the road up the hill. It was a rather desolate place, but not uncommon for the islands off Maine. Still, it made an isolated picture. Isolation was fine by me. I was tired of being around people who didn't understand.

The sun was lowering, sending brilliant orange and pink rays across the ocean to my left. On my right, a high stone fence rose up along the road and followed us, ending at a set of large, iron gates, complete with a gatehouse. It seemed a bit extreme, but I knew rich people liked their privacy and Aaron was obviously rich. I couldn't help but wonder what he did for a living. I should have asked Lewis more questions on the way here, but had been too emotional to think straight.

We paused at the closed gates. "Don't worry, it's mostly for show," Aaron said, giving me a reassuring smile.

I wasn't sure what he meant but nodded like I understood. Two guards came forward, glanced inside the car, then opened the gates for us. I noticed the guns strapped to their sides almost immediately. My stomach lurched. Lewis had said S.P.I. was a real threat. Was the fence here to keep S.P.I. out or us in?

The car rolled through the iron gates and Aaron's home came into view. For a moment I forgot my unease. "You're our honored guest. Anything you want, anything you need, we have it here. In fact, there's no reason to leave." Aaron laughed after he said that, as if he was joking.

I kept my smile in place, but it was hard to do. I was tired, I told myself, merely exhausted from the day's events. Yet, as the gates closed behind us, I couldn't help but glance back.

I might have been an honored guest, but I was a guest who was apparently going to have to get permission to leave.

Chapter 9

I felt like I'd slept on a cloud of soft loveliness. Last night the wind didn't seep through the windows and rattle the glass panes, keeping me awake. The floorboards didn't creak and moan. And I didn't have to listen to Grandma's kitchen noise. Even though I'd expected to feel odd in a strange house, I'd slept silently, deeply, wonderfully.

I lifted my arms above my head and stretched my muscles until they eased. The room was dark, only a sliver of light pierced the thick drapes that hung over the floor to ceiling windows. It was a large room, as big as our living room and kitchen combined. I pushed my down comforter away and rolled off my Queen sized bed. The warmth of my cocoon called to me, but the room wasn't chilly, even though the house was atop a hill and the wind was battering the island outside. They must have had some amazing heating system to keep this huge place warm when even the smallest of homes got cold during fall and winter in Maine.

I went immediately to the bedside table and picked up my cell phone. No messages. No one from school calling to ask why I hadn't arrived for history class. Not even Grandma had called. I dampened down my disappointment. That blue light of my cell merely mocked me.

Well, screw them. I wouldn't think about Grandma, I wouldn't think about school. I was starting over. Last night I'd had a wonderful dinner with Lewis and Aaron. We'd talked until midnight, discussing when I'd start my studies and what I'd learn. He'd even given me some CDs on meditation, apparently the first step on my road to success. I'd felt safe and for the first time in my life, I'd felt like a normal person…comfortable in my own body. No more hiding, no more pretending.

With a sigh, I set my phone down and walked toward the windows. Would anyone even care that I'd moved away? How would Grandma explain my disappearance? My feet sank into plush, white carpet. It was so warm I didn't need my typical double layers of socks. Managing to avoid the shadowy furniture, I gripped the thick blue curtains and threw them wide.

The rooftops from the buildings in the town below glimmered under the morning sun. And there, just beyond, the brilliant blue ocean shimmered, sparkling like a million diamonds trapped in a mermaid's net. The few trees sprinkled across the large yard wavered and weaved under the autumn wind. To the left the sky was gray. A storm was coming, but that wasn't uncommon along the coast. Here quickly and gone just as fast.

I started to turn away, when a sudden movement drew my attention back to the yard below. A small girl stood upon the brilliant green grass as if she'd appeared like some fairy from the books I'd read as a child. She couldn't have been more than eight. With blonde hair and a round face she was far cuter than I'd been as a gawky child. What was she doing down there alone?

The dress and jacket she wore wrapped around her thin legs, the material pulled fierce by the wind. As if sensing my attention, she tilted her head back and stared directly up at me. I pressed my hand to my heart, feeling her gaze as if she'd reached into my chest and squeezed my very soul. Who was she? Lewis had said Aaron took in people with our abilities, was she another Mind Reader? Or maybe his daughter?

"About time," an unfamiliar voice mumbled from behind me.

I spun around, the curtains falling back into place and shadowing the room in darkness.

An older girl, perhaps a year or two younger than me, sat in the wing-backed chair near my stone fireplace. Her jean-clad legs were curled up underneath her and a strand of her dark hair was between her lips. It wasn't surprising I hadn't noticed her until she'd spoken; she was dressed in black, even her hair and eye shadow were dark. She blended into the shadows like some sort of ghost in a haunted mansion. Another Mind Reader?

Daring to look away, I glanced back out the window. The little girl was gone, as if she'd never been there. I sighed in frustration. There was way too much mystery going on this early in the morning. I turned back toward my intruder. "Uh, hi."

She spared me a quick glance, then pulled the damp strand of hair from her mouth and began to play with it, twisting it over and over around her finger. "I'm Olivia."

She didn't look me in the eyes, only quick glances up, as if to make sure I was still there. "Cameron."

She unfolded her legs and stood. She was a couple inches shorter than me. "I know."

Taken aback by her response, I flushed. She apparently knew about me, but I didn't know a thing about her. "Okay." Why the heck was she here? Did everyone know who I was? Did I have no privacy? A million questions rushed through my mind at once.

"Aaron wants to see you in his office." She moved toward the door, only to pause and glance back. "You don't hide your thoughts very well."

Confused, I frowned. She pulled open the door and disappeared into the hall. It was only after she'd left that I realized I hadn't been able to read her mind.

"Oh God." Like Lewis, she'd learned how to block her thoughts.

I was so not used to having to worry. Annoyed, I opened my suitcase and pulled out a pair of jeans, a t-shirt and a green hoody. I dressed slowly, my mind spinning with the possibilities and irritation quickly gave way to wonder. The place had seemed so quiet last night, internally and externally, that I hadn't thought there was anyone else in residence. How many other Mind Readers lived here?

I moved into my huge, private bathroom, barely aware of the marble tile and massive tub that had so impressed me last night. As much as I wanted to enjoy my new day, two things nagged at me: the fact that I was basically locked inside a fence and the fact that people seemed to appear and disappear like haunting spirits.

I brushed my teeth, then pulled my hair into a ponytail. Usually I put on a little makeup, but I was too eager to know what Aaron wanted. Realizing my natural look would have to do, I moved into the hall, only to pause. Carpet ran the length of the corridor, and it was a long hall. Small, crystal chandeliers twinkled above. I was so tired last night, I hadn't gotten a good look. Now I could study every detail and one realization remained clear; Aaron had money, but how had he made his fortune?

I made my way down the wide steps that led to the foyer where more marble tile lay upon the entryway floor. I knew where Aaron's office was as we'd had dinner there last night. Still, I paused, feeling odd now that it was the bright light of day. Things seemed harsher, more real under the sunlight. As much as I wanted to belong, it would take a while for this mansion to feel like home.

Much to my surprise, the door opened and Aaron stood there. "Come in!"

I flushed again. Of course, he'd heard my thoughts. God, it sucked being the only person in this place who couldn't hide her feelings.

"We'll get to it."

Confused, I stumbled as I moved into the room. "What?"

He grinned, looking just as rich in jeans and a sweatshirt as he had yesterday in his button up shirt. "I know how you feel. But I promise we'll teach you how to block your thoughts. First, though, I have something for you."

I didn't have time to feel embarrassed because he left me standing in the middle of his office as he went to the bookshelves that lined the far wall. The room was just as beautiful as the rest of the house, with rich burgundy carpet, a dark wood desk and plenty of bookshelves full of novels. No pictures. Not of Olivia. Not of the young girl I'd seen outside. Maybe they weren't related.

He returned with a small box in hand. "For you."

Any worry gave way to excitement. Cradling the box in my arm, I lifted the lid. Photos. "Um, thanks." Polaroid's of people I couldn't identify. I didn't know what I'd expected, but not this. I lifted one yellowed picture and studied the two men standing side by side. Both were smiling, one was familiar, one not.

"You." I looked up at Aaron and pointed toward the taller man with blond hair.

He leaned against his desk and crossed his arms over his chest. "Yeah. And the other man…"

He didn't go on, but he didn't need to. My heart stopped for a brief moment as I realized who I was looking at. I suppose Mom might have had pictures of my dad, but she'd dropped me off at Grandma's when I was so young I didn't remember much. Grandma had nothing and I'd always supposed it was too painful for her.

My hand was trembling, I didn't realize that until the photo started shaking. "My dad?"

"Yeah," Aaron said softly.

He was right. I did look like my dad. Same dark hair, same hazel eyes. My lower lip quivered, my nose stinging as I tried to fight the tears.

Aaron took the box from my hands and set it on his desk, then led me to a chair. I let him because I was too overwhelmed to resist, overcome with emotions I couldn't seem to identify. How could Grandma not even give me a picture of my father? Vaguely, I was aware of Aaron sitting in the chair next to mine. When he took my hand, I let him. Even though I should have felt weird holding his hand, I didn't. His touch brought me comfort in a way I couldn't even begin to understand. Comfort I'd rarely felt before.

"There are so many things your father would have wanted you to know, Cam. He might not be here now, but I am."

They were the exact words I needed to hear. He reached into his pocket and pulled out a hankie, an actual cotton hankie, and handed it to me. "You don't know how long I've searched for you. I made a promise to your father that I would see you survive. That you would be proud of your ability and not shun your powers. That you could protect yourself and know who to trust."

Shun, which is what Grandmother had wanted me to do. I sniffled and dabbed at my eyes. This was where I belonged, where my dad would want me to be.

He smiled again, those perfectly straight teeth blindingly bright. "There are many things I'm so excited to teach you. Will you let me?"

I gave him a wavering grin. "Yeah."

He patted my hand. "Good. I'm here for you, Cameron. I'm not going anywhere."

The words I needed to hear. The same words Lewis had said to me that night I'd confronted Annabeth and changed my life forever...for the better.

"Now, Lewis is waiting for you in the dining room. You get some breakfast and if you're up for it, we'll start your lessons today."

I clenched the picture to my chest, excitement replacing my sadness. "Really?"

He nodded, laughing in delight. "So like your father."

I grinned, accepting the compliment.

"Now, go along and after breakfast I'll teach you how to block people's thoughts."

Block people's thoughts?

Silence. I'd hear pure, wonderful, silence. "My God, I'll know quiet."

He laughed again. "Only your own thoughts to keep you company."

Not that my thoughts would win me a Pulitzer anytime soon, but they were mine and only mine. I knew as I left his office that I'd done the right thing. This is what my father would have wanted. More importantly, this is what I wanted.

****

"Are you relaxed?" Aaron asked as he settled on the floor across from me.

I shrugged. As relaxed as I could be in a room with a man I barely knew and a guy I had a crush on. I slid Lewis a glance. He, too, was seated on the floor but a few feet away from me, half hidden in the shadows. He looked so serious and he was so cute when he was serious. Obviously he wasn't reading my mind or he'd be laughing right now.

"Okay," Aaron started. "Close your eyes."

I felt sort of silly, but I did as was told.

"Deep breath in, deep breath out. Again. Feel your body relax."

I knew I looked like some sort of meditative Buddhist with my legs crossed and my arms resting on my thighs, but I wasn't a very good Buddhist. I tried to sit up straight in an imitation of a beautiful lotus flower, as my meditative tape had suggested earlier. But sitting straight hurt and so I was sort of curved like the Hunchback of Notre Dame. So much for being a flower.

"Cameron." Was that a note of warning in Aaron's voice? Crap, he knew I wasn't paying attention. "I'm going to count backwards. Five. Deep breath in. Four. Breathe out. Three. Deep breath in. You're becoming more relaxed with each breath. Two. And one. Now picture yourself somewhere you love. Somewhere that makes you feel relaxed. A meadow, a lake, the ocean..."

Immediately, the ocean came to mind... the waves crashing against the shore... the very spot where Savannah was found. Her gray body flashed behind my cyclids. "No." I hadn't realized I said the word aloud, until Aaron reached out, resting his warm hand on mine, bringing me back into reality.

"Concentrate. You're here, at the estate. You're completely safe. Did you see the beach from your window this morning?"

I nodded, my eyes still closed, but my heart racing.

"Good, picture yourself on that beach. It's summer. It's warm. Yellow wildflowers are sprouting out of the dunes, white butterflies floating on the breeze. Do you see it?"

I saw it, everything he said. I wasn't sure if he was implanting those pictures in my head or not, but it didn't matter. The images called to me, calmed my racing mind.

"You're lying down in the sand, on a blanket. Do you hear the ocean waves? Roaring in...out...in...out. You've closed your eyes, the sun is warm on your skin." He was silent for a moment, letting the picture sink in. "You feel drowsy, but you're not sleeping."

I was there. The library room was gone. Lewis was gone. Aaron was just a vague rumbling voice in the background of loveliness that had become my reality. I didn't want to leave this place, not ever. I didn't want to think. I didn't want to do anything.

"Focus on those waves," Aaron said softly.

I did so easily. I'd always loved the sound of the beach, that soft roar that drowned out everything else in life. The mystery of the deep waters.

"Take a breath in, breath out." Aaron was suddenly gone, replaced with a deeper voice, an unfamiliar voice that spoke directly beside me.

Confused, but too numb to be afraid, I turned my head. My dad sat next to me, grinning down with a warmth that invaded every cell of my being. Startled, I sat up.

"Dad?"

"Breathe in, and out," he said. "Concentrate. I need you to concentrate."

I frowned. Was it my dad? Or was it Aaron…I wasn't sure. I didn't want to know. I closed my eyes and lay back down, focusing on the air coming in and out of my lungs.

"Now, I want you to picture a shimmering, silver wall in front of you. Nothing can get through this wall, nothing. You are protected."

Easy enough. The silver wall was there, hovering around me protectively.

"Now Cameron," Aaron was back, his voice replacing Dad's. "I'm going to ring for a maid. She doesn't know we can read minds. You'll keep your eyes closed when she enters. She thinks I'm teaching you to meditate. You'll hear her thoughts, but I want you to try and block them. The moment you hear her words, you'll picture your ocean. You'll smell the salt, you'll hear the waves. When her thoughts come at you, you'll push against that silver wall, push her thoughts back toward her. They will not penetrate that wall."

I think I nodded. I wasn't sure. I didn't care. I only wanted to continue to float into oblivion, in my make-believe world. There was a soft rustle of movement as he made his way to the door to call for the maid. My mind reached for the noise, wanted to focus on his movements and drag me back to reality.

Keep breathing, I heard Lewis's voice whisper through my head. *Focus on your breathing…focus on those waves.*

A few moments later I heard the door crack open.

She's here, Lewis said. Suddenly he appeared sitting on that blanket beside me, wavering in and out of focus through that silver wall. Was I imagining him, or had he placed himself in my mind? He looked gorgeous with the wind blowing through his dark hair, the sun warming his skin.

But don't focus on her, he continued. *Let your mind wander, listen to her thoughts but keep your eyes closed.*

"Sarah," Aaron's voice was low and calming as he spoke to the maid. "Can you make sure it's kept quiet today? We're meditating."

"Yes, of course," the maid replied, but I was more interested in her thoughts. *What is she doing? Sometimes I really don't understand these kids.*

I could practically feel the maid's attention on me. Her gaze burning into my face.

"And make sure the windows are cleaned by tomorrow."

"Yes, Sir." *I shouldn't be surprised, weirder things have happened here. But oh well, as long as he pays me.*

My mouth twitched as I resisted the urge to smile. The ocean was fading, that silver wall fading as I naturally focused on her thoughts.

Cameron, Lewis' voice pulled me back. *Focus on the ocean. Focus on your breathing. Focus on that wall. Picture the maid. She's standing in front of you. Now push on that wall, push her thoughts back to her.*

I took in a deep breath, in…out…in…out. As I focused on my breathing, their conversation faded…the maid stood before me, a woman dressed in black slacks with a white apron. Odd musical notes drifted from her head toward me. Her thoughts, I realized. The notes bounced off my wall and floated back to her.

Good. Keep picturing that wall. That silver glow around you, protecting you. Nothing can get through, nothing…the thoughts merely bounce off…

Lewis's voice faded. All sound faded. The only noise was the soft roar of the ocean, waves coming in, waves going out. I pushed my elbows under me and sat up on the blanket. The maid was gone. The wall was gone. Even Lewis and my dad were gone. A wonderful peaceful feeling settled around me, warm, comforting, like a blanket. No one existed, I wasn't sure if I existed. And oddly I didn't care.

Peace. I knew complete and utter peace.

I wasn't sure how long I sat there in wonderful, utter silence, but suddenly I felt a touch on my arm, a soft, warm touch. Reality invaded, cold and piercing. The ocean faded, blackness surrounded me. A rush of air brushed past my body, blindingly white stars blurred before me as I raced through space. Suddenly, I slammed against a mental wall.

Jolted, my lashes fluttered up. The walls wavered in and out of focus. I was back in the study. Lewis was sitting beside me, his face tense and serious. "Are you all right?"

Even though he spoke softly, his voice sounded unnaturally loud. "Yeah." I released a shaky breath and looked around. I felt as if I'd just woken from a super deep sleep. Aaron was sitting across from me again, the maid was gone.

"Did I...fall asleep?"

Aaron shook his head. His face was serious too. Nerves got the best of me. I felt like I'd done something wrong.

"No, you were in deep meditation," Aaron explained.

It sounded normal enough, but they were both watching me like I was some specimen in a museum, like they were looking to explain something they couldn't quite understand.

"Oh." I raked my fingers through my hair. I felt shaky, disorientated, as if I'd been thrown into a cold lake. "Was that supposed to happen?"

Aaron and Lewis shared a glance. "Yes, it's been known to."

Yet, they looked odd, unsure. They certainly didn't look happy. My insecurities came roaring back. "What happened? What'd I do wrong?"

"Nothing." Aaron smiled. "It's just..." His smile wavered. "Did you hear anything from the maid? Any thoughts at any time?"

I frowned, trying to remember, but my mind was fuzzy. "I heard Lewis inside my head." I shot him a glance, making sure I was supposed to tell, hoping he hadn't done something he wasn't supposed to. At his nod, I continued. "I remember..." I clawed my way through my murky memories, but it was hard. "I remember the maid coming in. She thought..." I blushed.

Aaron nodded. "Go on."

"She thought we...you...were weird, but she likes her pay."

Aaron laughed softly. "Yes, I know. And then?"

"And then Lewis...he was telling me to concentrate on the waves, on the silver wall."

"And..." Aaron urged me on, but there wasn't really anything to say. "Nothing else after?"

I shook my head. They shared another glance. Okay, they were totally making me paranoid. "What?" I demanded. I couldn't take not knowing any longer.

"Well…it's just that…" Aaron frowned. "The maid was here for a good ten minutes."

"Oh." I cheered up immediately. Why did they look so dour? I thought they'd wanted me to meditate well? "So I did it? I blocked her thoughts?"

Lewis nodded. But they didn't look as thrilled as I felt.

"And then another maid came in. Then, Lewis opened his mind and let his thoughts flow out…." Aaron studied me for one long moment. "You didn't sense or feel any of this?"

Lewis had opened his thoughts? Ugh, I wish I could have heard them. I tried desperately to turn my mind backward, but could remember nothing but the beach. I was starting to feel like a disappointment. I hated that feeling. "No, I didn't sense any of it. Should I have?"

"No." He laughed a merry sound that made me feel somewhat better. "No. It's wonderful."

"It is?" I looked at Lewis for confirmation. He was finally smiling too.

"Your concentration is wonderful. Your ability to block everything…amazing." Aaron shook his head. "If only you'd been taught meditation early on. Hell, if you'd done yoga it would have come out."

He took my hand and helped me to my feet. I still felt a little weak, but his praise gave me strength. "You're doing amazingly well, Cameron. So much better than I'd expected."

I nodded slowly, watching Lewis as he walked toward the windows. He stared outside, as if in deep thought. I couldn't help but wonder what he was contemplating. He seemed upset…or maybe just lost, confused, I wasn't sure.

"I've invited a few people from town, normal people," Aaron said, forcing my attention back to him. "In a few nights there will be a dinner party here."

Normal people? I didn't want normal people here. Normal people had made my life miserable. I wanted to be surrounded by people like me. "Okay."

Surely Aaron heard the reservations coming from my mind, but he didn't seem to care. "And during that party, I want you to try to block their thoughts. Think you'd like to try?"

I shrugged. I wasn't sure, but I didn't want to disappoint Aaron. I slid Lewis a glance. He nodded, as if sensing my unease.

"Sure, I guess."

Aaron smiled, a pride in his eyes that I'd never experienced before. The sort of pride only a father could give a daughter. I liked it more than I wanted to admit. "You'll concentrate, just like you did today. But don't worry, we'll practice more in the next couple days."

"Sure."

He cupped my shoulders and drew me close into a hug. "I'm so proud of you, Cameron."

Warm giddiness swept through my body, this deep sated need that was finally being filled. This is what it felt like to have your parent's approval. I squeezed my eyes shut and dared to hug him back. I knew, in that moment, I'd do pretty much anything Aaron asked.

Chapter 10

Two nights later I dreamt of my mom.

I'd rarely thought about her, forcing my mind to stay in the present. It was too hard to remember, what little memories I held. So the dream was surprising, to say the least. The images that flashed through my mind once I closed my eyes were odd, swirling images of color and emotions that made no sense. Images that confused me. That made me nervous.

The dream started like my meditation exercise and for a moment I thought I was back in Aaron's study. I was sitting on the beach, the sky an odd, hazy gray and orange, as if the sun was setting. The waves roared in, the tide rising, water tickling my bare toes, but I wasn't worried. I was calm, relaxed. I wore a long, blue sundress that wavered on the warm breeze. Sea gulls cried overhead, hovering on the wind. I was alone, but I wasn't afraid.

I glanced away from the softly roaring waves to the sky, brilliant, bright, too bright. Warmth came from not only above, but also to my right. Two suns, one at the top of the sky, the other a fiery ball on the horizon. How odd. I didn't have too much time to think on it before I felt a presence next to me. A shiver over my skin that told me I was no longer alone. My father, I assumed, for he was the one who had come to me first in my meditation. I turned, looking for the intruder. From the gray haze a form stepped closer.

But no. Not Dad.

A woman wearing a long sundress like me. She was a shadow against the brilliant sun. Unidentifiable, but somehow familiar. Slowly, she started toward me. Her long, dark hair fluttered in the wind. I didn't recognize her immediately, my mind was oddly numb. But the moment she settled beside me, everything fell into place. The familiarity of those full, smiling lips, that pert nose, those large eyes. My mom was beautiful. She was young. As young as she'd been the last time I'd seen her, twelve years ago. I knew she must have aged and I knew she wouldn't be here now. And so I realized she wasn't real.

"I missed you." She settled beside me, so close I could see the silver flecks in her blue eyes. So close I could smell the vanilla scent that was only hers. She wasn't real, but my heart didn't realize that. Emotions welled within, a lump that settled painfully in my chest.

"Mom?" I was too confused by her sudden appearance to be surprised. *"Why are you here?"*

She studied my face, as if trying to memorize every detail. *"Because I've missed you."*

I wanted to believe her, but couldn't. No, I wouldn't let her break my heart again. *"But you've never even called."*

Her smile fell. *"I couldn't find you, until now."*

My mind spun with confusion. I wasn't sure where I was, even who I was. I wasn't sure if I could believe her. *"You know…"* I looked around the beach. *"I'm here?"*

She nodded, smiling again. *"I've been looking for you, Cameron. I've been searching for you for so many years."*

I shook my head. I wouldn't let her make me care. I wouldn't let her break my heart again. *"No, no you left me."*

"I did, but it wasn't supposed to be forever." Only sincerity shone on her face. She was tan and healthy, she'd been pale and sickly looking before. How weird.

I wanted to believe her. My heart so badly wanted to believe her, but I knew I couldn't trust her. Grandma had told me that Mom was a druggie. Drug addicts couldn't be trusted. She would never come back for me. I had to let her go.

"No," I whispered. *"You can't do this to me. You can't make me care again."* I turned away from her and stumbled to my feet. Tears stung my eyes. I wouldn't look back. She wasn't real. I started down the beach, my feet sinking into the sand. I was barely aware of the sea gulls squawking their protest as I rushed through their flock.

"Just a dream," I whispered. *"I'm imagining this. It can't be real."*

"Cameron!"

I froze, even as my mind told me to keep going, my body wouldn't listen.

"This time it's different."

I didn't want to believe her, yet I turned, facing her. *"How?"*

"I'm coming for you, I promise."

I tried to pay attention to her words, but sand was falling down around my ankles. I was sinking. *"How strange."*

Sand, warmed from the sunlight, fell and pattered against my legs... faster, higher the sand grew. Confused, I looked up, searching for my mom. Fog was rolling in off the ocean, my mom a mere shadow some distance away.

"Cameron, I will come for you."

"Mom?" But she was fading... fading into the fog and the sand was pouring around me, the mound growing higher... higher... to my knees. I shifted, trying to move. The sand was too thick, too heavy. Panic tightened in my chest. *"Mom!"*

The sand came higher, up to my thighs, those little crystals falling and rolling over themselves as they tumbled down around me. I was sinking...sinking. *"Please! Someone help me!"*

The only response was the sharp cry of the gulls overhead.

I reached out, searching for something... anything to grab onto. The sand rose to my chest. I reached out, clawing at the tiny particles. It was coming higher... higher...

"Please!"

I jerked awake, my entire body jumping on the soft bed. My frantic gaze darted around the dark space as my mind tried to accept the fact that I wasn't being buried alive. The room. I was in my new room. I covered my face with my trembling hands.

My breathing was harsh in the quiet, dark room. It took a moment for my confused brain to work again. Even longer for my heart to stop its mad race.

"Just a dream," I whispered to no one, because no one was here. Not Grandma. Not my dad. Certainly not my mom. How I wished Lewis would hear my silent cry and come for me. But it would be ridiculous to go to him now and wake him because I'd had a nightmare.

I pushed aside the down comforter and settled my feet in the plush carpeting. As much as I wanted to, I couldn't stand. My body was trembling too badly, sweat made my t-shirt cling to my back. Why, after all these years, had I dreamt about my mom? What had the dream meant? Was it just some weird, random scene, or had it been something else... a warning?

But it wasn't real. It wasn't a warning. It was just my messed up head trying to come to terms with the fact that my life was changing dramatically. And yeah, sure, I was a little nervous. After all, I didn't really know Aaron or Lewis all that well and I was in an unfamiliar house. I'm sure it was totally normal to have a nightmare.

My body stopped shaking enough that I managed to stand. The silence of the place had comforted me when I'd first arrived, now it seemed spooky. This huge mansion with the many, many rooms that held who knew what. I grabbed my robe and shoved my arms through the sleeves. The worn cotton offered some warmth. Not that the room was cold. No, but my insides were chilled.

The window panes rattled, the wind fierce tonight. I glanced at the clock on my bedside table.

3 a.m.

Sleep felt as far away as my Mom. I raked my hands through my hair and started toward the bathroom door. The creepy sound of wind whistling through the trees raised the fine hairs on my body and reminded me of the cry of the gulls in my dream. I reached for the bathroom door when I realized the sound wasn't coming from outside, but from my bedroom door. I froze, confused.

Not a whistling, but something high-pitched. A cry. I tightened the belt on my robe and made my way to the door, opening it cautiously. Silence. Had I imagined it?

I stepped into the hall. The sconces that were attached to the walls of the corridor gave the hall a soft glow, just enough light to see.

There it was again!

A high-pitched cry, like the tearing of a soul. I turned right and started down the hall, following the sound. My heart hammered madly, the suspense too much after having had the nightmare. Not the cry of pain, no, the cry of sorrow. A child, crying. My steps hurried, my pulse thundering. I knew there were other children here, but this cry sounded young. Too young.

I turned a corner and stopped short. There, only five feet from me, huddled a small child. He wore pajamas with some sort of super hero on them. His scrawny legs were tucked to his chest, his back to the wall.

"Are you...are you okay?"

His little shoulders stiffened, but he didn't lift his head.

"Are you... lost?" Okay, it was a stupid question. The kid obviously lived here, where as I had just arrived. He probably knew the place better than I knew my cottage back home. "You want me to get Aaron?"

He lifted his head, his brown eyes wide and shimmering with tears. "No," he whispered.

"Sam," someone called from the shadows.

A blonde girl stepped into the light, her white nightgown practically glowing like a ghost. The girl I'd seen from my window the morning after I'd arrived. She reached out and the boy rushed to her side, taking her hand and obviously taking comfort in her presence.

"You're supposed to be in the dorm room," she whispered.

She was only a few inches taller than him, but seemed older. As one, they lifted their heads to look at me and I realized I was staring, my mouth hanging open like an idiot. Immediately, I reached out with my mind, trying to read their thoughts. Nothing. They'd obviously been taught to block them.

They didn't look afraid, but they did seem confused as to how I had gotten there. I was an adult. Well, would be in less than a year according to law, I should say something to make them feel better. "Are you... okay?"

She looked at me for a moment, as if judging my worth. Finally, she nodded. "We're fine." She turned, taking the boy with her, a little mother hen. "You need to go back to bed."

It took a moment for me to realize she was actually talking to me. "Wait!" I started after them.

The girl paused. "Go, Sam." She pushed him gently, until he scurried into the shadows toward the direction where she'd appeared.

"Why was he crying?"

She shifted, clutching her small hands together in front of her and looking completely uneasy. "Homesick, is all." She turned and started after the boy.

Homesick? "But, wait!" She was gone, fading into the darkness. After a few moments her soft footsteps quieted and silence settled in the hall. If he was homesick, why not go home?

"Cameron?"

Startled, I spun around. Lewis stood there looking as confused as I felt. So close I could feel the warmth of his body. His hair was mussed, his eyes half-closed. He wore only athletic shorts, no shirt or shoes and had obviously come from bed.

"Did I wake you?" I asked, embarrassed to be caught, although, why I wasn't sure.

His gaze shifted from me to the dark hall behind me where the girl and Sam had disappeared. "What's wrong?"

Flustered, I wasn't sure how to explain. "Crying," I said, raking my hands through my hair, hoping I didn't look a total mess. "There was a little boy crying."

He frowned and reached out, taking my hand. "They do, sometimes."

I allowed him to lead me back toward my room. "But why?"

He shrugged. "They're sad; they miss their families."

I pulled away from him, too upset to take comfort in his touch. "Are you saying their families are... dead?"

"Some." We paused outside my door. Lewis leaned against the wall. "Some just don't want them because of what they can do."

The words hit home, pierced my chest.

"What is it?" He cupped the side of my face, forcing me to look at him. He had a shadow of whiskers on his cheeks. It made him look older, rugged. Gorgeous.

"Nothing." I forced myself to smile. "I'm being silly."

"Tell me." His palm was warm. So warm, so comforting. He shifted so his body was closer to mine. How I wanted to sink into him!

"It's just... I understand. My mom didn't exactly want me." My mom, and there she was again, hovering on the edges of my world.

His blue gaze grew soft. He grasped my shoulders and pulled me against his warm body. Tossing my nerves aside, I wrapped my arms around his waist and allowed him to hug me tight.

"You don't have to worry about that anymore," he said. "I want you here. We want you here. You're home Cameron. Exactly where you belong."

****

I couldn't sleep after Lewis had left me at my door, which was why, at six in the morning, when it was still dark, yet the morning birds could be heard, I made my way down the hall where I'd seen the blonde girl and Sam disappear. For some reason, this close to dawn, the house wasn't as intimidating. I stuffed my hands into the pockets of my hoodie.

Home. Lewis had said I was home. But this massive mansion didn't feel like home. Not yet. I turned the corner, expecting… I don't know what. But I wasn't expecting more silence, more emptiness. A short corridor, two doors and a narrow staircase that went down to the first floor and up. I looked behind me, making sure I was still alone. Had the children gone down the steps, or up? A few hours ago, it had been too dark to see. It was an old house with one of those massive attics, or so Lewis had said. What could possibly be up there? But it was still too dark and my nerves got the better of me. Maybe Aaron was awake. I swore I could smell the scent of pancakes coming from somewhere below.

I started toward the first floor steps, but something made me pause. An invisible line that practically pulled me toward those stairs leading up to the attic. Slowly, I turned. At the top of those steps was a door. Aaron had told me that his home was mine. Still, I doubted that was a pass for snooping. But what was the harm in looking in an attic? I started up the stairs, each step creaking so loudly I thought surely someone would hear, but no one came running.

When I wrapped my fingers around the ancient looking porcelain handle, I expected the door to be locked, but it opened easily under my touch. As Lewis had said, the attic was huge, running the length of the house. It took a moment for my eyes to adjust to the dark light. Windows lined both long walls, gray squares allowing the dull, morning light to enter. It was your typical attic with boxes and trunks stacked like small mountains around the room. I wondered why Aaron would have so much junk. He didn't seem the hoarder type. Although half the room was in shadows, I felt oddly comfortable here.

Not ready to return to my room, I moved across the creaking floorboards and to the windows. The ocean sparkled below under the quickly fading moonlight. Dawn was turning gray skies a brilliant orange. A few gulls hovered in the air, their screeches high pitched, but comforting in their normalcy. Everything was as it should be, so why couldn't I shake the feeling that something was off?

I started to turn when a whispered warning caressed my skin. Someone was here. My heart slammed wildly against my ribcage. "Hello?" my voice quivered.

A shuffle interrupted the quiet, like mice scurrying from a cat. From behind a pile of boxes a small form stepped into the light. Golden hair glinted under the rising sun coming in through the windows. The girl who had come for Sam. "You," I said, realizing how stupid I sounded, but I was too surprised to care. "I didn't get your name."

She wore a blue woolen dress that came to her knees and white tights. Her hair was pulled into a lopsided ponytail, her long bangs hiding her eyes. My fingers curled as I resisted the urge to reach out and fix her hair. She'd obviously done it herself. I wasn't sure how old she was, maybe seven or eight. Too young to be without a mother.

She didn't look surprised in the least to see me and settled down again, hidden behind her box. "I'm Caroline," she whispered.

I moved around the boxes to see her better. She had an entire little world set up here in this dingy, dusty attic. An old, stuffed bear sat in the corner, his button eyes hanging on by loose threads. She'd propped a box up for a doll house. I supposed most kids would have loved their own little hiding place, but for some reason this just felt sad.

"Hi Caroline, I'm Cameron."

"I know," she whispered, not looking at me as she picked up a little doll. She smoothed its hair from its porcelain face.

"What's your dolls name?" I settled on the ground beside her.

"She's not mine."

"Oh."

"I… found her."

Was she nervous I'd take the toy away? "Well, I'm sure no one will care if you play with her."

"Maybe not." She held out the doll and looked at me expectantly.

"Uh, thanks." I took the toy, cradling it close. I'd never played with toys much as a child. Maybe because I'd had to grow up too fast. I realized, as I held it close, that the doll was old. The lace dress was stained yellow with age. Her pale, porcelain face was crackled, the paint flaking.

"It's the mother and this is the child." She picked up another doll, as old as the first.

"Neat," I said, handing her back.

While she settled them down near their house, I studied her little area. Under the rising sun it was easier to see and I was startled to notice a blanket in the corner of her nook. "You don't sleep here, do you?"

She shrugged, glancing at me through her lashes, as if judging my reaction. "Sometimes, but only if I need to be alone."

"Alone?"

She sighed, her narrow shoulders sinking. "There are so many. Sometimes they cough, or sneeze and they wake me up."

"They? Who?"

"The other's like me. Like you."

Her gaze was so sincere I didn't dare doubt her.

Others? Dear God. I knew there were others, but I figured two, three at the most. "And how many are there?"

She shrugged. "I don't know." She tucked her dolls into their house. "He's awake, you should go."

"He?" I stumbled to my feet. Nervous, although why, I wasn't sure.

"Lewis, he's looking for you."

"Oh." I looked back at the door. I didn't exactly want to be caught snooping. "You know because…"

"I'm like you."

That didn't really explain, but I didn't have time to ask more questions. If I didn't want to get caught snooping, I needed to hightail it out of there. "Well then, I'll see you around."

She nodded, watching me as I made my way to the door.

"Cameron," she called out.

"Yeah?"

"You won't tell? About my secret hiding place?"

I shook my head. "No, promise."

She nodded, looking relieved. Pausing, I rested my hand on the wooden railing, worn smooth with age. I couldn't help but wonder why she didn't want me to tell. Merely because she didn't want other people stealing her hiding place, or because she'd get in trouble? She turned back to her dolls and began to hum some song, dismissing me.

I felt odd leaving her alone, but she'd lived here longer than I had. Maybe Aaron didn't care if she was there. I glanced back one last time, seeing her placing her dolls in their house, then made my way down the steps.

I was out of breath by the time I'd made it to my room. As if sensing me, just as I reached for the handle, Lewis' door opened.

He was dressed in jeans and a t-shirt, his hair no longer messy. He looked perfect, too perfect, and I realized I preferred him rumpled and warm as he'd been last night. His guard down.

"Hey! There you are." He smiled, that dimple flashing and my insides warmed. "I was looking for you." He was watching me curiously.

"In the bathroom," I blurted out. "I...didn't hear you knock."

It was a lie, obviously.

He nodded. "We'll have breakfast, then do some more meditating, if you're up for it."

"Yeah, sounds great." I smiled too and followed him down the hall toward the front of the house.

"Did you sleep well?"

I nodded, but the entire way down that impressive front staircase, I couldn't help but wonder why I'd lied about being in the bathroom. I was only in the attic, it wasn't as if I was working on a plan to take over the world.

Lewis chatted amicably beside me as we made our way toward the breakfast room.

He was cute. He was kind. He cared about me.

Yet, something niggled at the back of my mind, something that made the smile on my face quiver.

I trusted Lewis, didn't I?

Chapter 11

I'd never really had the opportunity to dress up. At last year's prom I had pretended I'd be out of town, partly because I couldn't afford a dress, partly because I was afraid no one would ask me. Hearing about how much fun everyone had had made me wish I'd gone. I'd been planning to go this year. Now…well, I was no longer a student and the realization that I'd miss out on something so major made me somewhat sad. That is until the dress Aaron had bought me for the dinner party arrived.

Instead of prom, I tried to focus on the fact that I was wearing a totally cute dress with a halter type neckline and an A-line skirt that landed at my knees. It was more mature than I normally wore, but not too sexy. When I'd put the dress on, I'd noticed the tag said Louis Vuitton. I was no fashion expert, but I knew expensive clothing when I saw it. Once again I was aware that Aaron had money. But how? From what I could see, he didn't work.

I pulled on my Gucci high heels. Blue, to match the dress. The heels weren't high, but it didn't matter. I wasn't used to wearing dress shoes and for a moment, I wavered on my feet.

"Must be nice."

I spun around, teetering as I did. Olivia stood in the doorway, chewing on a strand of her hair while she glared daggers at me.

I resisted the urge to grimace. I'd only been here a few days and already had an enemy. "What must be nice?" I grabbed onto the post of my bed, regaining my balance.

She slumped against the doorjamb. She was wearing a black sweatshirt and jeans, apparently her normal garb. "I said it must be nice to be Aaron's new favorite toy."

I bristled at her comment. "I don't know what you mean."

She laughed, but didn't look me in the eyes, instead focusing on the floor. "Right."

She was jealous, obviously. I didn't blame her. Aaron was awesome and I was taking his attention away from her. But she probably had no idea that Aaron was practically an uncle, so of course he felt a connection with me. "Listen, Aaron knew my dad…"

Her black eyes darted up to me. "So?"

So I can't help it if you're jealous.

She narrowed her gaze into a glare. "I'm not jealous, for your information." She took a step back. "Just be prepared when he tosses you aside for someone new."

She left me standing there in shock, hugging the bedpost. Surely Aaron wouldn't toss me aside. We were practically related. She was just jealous, I repeated to myself. In fact it made me feel a little good, in a twisted way, that finally someone was jealous of me. Aaron thought of me as a daughter, it was obvious. And little miss dark and dour couldn't stand that.

"You ready?" Lewis appeared in the doorway looking like a model in a magazine.

Butterflies fluttered in my stomach, sighing with oppressed lust, those little sluts. He wore a black suit that made his blue eyes pop. I noticed almost immediately that the blue shirt underneath matched my dress. Had he worn that shirt on purpose? I took my lower lip between my teeth. Dang, he looked great. I was gawking, I realized and quickly looked away.

"Yeah, I'm ready." My voice came out a little breathless. I wished I could read his mind, wished I knew what he was thinking…

He cringed, his hands jerking to his head.

"What is it?"

"Nothing, just…a little headache all of a sudden." He frowned, his gaze piercing mine. "Did you try to read my mind?"

Confused, I shook my head. "I don't think so." I'd wanted to read his mind, but I hadn't, had I? So why was I flushing like I was guilty?

He smiled, but it didn't quite reach his eyes. "It's nothing, it's gone. Come on." He took my hand and I practically fell into him. My body hitting his in an embarrassing display of awkwardness.

"Sorry," I muttered, pushing away. "I'm not used to heels." I blushed at the admission and seeing my red face, Lewis laughed.

"All right, then just hold onto me."

Yes, sir, no problem there. I'd gladly cling to Lewis. I looked down at the carpet and slipped my arm through his, my hand sliding over the smooth, cool material of his jacket. "I didn't realize this would be so formal."

He shrugged and led me into the hall. "We're always kind of formal."

In other words they were rich. Rich people were always formal, at least in my experience. I frowned. "What, exactly does Aaron do?"

"You mean for work?"

"Yes."

He shrugged. "To be honest, Aaron comes from family money. His parents were rich, his grandparents. Railroad, oil, something or another. But don't worry, I mean...no one's a snob or anything."

"Oh, okay." But it wasn't okay. I wasn't used to dressing so fancy, or using more than 3 pieces of silverware at dinner. I'd look like a total dork. Even now I could barely stand in heels. And please, I knew more than anyone how snobby people with money could act.

Lewis rested his hand on mine, drawing my attention to him. He looked confused for a moment, his dark brows drawn together. Our steps slowed as I waited to see what was bothering him. His lips parted as if he was going to say something, but instead he shook his head, remaining stubbornly silent.

"What?" I asked, feeling completely self-conscious. "Why are you looking at me like that?"

He gave me a half-smile, his cheeks flushing. "It's just...I'm not used to reading body signals."

We paused at the top of the steps. "What do you mean?"

He looked away, as if he was suddenly shy. "I'm not reading your thoughts and I meant it when I told you I'd stopped. But...now I'm wondering what the heck you're thinking and I don't like not knowing. Are you flushing because you're nervous? Excited?"

I grinned, relieved his problems weren't anything more serious. "Now you know how I felt when I met you."

We started down the steps slowly, both of us wanting to prolong the moment. "So, I guess we're even then."

I bit my lower lip to keep from grinning. I loved when he teased me and we'd been so serious studying meditation and blocking thoughts the last few days that it hadn't happened often. "I guess so."

"Cameron, Lewis," Aaron called up to us. "You ready?"

I was disappointed that my time with Lewis was over but eager to try my new ability. More eager to impress Aaron. I'd been meditating a few times a day, but still, I felt the tingle of nerves as Lewis and I arrived in the foyer. They treated me like some sort of prodigy. I wasn't complaining…much. It was odd going from being ashamed to proud of what I could do. But I couldn't help but worry I'd disappoint Aaron and then…who knew. He'd toss me from the house in shame? Find a new toy, as Olivia had said?

"You look lovely," Aaron said and kissed my cheek in a fatherly show of affection.

I flushed. "Thanks."

He pulled back, but his spicy cologne lingered around me, comforting in some way. "Now, there are only a few people here, no need to worry. Lewis will help you out."

I nodded, nerves making my stomach churn.

Aaron took my hand, pulling me away from Lewis. "You'll be fine. Just make polite conversation and try to keep that wall in place." He wrapped his arm around my shoulders and led me toward the living room, or parlor as they called it here. I looked back, needing to see Lewis. He smiled at me, his presence giving me strength.

Before we made it into the room, a tall woman in a short, tight black dress came toward us. She didn't seem to have any problem walking in her heels, which were a good inch taller than mine. She was thin with tanned skin and long black hair. Indian? I wasn't sure. She was gorgeous and could've easily been a model. Was everyone here beautiful? I shifted in unease, my stupid insecurities rushing back.

"Cameron," Aaron started. "This is Deborah, she helps around the house, sort of a dorm mom. If you need anything, she'll be happy to help you."

Dorm mom? As if I'd believe that this woman, with her supermodel looks, was a glorified nanny. And how many children were here, anyway? Besides Caroline, Sam and Olivia, I'd met no one else. She smiled, but her dark eyes remained cold. Without a word to me, she leaned closer to Aaron and whispered something I couldn't hear. The way they whispered, the way she slipped her arm through his, I couldn't help but wonder if they were dating. She sashayed away without a goodbye or nice to meet you and I was left to wonder who she really was to him.

Aaron took my arm and pulled me into the room. Lewis had said only a few normal people would be here, but there were at least ten guests gathered in the large room. I swallowed my nerves and pasted a smile upon my face. A rush of thoughts and conversation bombarded my mind. After having gone days in silence, the sudden invasion was almost too much. My skull seemed to expand, my brain aching.

I would have staggered back if Aaron hadn't been holding me upright.

"You all right?" Lewis was suddenly by my side, his face showing his concern.

When he held out his hand, I took it. "Yeah, just not used to all the thoughts. Didn't sleep well last night. I heard someone crying…"

"The wind," Aaron said, smiling. "It's a creepy sound sometimes. But you'll get used to it."

He was lying, or maybe he really thought it was the wind.

Lewis gently squeezed my hand, drawing my attention to him. Stay by me, all right?

I nodded, pushed away from Aaron and made my way into the space. Needing time to gather myself, I looked away from the elegant guests and studied the room where I'd done my meditation exercises with Lewis and Aaron. A fire was crackling warmly in the large stone hearth. The curtains covering the floor to ceiling windows were tied back, showing the quickly setting sun and the expanse of the front yard.

In the background the soft sound of classical piano music played on hidden speakers, combining with the chatter of conversation. I tried to focus on that music instead of the thoughts bombarding me, fighting for attention. Aaron had moved away and was already engaged in conversation with a short, round man with a bald head who reminded me of Humpty Dumpty.

As if sensing my attention, Aaron turned toward me. "Cameron, I'd like to introduce you to Dr. Carl." Aaron was smiling, but his gaze was all business. "He and his wife vacation on the island."

The bald man nodded. "Lovely to meet you." When he held out his hand, I took it automatically. His palm was cold, damp, kind of gross.

I want you to focus on his thoughts, Lewis said. *Dr. Carl is your target.*

Target? Like I was some secret agent. I frowned, barely listening as Dr. Carl and Aaron talked about his plans to return to the mainland. *Doesn't focusing on his thoughts defeat the purpose of blocking them?* I asked.

Lewis grinned, his blue eyes twinkling. *Just trust me. You have to focus on the thoughts first, focus on the person you want to block, before you can start blocking them.*

Okay. I looked at Dr. Carl, focused on his faded blue gaze, the lines at the corners of his eyes, the way his lips were moving, smiling, then frowning, smiling again. He smelled odd, like cologne and old man.

Did I pay the mortgage? Shit, I can't remember, he thought as he took a sip of the champagne he held and glanced around the room. Of course he hadn't a clue his thoughts were entering my mind, punching me over and over in the gut. *Is there enough money in my account? If Karin finds out that I've lost everything she'll leave me. Does she look suspicious? She does, she's frowning...*

A heavy sense of sadness weighed down upon me, sucking the energy from my body. His sadness. His gaze settled on the woman across the room, a woman much younger and better looking than him. His wife Karin. He loved her. But it wasn't a true love he felt, but more like an obsession. She was using him for his money, and he knew it, but didn't care as long as he had her.

"And how are you enjoying your time on the island, my dear?" He glanced at me.

"It's very nice," I muttered, trying to keep up my concentration as well as talk to the man. Aaron drew him back into conversation and I was left blessedly alone.

Okay, Lewis said. *Keep focusing on him, but this time imagine that ocean you brought to mind so well the other day.*

I took a deep breath in, out, in…out. Quickly enough my body began to relax. The room faded, the people and the noise morphed into ocean waves, roaring in and out with the tide. Dr. Carl appeared before me. Instead of his suit, he was sporting a Speedo, his huge gut hanging over the tight swimwear. Why wasn't I surprised in his choice of swimwear? He smiled down at me. I cringed, grossed out.

Be gone, you fool, I muttered and pictured that wall. Those music notes coming from his head bounced away. I laughed. I couldn't help myself. He looked so ridiculous wearing a Speedo while those notes hit him in the head. Soon enough, he faded too and I was left on my ocean island paradise alone. I was free here, in my little mind world, free to relax, free to breathe and hear what I wanted.

A sudden hand on my arm jerked me back into reality. The parlor came harshly into view, the noise of conversation overwhelming.

I blinked up at Lewis, he was frowning. *Only block his thoughts. Keep focused on mine. You're fading completely away. I want you to focus on my thoughts and not anyone else's.*

I rubbed my head, my skull aching some. How? This was more difficult than I'd thought and I was growing quickly frustrated. Since my wall was gone, thoughts came rushing back in and I had to wade through them to find Lewis's familiar voice.

Who do you hear? he asked.

Everyone.

He settled his hand on my back, the warmth of his palm comforting. *Right, so just focus on me, much like you did on that ocean last night. Focus on my thoughts. Not my voice, but my thoughts.*

Startled, I looked up into Lewis's blue eyes. He was seriously going to let me read his thoughts? There was no mirth in his sincere gaze, his face completely serious. I admit the idea had me practically foaming at the mouth. To be able to read his mind, to know what he was thinking.... I felt the subtlest shift, a pressure released, and then heard,

God, she has gorgeous eyes.

I blushed, but didn't look away. My heart was hammering madly in my chest as I realized the importance of this moment. For the first time, I was reading his thoughts. He'd opened up to me, trusted me. It was easy to remain focused on Lewis because I was so interested in what he had to say.

His gaze slipped to my lips.

What does she taste like? Are her lips as soft as they look?

Heart swirled low in my belly. He wanted to kiss me. He was going to try soon. How I wanted him to! In that moment, no one else mattered. No thoughts entered my mind but his. I had total control.

Aaron rested his hand on my arm, breaking me from my concentration. "Ah, and here comes your lovely wife now." He was looking at Dr. Carl, but it was obvious he wanted me to pay attention. Ugh, I didn't want to pay attention to Dr. Carl's lame thoughts. I wanted to know more about Lewis.

Block Lewis and practice on the woman's thoughts. She's coming now. I was surprised to hear Aaron's voice in my head.

My brain was thumping again. There were too many people telling me too many things. I didn't want to know what Dr. Carl was thinking, or his plastic-looking wife. I wanted to focus on Lewis and what he thought about me.

Dr. Carl's wife Karin came sashaying toward us in a tight red dress that showed off every inch of her fake boobs and probably fake butt. I realized this would be Emily five years from now; sexy, beautiful and completely self-centered.

"Hello, darling," she slipped her arm through her husbands and leaned close to him. *I can't believe I have to be here. Ridiculous, talking to children.* Her eyes narrowed ever so slightly on me. *Why is her dress better than mine? How the hell can she afford something like that? Please tell me she's not sleeping with Aaron.*

I almost grimaced at the disgusting thought, but managed to force my lips into a smile. "So nice to meet you," I said with mock sincerity.

Really, Lewis asked. *Is it really nice to meet her?*

I slid Lewis an annoyed glance. He grinned down at me. *You know, I could totally see you two being B.F.F.'s. Slumber parties, braiding each other's hair. You're about the same age.*

I pressed my lips together to keep from laughing. *Would you shut up?*

Ready to try again? Aaron asked, interrupting. Was it my imagination or did he sound annoyed?

I gave a discreet nod and focused on Karin, pushing everyone else's thoughts to the side.

Why doesn't she love me? Pathetic Dr. Carl slipped through the cracks.

How will I pay my bills? Someone else was thinking.

Wonder if this winter will be cold.

Ugh! I took a deep breath in and out, and focused on my beach, on the roar of the waves, while staring blankly at the crowd in the room.

Okay, Lewis's voice broke through my defenses. *Now let's switch. Focus on my voice. Just my voice.*

Then talk to me, I begged. I couldn't do this alone. I needed help. I know they thought I was some genius prodigy, but I wasn't and eventually they were going to realize I couldn't do what they wanted me to do. Might as well be now.

Okay, Lewis started. *I'll talk to you, about you, because you like when I think about you.*

I flushed and looked away from him, taking the cup Aaron handed me, but barely noticing the man. The other voices around me dimmed. Breathe in…out. Focus on Lewis. It was so easy to focus on Lewis.

And? I asked.

And…and I like your laugh. It makes me want to smile.

I bit my lower lip, feeling giddy and warm. I couldn't look at him, afraid I'd break down and throw my arms around his neck. I took a sip of the champagne. I'd tasted alcohol before, but rarely. It was bitter and bubbled oddly on my tongue. I wasn't sure if I liked it.

And, Lewis continued as he gazed casually around the room, *did you know that when the sunlight hits your hair, it has a red tint?*

Red? I jerked my gaze toward him.

He grinned. *I like it. And...I like you.*

I couldn't look away from him. I felt like I was drowning in his blue eyes and I welcomed the death. Vaguely, I knew the entire room had grown silent, no thoughts seeping into my brain. The only sound was my heart beating, his heart beating. I heard no thoughts but his...I'd succeeded and didn't care.

A warm hand suddenly touched my arm. I jumped, glancing up at Aaron. He was smiling down at me, pride shimmering in his eyes as if he'd realized the importance of my success even if I hadn't.

Aaron winked down at me. *I think you deserve a break.* "Would you escort Mrs. Carl to the restroom?"

I set my glass on a side table. "Sure."

"I'll go with," Lewis said immediately.

Aaron seemed surprised, his brows drawing briefly together. But before Aaron could object, Lewis latched onto my arm. I had to give him credit for not cowering under Aaron's obvious disapproval. We started into the hall, Mrs. Carl following.

"I like your dress," I said mostly to make conversation.

She smirked down at me like I was all of five years old. "Of course you do."

I slid Lewis an amused glance.

This place is way nicer than ours. How much longer do I have to stay with Carl? Perhaps I should test Aaron. Of course he's interested in me, but how long before I could move in after divorcing Carl? Aaron obviously has money, I am not going to let some teenager get what I deserve. She slid me a look of disgust after she'd thought those vile thoughts.

Lewis and I shared a glance of disbelief. My God, the woman was arrogant and disgusting. Lewis grinned behind the woman's back, finding her more amusing than repulsive. "Right through this door," he said.

Without a thanks, she sashayed into the bathroom.

I shook my head, turning toward the living room. "What a b—"

Lewis grabbed my hand and jerked me around. "Lewis, what are you doing?"

He started running down the back hall, dragging me with him. I tripped over my heels, passing gawking servants, and laughing so hard I could barely stand. "Lewis! Where are you going? Aaron is waiting for us!"

He shoved open the back door and we stumbled outside. "He won't notice." He paused and I fell into his chest. My legs were weak, my balance off. I wasn't sure if it was because of the heels, or because I was so close to Lewis. Our laughter faded as a sense of solitude wrapped around us. Only us. His face was serious, his gaze warm under the soft glow of the backdoor light.

"You're cold," he said softly.

"I'm all right." Even though I wasn't, I was afraid if I told him I was cold, we'd return to the party. It was freezing and the wind was doing quick work of pulling down my hair from the pins I'd secured it with earlier.

He shrugged off his jacket and placed it around my shoulders, his warmth and scent clinging to the material. It was totally romantic and my heart swelled with the act. He pulled the edges of the jacket closed, at the same time tugging me closer to him. I knew if I looked up into his eyes, he'd kiss me. My heart hammered, warring with my rational mind. *Don't do it,* my mind said. *What if he pushes you away? Screw you,* mind, my heart thought.

I looked up.

For one moment we merely stared at each other. Finally, just as I was getting ready to bite the bullet and kiss him, he lowered his head. My eyes closed and I held my breath, waiting. His lips met mine. A soft kiss, a wonderful kiss. My toes curled in my shoes, my heart jumping madly against my ribs. I'd been kissed before, but never had it felt this…soft, warm, intense.

All too soon, he pulled back, then just as quickly, leaned forward and pressed his mouth to mine again…as if he just couldn't help himself. I wanted to sink into him, to hug him close, to kiss him again and again. When he pulled back the second time, I let him, too shy to ask for more.

He stared at me for one long moment and I wished more than ever I could read his mind. But I didn't dwell on the fact that I didn't know, instead, I savored the quietness of the moment. I savored the feel of his warm hands on my waist while the cold wind bit at my body. I savored the taste of him on my lips.

He smiled down at me, a personal smile, a smile that said we'd shared something amazing. "We should get back inside."

"Yeah," I whispered, knowing our time was up, at the same time knowing that while I was here we'd have plenty of chances to be together. I slid my hand into his, following him into the house.

Chapter 12

There was no one in the breakfast room when I came down the next day. To say I was disappointed would be an understatement. I hadn't had a chance to talk to Lewis since our kiss. Part of me was a little nervous; what if he regretted it? Blamed it on the spur of the moment? Told me I was disgusting and he never wanted to see me again? Another part of me wanted to see him face to face hoping to understand what had happened.

Aaron's breakfast room was as impressive as the rest of the house and although stylish, I wouldn't call it comfortable. A side table held a variety of food placed on silver platters that mysteriously arrived before anyone else did, yet the food was always warm. Piling some eggs and fruit onto a porcelain plate, I settled at the end of a long cherry wood table, and glanced at the many chairs. I felt lonely, staring at those empty seats, sitting in this oddly quiet house. Lewis said the other, younger children were kept in the dorms below, or they'd run rampart through the house. At the moment, I didn't think I'd mind the craziness.

My plate of fruit and eggs was suddenly unappetizing. I was too damn nervous about seeing Lewis to eat. I wasn't wearing my typical zip up hoody. Instead, I'd actually made an effort and was wearing skinny jeans, a green sweater and make up. I'd even left my hair down, allowing it to fall in waves around my shoulders. I hoped I didn't look like I was trying too hard.

"Hey," Olivia came into the room and settled a few chairs from me, pouring a glass of orange juice from one of the pitchers on the table. She was sulking, crouched over her glass like a caveman…or cavewoman. She was wearing black again, a sweatshirt and dark jeans. She didn't look like she wanted to talk, but I couldn't help but be relieved I wasn't alone any longer. My relief quickly gave way to curiosity. How long had she been here? What had happened to her parents?

"Two years." She looked up at me, bringing that lock of hair to her mouth. Under the bright morning light streaming through the open windows behind me, she looked even paler than before, dark circles under her eyes, as if something was keeping her up at night.

I drew my fork through my eggs. "What do you mean?"

"I've been here two years. You were wondering how long I'd been here." She didn't look at me as she answered but picked up her glass and drank.

I frowned. Okay, maybe being alone was better than having company. "It's not polite to read my mind."

She looked at me, her dark brows drawn together in confusion. "Why? Haven't you read minds your entire life? How is it any different?"

"Because...just because it is." I set my fork down, the metal clanging against the porcelain plate. I was annoyed with her because I knew she was partially right. "Lewis doesn't read my mind."

"Aww, Lewis is it?" She laughed, a harsh, sarcastic sound that bit at my nerves. "So you and Lewis are together?"

I flushed, wondering how the heck I'd answer that question. I mean, we'd kissed, but it wasn't like we were registering for his and hers towels. And even as I thought the words I flushed with embarrassment, knowing she now knew.

"You don't have to answer." She sipped her orange juice and smirked at me over the rim of her glass. "You think you're the first one Lewis has led on?"

Her words hurt, but even as I cringed, I forced myself to focus on the fact that she was jealous. After all, how often could Lewis really date when he lived on an island with a total population of three? "Listen, I get it, you were the only female here for a long time..."

She laughed again. "You think I'm jealous?" She shook her head and stood, her movements jerky and stiff. "I'm warning you because I'm nice. You're a pretty, new toy and just like all toys, he'll grow bored with you."

Anger replaced my hurt. "If it's so bad, why are you still here?"

She shrugged and picked up that damp lock of hair, leaving her glass on the table. "Free room and board. Besides, I've no place else to go." She slipped that lock of hair between her lips, chewing on the strand as she left me sitting there alone.

Perfect start to the day. I took a bite of eggs, barely tasting the food. I wanted to ignore her remarks, but they bothered me. Not only had she implied that Aaron was using me, but that Lewis was going to dump me for the next available girl who came along. She was wrong, just jealous. Yet…what if she wasn't? How well did I really know Lewis or Aaron?

"Hey." Lewis appeared in the doorway as if I'd conjured him. Wearing a blue vintage t-shirt that matched his eyes and dark jeans, he looked totally hot. Way too hot for me. I didn't know if I wanted to throw my arms around him or cry. God, Olivia was right.

"Hey," I muttered, dropping my gaze to my plate.

He moved to the chair right next to mine and plucked a grape from my plate. His warm, clean scent swirled around me, turning my insides to mush. Screw Olivia, what did she know about anything? His hair was damp, as if he'd just taken a shower. He looked and smelled so good I had to curl my hands on my lap to keep from reaching out to him.

"About…last night."

Surprised, I stiffened. Was he really going to bring up the kiss? I held my breath and waited, part of me anxious the other half terrified.

"I…We…" His cheeks flushed and his thick, dark lashes lowered as he stared at the tabletop.

Please don't say it was a mistake, please don't say it!

"Will you go out with me?" He looked up, sincerity in his gaze. "I mean, on an actual date." He smiled and my heart did an odd flip. "We can't really leave the island, but there's a nice restaurant—"

"Yes," I blurted out.

His smile widened and he grabbed another grape. "Good. Tonight then?"

I nodded, too giddy to talk. Olivia had been wrong, the little witch.

We didn't speak, merely sat there, staring shyly at each other. I wasn't sure how long, but it seemed like it hadn't been nearly long enough when Aaron suddenly appeared, totally ruining the mood. He was smiling like always, but when he saw us sitting so close, his smile wavered. I scooted back from Lewis, embarrassed, although why I wasn't sure. It's not like we'd been doing it on the table.

"Lewis, can you leave us for a moment?" Aaron asked.

My heart plummeted. This couldn't be good. Lewis slid me an unreadable glance then stood and left the room. I gritted my teeth, resisting the urge to call out and beg him to stay.

Aaron took Lewis' vacated seat, his face fatherly serious. "Listen, I know you and Lewis have something going on."

Heat shot straight to my cheeks. "Did Olivia tell you?" I demanded a little shrilly.

He brushed his hand through the air, dismissing my comment. "No, I…I read it, you don't keep your thoughts to yourself very well."

Not the first time I'd heard that. I frowned, dragging my fork through my eggs. Oh God, what else had he read? I guess I'd known all along that he could hear my thoughts, but I hadn't really figured he would. I sure as hell hadn't liked it when Grandma read my mind and I didn't want Aaron to either.

He rested his hand atop mine, stilling my movements. "I know you like Lewis, but I think you need to take things slow."

My gaze jumped to him. Was he seriously having a father daughter moment with me? I had the sudden urge to glance back to make sure he wasn't talking to someone else. It was an odd feeling, like I was watching a play. It was certainly something I'd never experienced before. My annoyance and embarrassment gave way to curiosity. I was like some anthropologist, trying to decipher how monkeys lived in the wild.

He released his hold and leaned back in his chair. "I just think you're young. There are other things you need to focus on, like school and…" He stood and paced, obviously nervous. I smiled, having the sudden urge to laugh. This is what girls at school complained about? I found it rather…endearing. "And your abilities. And…"

"Okay," I readily agreed. After all, it's not like Lewis had asked me to be his girlfriend or anything. We hadn't even been on a date…yet. I smiled at the thought of going out with him tonight. What would I wear?

Aaron arched a brow. "A date?"

I flushed and looked at my plate, trying to dampen down my annoyance. Aaron cared about me, I should be flattered. But I wasn't. "Just one."

He sighed. "All right. Fine."

I grinned, hiding it by taking a drink of my water.

He rested his hands on his hips and looked at me, all stern-like. "But be back by ten."

"Okay." I picked up a slice of red apple, unsure how to continue. I'd never had a curfew. Grandma pretty much let me go wherever I wanted whenever. As long as she knew about it.

"Well then." He started toward the door.

"Aaron?"

He turned and looked at me. Was that nerves that made his face all tight? Or was something else worrying him? "Yeah?"

I looked at the tabletop, wondering how to say what I wanted to say without offending him. "I don't…I mean…is there a way for you not to read my thoughts?"

He frowned, silent for a moment. The grandfather clock in the corner of the room ticked the seconds by. "You don't like the invasion?"

"Would you?" I asked bluntly. When he didn't respond, I quickly continued, afraid I'd pissed him off. "It's just that my Grandmother read my thoughts and it drove me nuts."

He leaned against the door jamb and stroked his chin thoughtfully as if the idea that I might be offended over his intrusion had never crossed his mind. "I understand." A smile spread across his mouth. "Sure, I can do that. But actually, before I forget, I'm here for another reason too. You have a lesson today."

My embarrassment gave way to excitement. I pushed away from the table, standing. "Oh, okay." I was eager to learn more, whatever it was he had to share. "What about?"

"Ironically, how to block your thoughts."

"Are you serious?"

He winked. "The most important thing you'll learn." He took a step back. "Now, eat up. It's going to be a long day."

****

"We call it lockdown," Aaron explained.

"Lockdown?" I was settled on the floor again, sitting cross-legged. Aaron sat across from me, and Lewis was sitting a few feet back. It was hard to concentrate with him in the room, at the same time, he was the one who could make me focus like no other.

"Whereas before to block others' thoughts you projected out, pushing their thoughts away, this time you'll project in, pulling your thoughts toward you. So the wall won't be pushed out, but pulled in, close to you. A steel wall."

I tried to concentrate on Aaron's words, but felt off today. Was I excited about tonight's date, or was it Olivia's warning ringing through my head? It was an odd jumbled mixture of highs and lows and now that I had time to sit and think, I found her annoying comments were pushing to the forefront.

"Cameron," Aaron's deep voice shook me from my thoughts.

I blinked up at him. "Yeah?"

He leaned forward, his blue eyes twinkling with laughter. "Are you listening?"

I flushed. Crap, he was reading my mind. He'd warned me he would for this lesson only. "Yes, yes of course."

He smiled, knowing very well I hadn't, but being too polite to call me out. "Good. Now then, close your eyes."

I did, but the moment I closed my eyes, I thought of Lewis. The other night flashed to mind. Lewis grinning at me. Lewis pulling me toward him. Lewis pressing his lips to mine...

"Cameron," Aaron's sharp voice was my second warning.

"Sorry," I muttered, even as my face grew horrifyingly hot. *Concentrate, concentrate.* Right. Sure, I could concentrate.

Thunder rumbled menacingly outside, rattling the glass in the windows, so easily drawing my attention. *Concentrate. Concentrate on the thunder.* Our little cottage would be freezing right now, wind seeping in through the windows. Was Grandma warm? Or was she being stubborn and keeping the temperature at 65 degrees because she didn't want the heating bill to be high?

Concentrate, Aaron's voice whispered through my mind. "I'm going to count backwards from five. Just keep breathing. Five."

I released a breath. A storm was coming. I could practically feel the energy in the air. I imagined the waves crashing against the shore, could practically feel them pummeling the island.

"Four."

Concentrate. Breathe in and out.

"Three. You're feeling very relaxed. Two. And one."

Aaron paused as I took in a deep breath, my body oddly weightless.

"You're in a room," Aaron's voice was soft, calming. I'd grown used to that deep voice. Almost as used to the tone as I was to my own. "The walls are steel, metal. But you're not afraid. You feel safe in this room. Do you see it?"

I was in the room. It came unbidden to mind, not forced, and easily accepted. It was coming so quickly now, this meditation thing, as if I'd always done it.

"Nothing can get into this room. No one can hurt you when you are in this room."

The warm sensation of peace settled around me. Slowly, the imaginary me turned around, studying the steel area. It had soft carpet, a big fluffy couch, but no doors and no windows. For some reason that didn't bother me. I settled on that couch, sinking into the cushion. I imagined feeling safe, protected. I could hear the thunder and wind outside, but it didn't reach me. Nothing could reach me.

"Now think of those walls as being completely steel. Think of your own mind as steel, as impenetrable. Nothing can get through your mind unless you let it. Pull your thoughts in, hug them close to you. They're in that room with you. Can you see them?"

I breathed deeply and did as he said. I thought of Lewis. He appeared inside the room with me. Easy peasy. My many other thoughts weren't so quick to catch. They flittered and floated around me like a thousand butterflies on the wind.

Did Lewis really like me?

Did Aaron?

Was I doing well here?

How was Grandma?

Did anyone at school miss me?

Each thought fluttered around me, annoying and persistent. I jumped up, grabbed hold of one butterfly and held it close; a tiny, white butterfly nestled on my palm. An odd, calming sensation settled over me like a warm blanket. There was a soft swoosh, like a falling star, then another and another. Suddenly, the butterflies danced around me, landing softly all over my body, their delicate wings tickling my exposed arms and neck.

"Think of something…anything," Aaron's voice intruded.

My father came unbidden to mind. I saw him as I'd seen him in the photo. Young and happy, full of life. But seeing him didn't thrill me as it had before. My sadness weighed down, heavy and suffocating. I'd never met him, never truly know him, and never would.

"Hold that thought," Aaron whispered.

I did, kept thinking of my dad, even though it depressed me, even though there were a million other things I'd rather think about. My room shook slightly, sending me stumbling off balance. I frowned, glancing up at the walls, but they were still there. What had just happened?

"Do you feel it?" Aaron asked. "The ever so subtle pressure of my mind delving into yours?"

The room shook again, sending me stumbling backwards. Almost immediately I felt an odd pulling sensation on my body, as if someone was inside me, moving, tugging at my brain. I froze, standing my ground. My heart hammered madly in my chest as I waited for what would happen next.

A crackle of electricity branched across the ceiling. The lightning burst anew, reaching out and stabbing me. Fire exploded inside my body. I gasped, stumbling back. I'd been shocked, the tingling sensation was still there. I was under attack. The walls suddenly disappeared and I was surrounded by empty blackness, floating in nothingness.

"Aaron!" I screamed.

That's me, Cameron, Aaron warned. *I'm in.*

Frustrated, I wanted to give up, but my pride wouldn't let me. I felt my thoughts burst into the universe, like stars flying past me. It felt good to let go, as if a pressure had been released. Yet, I scampered to pull those thoughts back to me, knowing I needed them.

"Now, I want you to push me away, push me out of your universe and throw up those walls."

And if I didn't, would there be more pain? I gritted my teeth, rolling my shoulders to relax my body. Keeping my eyes shut, I gave up on trying to recapture my thoughts; those damn stars were long gone. Instead, I pictured my steel room. The walls appeared.

"Good, you've set up the walls again; you're keeping your thoughts inside. Now keep your thoughts close."

I looked around my room. Same metal walls. Nothing out of the ordinary…except for the little girl who was sitting on the couch. Startled, I stumbled back a step.

Hi, Caroline whispered, watching me with those large, knowing eyes.

I froze, Lewis and Aaron forgotten. *How'd you get in here?*

She plucked at the hem of her green dress and shrugged. *Will you visit me again?*

"Keep your eyes closed and relax," Aaron interrupted our conversation and I realized that he had no idea this child was here. "I'm going to try to break through your walls. No matter what, do not let go of your thoughts."

No, wait, I muttered. But Caroline had disappeared. *Damn.* I spun around, looking for her. I even tried to imagine her in that room. It didn't work. Then I felt it and I had no more time to dwell on the girl…that subtle pressure that said Aaron was attempting to break through.

Picture the walls, Lewis said, his voice urgent. *Push against those walls.*

So I did. I pictured that steel room, those steel walls. I felt the tentative push on my brain, the slight shock of someone trying to invade. Panicked, I rushed to the closest wall, settled my hands on the cold steel and pushed back. An odd tingling sensation rippled up my arms, electricity branching through my body. I bit my lower lip, squeezed my eyes shut and pushed back. A cold sweat broke out on my forehead. My arms were trembling. A sharp pain pierced my head. It was too much. All too much. My knees folded.

"Hold it," Lewis urged, speaking to me out loud, his voice so demanding, I didn't dare refuse.

I squeezed my eyes more tightly shut and focused on that room, focused on the walls, focused on my trembling arms pushing back. Hot tears stung my eyes and I had to bite my lower lip to keep from crying out. The pain pulsed through my body, streaming through my veins, an electrical burning sensation that ate at my flesh.

"She's had enough," I vaguely heard Lewis say.

I ignored his words, tried to stay focused on those walls. I couldn't fail. If I failed, they might send me back. I felt Aaron pushing; I knew it was him now. Sweat trailed down my temples. I felt this insane desire to win, to prove to myself and to them that I was the prodigy they seemed to think I was.

"She's in pain," Lewis snapped.

True, but I didn't care. Besides, I'd had worse headaches. Perhaps I should have been grateful he was concerned about me, but I wasn't. I wanted to prove my worth and I didn't want him screwing it up. So I ignored the pain and I tried to ignore Lewis.

I took in a deep breath, gritted my teeth and with an internal roar, I pushed as hard as I could. The pressure gave way instantly. The shock moved from my body and I was left cold, alone in my steel room. For a moment it felt as if I floated. Then I heard the cry. Not in my mind, but outside my body. Shocked, I jerked from my dreamland and dove back into cold reality.

I opened my eyes, my breathing harsh. The room wavered in and out of focus. For a brief moment, I wasn't sure where I was; I wasn't even sure who I was. There was a movement across from me and it all came rushing back.

Aaron lay on his back, staring up at me with wide, unblinking eyes. His face was pale, sweaty. For a horrifying moment I thought he was dead.

"My God," he whispered. "That was…"

"I'm sorry." I crawled toward him, my body too weak to walk. "Did I hurt you? I'm so sorry."

He laughed, sitting upright. "No. Don't be sorry." He paused for one long moment, breathing as harshly as I was. "That was unbelievable. I wasn't using full strength, but close."

Tucking his feet underneath him, he stood, his body trembling with the movement. I jumped to my feet, searching the dark room for Lewis. He stood back in the shadows, his face unreadable.

"Seriously, I'm so sorry," I said, hoping he believed me.

"Don't be. Are you kidding? That was amazing." Aaron looked at Lewis, but Lewis was looking toward the windows. "Did you see that?"

"How much did it hurt?" Lewis asked, ignoring Aaron and glancing back at me.

I pressed my hands to my temples. They were thumping slightly, but it wasn't unbearable. The numbness in my body had given way to an odd shimmering current. "I'm okay. Just a slight headache." Is that why he was frowning?

"You sure you're okay?" he asked.

Aaron laughed and thumped Lewis on the back. "She's fine, in fact, she's great."

He clasped my shoulders. "I knew it; I knew you'd be just like your father."

Shockingly, he pulled me close for a tight hug. Although I should have been embarrassed, I liked his affection, craved the attention like some pathetic druggie.

I sank into his body. And I wanted to be thrilled, I should have been thrilled, but when I looked over Aaron's shoulder, I saw that Lewis was still frowning.

Was he jealous? Worried? Or was there something more to that dark look?

Chapter 13

The drive to town seemed to take forever, every moment lasting an eternity. I wasn't sure what to talk about and apparently neither was Lewis as we remained awkwardly silent. I still had a little bit of a headache, but the thrill of being on a date overrode the pain and I didn't want to be home right now.

"You're doing really well, Cam," Lewis said, finally breaking the silence.

I smiled, but I didn't want to talk about my abilities or lack thereof. Besides, if I was doing so well, why had he looked so dour after I'd thrown Aaron on his butt? "Thanks."

No, I didn't want to talk about me, and I didn't want to talk about Lewis's odd reaction. I couldn't stand the thought that he might be jealous of my powers. There was only one thing I wanted to know about and that was Lewis himself. I wasn't sure where he'd come from, who his family was, nothing. Of course I couldn't read his mind, so that didn't help.

"Headache?"

"Huh?"

He looked pointedly at me and I realized I'd been rubbing my temples. I lowered my hands to my lap. "Maybe a little."

He shrugged, slowing the car as we entered town. The street lights flashed across his face. Was it my imagination or did he look a little pale? "When I first learned how to block my thoughts I'd get headaches."

My interest piqued. I knew Aaron had taken him in, but at what age had he started training? "Oh, yeah?"

"It will get better soon." He stopped in front of a large Victorian inn and restaurant. The place was glowing with lamplight, behind it the setting sun sent brilliant orange rays across the bay. It was gorgeous. Romantic. So, why was I suddenly uneasy to be here with him?

Because while stepping out of the car, the cool night air tugging at my hair and the skirt of my dress, I remembered this was a date…a real date. I hadn't been on a date in forever. During my junior year, I'd started going out with my first real boyfriend. A month later, when he'd realized he wasn't going to get laid, I'd heard he was going to dump me. So I dumped him first. To be honest, I'd only gone out with him so I could double date with a friend. But it still stung. Now…my God, now I was on a date with a guy who actually liked me. Then again, if what Olivia said was true, he only liked me for now…until the next woman came along.

His warm hand rested at the small of my back as we made our way up the wide wooden steps to the restaurant. Only a few people were in the building, most tourists having gone to dry land for the winter season. The inside lobby had a large antique desk. Flowered wallpaper decorated the walls and a golden chandelier dangled from above. Yep, definitely a date.

"Lewis!" A gorgeous hostess wearing a short black skirt rushed forward with a ready smile on her face. Startled, I stepped aside. She gave Lewis a tight hug and Olivia's annoying comment came roaring back.

You think you're the first one Lewis has led on?

I stood there awkwardly as they talked about where Lewis had been. He brushed off her comment with an answer about visiting friends on the mainland. I had to resist the urge to push myself between them and say, "Here I am!"

It seemed like an eternity before he finally looked at me. "This is Cameron." He took my hand, pulling me forward.

She seemed sincere when she smiled and her thoughts were only pure friendship. Her kindness made me feel somewhat better. It didn't last. "You want your usual table?"

Usual? In that he came here often… with other girls? This date was quickly turning into a nightmare and the worst part was that I knew I was being ridiculous.

"Yeah, near the windows."

He led me toward the back of the restaurant, a large open area that had obviously been added onto the building at a later date. He was still smiling, completely oblivious to the fact that I'd turned into a silly, jealous girl. And I was being silly, I knew that, but I couldn't seem to stop myself. He pulled out a chair for me, the perfect gentleman. The chatter in the room was a soft murmur that I barely heard, I was too intent on knowing what Lewis was thinking, secretly hoping his wall would slip and a thought would seep out. I know, I was pathetic.

"I love this spot," he said. "You can see the bay, the boats coming in, the sun setting. Perfect."

"Yeah." I swallowed hard and looked out the large floor to ceiling windows, but the beauty of nature was completely lost on me. "You come here often then?"

He shrugged, unconcerned by my question. "There aren't many other places to go on the island."

I suppose he was right. But Olivia's comment was still there, taunting me. Why was I letting her get to me? But I knew why, because deep down I couldn't believe that someone like Lewis would really like me. God, I was no better than Annabeth. I'd been playing second fiddle to Emily for way too long. It had destroyed my self-confidence.

An older woman dressed in black with a white apron took our orders, leaving us with a basket of bread. The moment she left, Lewis leaned across the table.

"So," he said, staring at me intently. "What's wrong?"

"Nothing," I replied a little too quickly.

He nodded slowly, but I could see he had his misgivings. "You sure?"

I unfolded the white napkin wrapped around my silverware. "Yeah, fine." I laughed, but it came out sounding a little manic. Olivia had turned me into a crazy woman, which is probably what she was hoping to do. "Where's your family?"

He blinked, surprised by the sudden change in topic. Good, I wanted to catch him off guard. "Ummm, dead."

I wanted to sink to the floor with mortification. I was such an idiot. "I'm so sorry."

He shrugged and looked out the windows again. "I was young, it's been a long time."

I played with my cloth napkin, heat rushing to my cheeks. I'd never felt more horrible, yet I had this odd, totally inhumane desire to ask more. I felt this frantic need to know everything I could about him. Maybe not everything, just his deepest darkest secrets. I guess I hoped the more I knew, the closer we'd be. "How'd it happen?"

He looked at the wooden tabletop, taking his own napkin and placing it on his lap. He didn't say a word and didn't look like he wanted to speak. His reaction left me cold.

"You don't have to talk about it. I'm sorry I brought it up."

He shook his head. "No, it's just…" He looked at me, his gaze so warm and intense that my heart skipped a beat. Yet there, in the back of his eyes, lurked something more… secrecy.

"What?" I asked.

"It happened the same time your father died."

I hadn't been expecting that and for one long moment I merely stared at him, wondering if I'd misheard. "How?" I whispered.

He lifted his glass of water. *Your father, my parents were being used. They didn't want to be used anymore. They decided to break out of the S.P.I. encampment, along with a few other people. Our parents didn't make it.*

Why did I have a feeling there was more to this story? More he wasn't going to tell me at the moment? But why would Lewis keep secrets from me?

He smiled, but it didn't quite reach his eyes. "Don't worry about it, okay? We're protected. Safe. They can't get to us."

"But where have you lived all this time?"

He sighed, realizing I wasn't going to shut up. I probably should have, but I couldn't help myself. "First with an uncle, then when he died, Aaron came for me. I was eight when I moved here."

"You've been here since you were eight?" He nodded and I continued with my third degree. "What about schooling?"

"I home schooled."

It sounded lonely to me, stuck on this island as a child. "And college?"

He shrugged. "Why go to school when I have the ability that I have?"

I didn't see what reading minds had to do with college and getting a decent job, but was waylaid from asking more when the waitress arrived with our plates. On the way to the restaurant I'd been starving, now I could barely think of food. There were too many thoughts, too many questions rushing through my head. But foremost was the fact that our parents had died together. We were like some sort of weird retelling of Romeo and Juliet in which we survived and our families died. I could certainly understand Lewis' need to see S.P.I. pay for what they'd done. Although I hadn't truly known my father, even I felt the need to avenge his memory.

I lapsed into silence as we ate our food. As ridiculous as it sounded, I couldn't help but wonder if we were destined to be together. I felt connected to Lewis like I had with no other. But did he feel the same way? Or was I just another girl in a long line, as Olivia implied.

"Lewis!" As if the Universe was playing some cruel prank on me, a young woman came rushing toward us. She didn't have trouble walking in her high heels and slinky black dress. Her hair was as red as the lipstick she wore. Lewis stood as she reached the table. He didn't look ashamed or embarrassed when she threw her arms around him. He sure as heck didn't push her away, as I'd been hoping.

"When did you get back?" she asked.

"Few days ago."

She pulled away, not bothering to glance at me. "Thank God, it's been so boring with you gone."

Heat slowly burned my cheeks as realization dawned. While I'd lived on the mainland, wasting away because no one understood me, Lewis had been perfectly happy here. He had friends and a life, while I'd been living this pathetic half-existence. It didn't seem quite fair.

"Call me soon," she said. "We need to go out."

"Sure." Lewis settled back in his chair and the girl flounced away. He hadn't even introduced me. I dragged my fork through my rice, staring hard at my plate. I would not cry. I was being irrational, ridiculous. I refused to be another Emily.

He slid me a glance. "You're thinking something again, something I can't hear, but I can see it on your face."

I forced myself to laugh. "No, nothing."

He was silent for a moment, so silent that I worried about what he was planning next. "I don't date a lot. I don't come here with a long line of women."

The blood drained from my face. I felt cold. Then just as quickly, heated embarrassment rushed through my body. "I…how'd you know?"

"Your thoughts—"

"You said you weren't reading my thoughts!" I realized I said that a little too loudly and glanced around to make sure we hadn't been overheard.

"I stopped blocking when I thought you were controlling yours. But they're slipping through your defense." He seemed frustrated, disappointed in me.

Well, screw him. I started to stand, embarrassed, humiliated. "I'm leaving."

"What?" *Unbelievable. Why are girls so irrational?*

I froze, shocked by the sudden invasion of his thoughts into mine. My God, did he even realize his thought had slipped out? The question quickly gave rise to the realization that he thought I was irrational. I'd had to watch him practically make out in front of me with two other girls and he was annoyed with me?

I tossed my napkin to the tabletop and pushed open the closest door. I found myself on a boardwalk that led to the beach. The air was chill, the wind bitter. I'd freeze out here, but couldn't seem to care at the moment. My heels sank into the sand as I made my way to the shore. Too much. I kicked off my shoes. It was all too much, too soon. God, what was wrong with me?

"Cameron!" Lewis was coming after me.

I didn't want him to. I wanted to be alone. I wanted…I didn't know what I wanted. I sank onto the sand, pulled my legs to my chest and rested my head on my knees. A tear slipped down my cheek, then another and another. God, I was crying and I couldn't seem to stop. It was supposed to be the perfect date. But then Olivia had ruined it, and those girls had hugged Lewis, making me doubt him. He'd practically ignored me. The worst part was realizing that my dad…his parents…they'd been murdered together. Knowing the facts made it too real, all too…real.

My dad had died.

"Cam," Lewis settled beside me, his body touching mine. He was warm and I had to resist the urge to sink into him. "What's wrong?"

"Nothing. I don't know." I stared at the sand, too embarrassed to look up at him.

I didn't know how to explain my tears because I wasn't sure why I was crying. He'd think I was insane...then again he probably already did. I took in a deep breath and lifted my head, staring at the ocean. The sun had almost set, the water growing dark. He couldn't read my features, couldn't see the tears. The darkness gave me courage. I closed my eyes and opened my mind, taking down that steel wall Aaron had taught me to build.

My dad is dead. I'm afraid of my powers. What if Lewis is using me?

The thoughts tumbled from my mind, into the dark world, into his mind. I felt his body stiffen. I knew he'd heard my thoughts and for a moment I regretted being so open. I turned my face away, too embarrassed to look at him directly.

Lewis was silent for a long moment. He didn't say a word, nor did he open his mind to me. I closed my eyes and closed my mind. I'd told him what he needed to hear. No need to let him know how utterly humiliated I was at the moment.

"I guess it's normal," he finally said, "for you to be afraid. It's all new to you. You didn't realize what you were capable of."

I nodded slowly, so relieved he was talking to me, at the same time leery of what he'd say. He wrapped his arm around my shoulders and I sank into his side, soaking up his warmth. "I vaguely remember when I came here. It was...overwhelming. I was younger, it was easier for me to handle it."

I drew my fingers through the sand, the gritty bits clinging to my skin.

"And as for your dad...I'm sorry."

Of course he was, and of course he knew exactly how I felt because he'd gone through it. "How'd they die?" I dared to look at him.

He swallowed hard, staring out at the dark waves. I wasn't sure if I'd gone too far, if perhaps he'd change the subject. But finally he looked down at me.

"I was there right before it happened."

My heart stopped. The pain I felt for him was almost unbearable. Compassion took hold of my chest and squeezed.

"They worked for S.P.I., supposedly. We're still not sure if S.P.I. is even a legitimate branch of the government. But anyway, they were draining them. That headache you have is nothing compared to what they experienced. One night they decided to break out. But S.P.I. found out. While they were escaping, they were captured."

I rested my head on his shoulder. I didn't need to know more, but I did wonder how much he'd seen. I prayed he hadn't been there when his parents died.

"Cam," he said softly. "I didn't introduce you to that woman because she's worse than Emily."

Relief was sweet. "Oh."

"When I see her, she always tells me to call her, I never do. She's a fake and it's easiest just to play along."

Wonderful, he'd read those thoughts as well. Still, I smiled, the tension in my body easing some.

"The hostess who checked us in is dating a friend of mine; that's how I know her."

Heat shot to my cheeks. Okay, maybe I shouldn't have let him read my mind. I was beginning to look like a total idiot.

"And Olivia…she's…I don't know."

But I did. She was jealous. Just as I'd assumed, so why didn't I go with my gut? Why had I let petty insecurities get the better of me? "I'm sorry," I sighed. "I hate not knowing what you're thinking. I'm not used to it, you know?" I looked up at him and he nodded.

"I've felt the same about you. I don't have a clue what you're thinking and it's frustrating as hell and interesting at the same time."

I grinned, a teasing smile. "You find me interesting?"

He smiled back, reaching out and tucking a loose lock of hair behind my ear, letting his fingers trail down the line of my jaw, light as a feather. "Yeah, you could say that."

I rested my hand on his drawn up knees, turning to get closer to him. "If you want to know something about me, just ask."

The wind ruffled his hair, and his gaze dropped to my lips. "You'll answer? No matter what the question is?"

"Sure," I said, wondering if I'd regret my ready reply.

"Well, I've been wondering…" He leaned closer to me, his mouth next to my ear, his breath warm on my skin. "If you liked our kiss."

Heat swept through my body. I couldn't believe he even had to ask that question. I was blushing, but fortunately it was too dark to tell. At least I hoped it was too dark. I didn't want to seem like some inexperienced loser.

He pulled back and looked directly at me. "Well?"

"Yes." I smiled. "I liked it, very much."

He drew his finger down the side of my face, a gentle touch. A buoy dinged somewhere out on the ocean, an eerie, magical sound. "And would you mind, very much, if I kissed you again?"

My heart squeezed. "No, I don't think I would."

He grinned as he leaned closer to me. Before his lips touched mine, he paused, his breath warm on my lips. Savoring the moment, I closed my eyes. An unsteady heartbeat later, I felt him lean into me and then his lips met mine.

His mouth was warm, firm. Lovely. His arm tightened around my shoulders, drawing me closer to his chest, while his other hand cupped the side of my face. I wanted to touch him, to pull him even closer, to do anything possible to keep him from moving away. I slipped my hands up his chest, my palm lingering over his heart, the beat steady and strong. My entire body tingled, from my toes to my fingertips. When his tongue slipped across my bottom lip, I shivered. I could kiss him forever.

"Well, how sweet. Young love," the unfamiliar voice was like a foghorn.

Lewis jerked back, his breathing harsh. His narrowed eyes were focused on some point behind me. Startled, I spun around. A man stood near the shore, only feet from us. It was too dark to make out his features, but I could tell he was older, maybe Aaron's age. He wore a dark suit and a smirking grin. My shock gave way to embarrassment. Slowly, Lewis stood, taking my hand and pulling me to my feet.

"How are you, Lewis?" the man asked. His gaze slid to me. "And who is this?"

Watching him warily, I swiped the sand from my clothes.

"No one you need to be concerned with." Lewis' grip stung almost as much as his words. I tried not to take his tone to heart. I knew he was upset, although why I wasn't sure.

He started up the dune, tugging me along. I had just enough time to pull on my shoes. His steps were fast and hurried, determined. In my heels, I could hardly walk, let alone at his pace. Stumbling, I glanced back. The man was following.

"Why the hurry?" he asked, his long legs easily catching us.

Who is he? I demanded, asking Lewis with my mind.

He didn't respond.

"Lewis," I tried speaking out loud. Still, he didn't answer, but merely stared straight ahead, as if I wasn't there, as if the man following wasn't there.

"Running away only makes you look guilty," the man said.

Guilty? What the hell was going on? Lewis stopped on the deck. I ran into his back, my face pressing to his hard shoulder. For one long moment he didn't say a word, then slowly he turned. He didn't look down at me, but kept his hard gaze focused on the man in the suit. He was pale with brown hair, I could see that now under the lights from the restaurant.

"What do you want Rodgers?" His hand was tight in mine, his anger palpable.

Rodgers smiled, his thin lips and wide nose stretching. "You remember my name, I'm honored."

"Cut the bullshit," Lewis snapped.

I stepped back, surprised by his hard tone. I'd never really seen Lewis angry, I'd rarely heard him curse. It confused and worried me more than I wanted to admit.

"Now, now, there's a lady present. We should watch what we say." The man shook his head, as if disappointed. I could see his features now that we were close to the light from the restaurant, but there was nothing familiar about his face. "Who is this young woman, by the way?"

"A friend."

Rodgers looked directly at me and I felt his black gaze shiver over my skin, as if he could read my very soul. "And does your friend have a name and a voice?"

"Cameron," I said.

"Cameron, so nice to meet you." He held out his hand.

I paused for only a moment, but realized it would be too rude to ignore him, so I slipped my hand into his. His fingers were firm and warm, but his touch made me oddly cold.

I drew back, stepping closer to Lewis.

Rodgers was back to staring at Lewis. "You've been gone for a while."

"Yeah, I can leave the island. I'm not a prisoner."

He clasped his hands behind his back. "Didn't say that. My, you're paranoid."

"I'm not paranoid, I'm late." He gave the man a stiff smile. "We have to go."

"Sure, don't want to break your curfew." He seemed amused by that.

Lewis didn't respond, merely tightened his hold on my hand and led me around the deck, toward the front of the building.

"Lewis." He was walking too fast and my voice came out breathless. "Who was he? What's going on?"

He released my hand and moved around to the driver's side. "No one, get in the car."

I pulled open the door and slipped inside, waiting for him to explain. No way was I letting him get away with that pathetic answer.

He was quiet as he settled in the seat and we pulled out of the parking lot. It was only once we'd made it through town that I asked him again. "Lewis, come on. What's going on?"

"He's one of them." He didn't look at me as he said that. He was upset, and it was worrying me. His knuckles were white as his fingers gripped the wheel. His hard gaze remained pinned straight ahead.

"One of who..." My blood went cold. "He's with S.P.I.?"

He nodded. We were silent as he drove up the hill, my thoughts in turmoil. I thought I'd be safe here, they'd promised I'd be safe. But how safe could I be if S.P.I. knew where we lived? Lewis stopped as we waited for the gates to open.

"But...how do you know for sure?" I asked, deciding to be calm, rational.

Lewis drove through the gates and onto Aaron's property. As the gates closed behind us, I admit I did feel somewhat safer.

Which was ridiculous. I mean, we couldn't live behind these gates forever. "He's been sniffing around here for months."

Panic set in, bitter on my tongue. Months? "Why? How'd he find you?"

He finally looked at me, his eyes softening with compassion. Maybe he'd read my thoughts, or maybe the panic was obvious on my face. "Don't worry, he can't hurt us. He doesn't have any reason to search our home."

He could find a reason, I had no doubt. If he really wanted to, he could get in. They told me I'd be safe. They said I was a sitting duck if I stayed in my hometown. I'd believed them. But for the first time since arriving, I wondered if I was any safer here than I'd been with Grandma.

Chapter 14

"Cameron, wake up."

I snuggled further down into my warm, soft bed, thinking maybe I was dreaming. I could have sworn I'd just fallen asleep. No way it was already morning. Besides, I didn't want to wake up. I wanted to sleep. Sleep was good. Very good.

Vaguely I was aware of the sound of wind battering the windows, rain tapping at the glass. It was bitterly cold outside. A storm had arrived. Yes, it was definitely a good idea to stay in my warm bed.

"Cameron." Someone gently pushed at my shoulders.

Suddenly fully awake, I bolted upright. "What's happened?" My voice was mumbled, sleepy.

Aaron stood next to my bed, the lamplight on the bedside table highlighting his tense features. He wore a sweatshirt and jeans, not his normal dress clothes, and his hair was all messed up. I'd never see him so out of sorts.

"What is it?" I asked, sudden panic gnawing at my gut. What had happened? Why wasn't Lewis here? My thoughts were a jumbled mess of feelings I couldn't control.

"Shhh, Lewis is fine. Come with me. I need your help."

I pushed my comforter away, my body shaking from the sudden dive into the conscious world. I was aware, even in my whacked-out state that once again Aaron had read my mind when I'd asked him not to. But I didn't have time to dwell on that, I was too worried about what the heck was going on. Aaron handed me a hoody and I pulled it over my head, cuddling into its warmth.

"I don't understand." I glanced at the windows. No light came through the cracks between the curtains, so it wasn't morning. I'd gone to bed almost immediately after Lewis and I had returned home. The house was still silent, which meant everyone slept. I turned and glanced at the clock. 3 a.m.

"Ugh," I said, brushing my hair from my face.

Aaron didn't seem to notice, merely handed me my tennis shoes. I took them reluctantly. "Are we going outside?"

"No." He started toward the door. "Hurry."

I slipped my feet into my shoes and followed him into the hall. "Aaron, what's going on?"

"Shhh, everyone's sleeping. Block your thoughts. If the others hear your thoughts, you might as well be yelling out loud. They're vulnerable when they sleep. It will wake them."

I tried to meditate as he led me down the steps, but worry and exhaustion made it difficult. I imagined that steel room, keeping my thoughts contained.

"Good," I was vaguely aware of his voice as my walls went up.

We'd made it to the first floor and were headed down a back hall. Too busy concentrating on my mental steel room, I was barely aware of where he led me. At the back of the house, Aaron pushed open a door that led to a long flight of stairs. Only a dull light highlighted our descent into the dungeon.

Surprised, I paused. "What's going on?"

"No time to explain, come on. I need your help." He took my hand, his grip warm and strong, and pulled me down the steps. It was your typical basement with stone walls, stone floor, empty of boxes, dreary and creepy looking. What was surprising was the very fact that he had a basement on an island, as usually the water table was too high for even a crawl space. Only one light was on and I couldn't see the entire area to know how far the basement ran underneath the house.

To say I was nervous would be an understatement. We paused at a steel door that ironically reminded me of the steel walls in my mind. I reinforced those mental walls, pulling my thoughts inward, keeping them close as Aaron punched in a code on the panel next to the door. I made out a one and a three on the keypad before he shifted, blocking my view.

The door slid open to reveal a dingy, stone room. Caroline stood there, trembling in her long, white nightgown. She looked so small, so lost. Her pale face turned toward me, those eyes wide, empty, almost.

"Caroline?" I started toward her, Aaron moved in front of me, blocking my entrance.

"Caroline, Sweetheart, go to bed. You've done what you can."

The child moved around him. She slid me a glance, something…something in her eyes… a silent message I wasn't getting.

"Why was she here?" I demanded the moment she left the room.

"She was helping. She's fine, there's nothing to worry about. Caroline is quite powerful."

But it didn't seem right, something wasn't right. A child here… in this dingy cell. No windows and only one single light bulb hanging from the ceiling. But it was the man sitting on a chair in the middle of the small space that drew my immediate attention. No, he wasn't just sitting; he was tied to that chair. His arms were pulled tightly back behind him, his biceps bulging underneath his white dress shirt. His wrists tied to the spindles on the back, while his ankles were tied with white ropes to the legs of the chair.

Any lingering sleep disappeared; my mind was no longer muddy. Shocked, I froze while Aaron went inside, strolling toward Lewis. Yes, Lewis was there, standing casually to the side like they hung out in stone cells together often.

"What the hell's going on?" I demanded, but he didn't bother to answer.

Was I dreaming? It was like some bad horror movie. With quick assessment, I took in what I could of the situation. A cot was placed against the far wall, no sheet or blanket. Obviously he was a prisoner of some sort. Was he S.P.I.? As if sensing my question, he slowly lifted his head. A gag bit into his mouth, the white material contrasting against his tanned skin. His gray eyes met mine, mutinous gray eyes that pierced my skin, seared my soul. He hated me with a hatred that was almost tangible.

I sucked in a sharp breath. Although he was tied and unable to move, it didn't make me feel any better. His skin had an unhealthy ash color to it and his hair was matted with sweat and dirt. But even in his animalistic state, I could see he was gorgeous. As ridiculous as it sounded, I wasn't expecting that. Weren't evil people supposed to be big, bully men...not freaking models?

Twenty, twenty-one? I wasn't sure about his age. The white button-up shirt he wore was filthy and ripped on the left sleeve, as if he'd been in a fight. His gray slacks were just as rough looking, caked with mud at the cuffs.

"What happened? Who is he?" I demanded, my voice harsh with emotion.

"This," Aaron nodded toward the man, "Is part of the group who wants us dead."

This? As if he wasn't a real person? I looked at him again. He seemed so young, so harmless. So human. Did he really work for S.P.I.?

"This can't be legal," I whispered the obvious.

The man narrowed his eyes into a glare, as if agreeing with me. I had to resist the urge to step back, intimidated by his stare. He was broader in the shoulders than Lewis, taller than Lewis, angrier than Lewis and Aaron put together. I didn't blame him. I didn't like this situation. It didn't feel right.

"Aaron," I whispered.

Aaron waved me over and as I stepped inside the small room, he shut the door behind me so that I was trapped as well. "We caught him lurking around the property."

The man mumbled something indecipherable through his gag, but I could imagine it wasn't pleasant introductions.

"He works for S.P.I., the very people who killed your father and Lewis's parents."

I glanced at Lewis. He was merely standing there, arms crossed over his chest, glaring down at the man. He didn't bother to glance my way. No, he was focused on the S.P.I. agent, like a dog wanting to go after a squirrel. I didn't know or understand this angry Lewis. The Lewis I'd been introduced to on our date was back.

"We need to find out what he knows," Aaron explained.

I brushed aside Aaron's comment. At the moment it didn't seem important. No, what was more important was that we had someone illegally restrained in the basement. "How long has he been here?" I should have felt angry toward the man who worked for S.P.I., the people responsible for my father's death. But all I felt was sick.

"A week."

Startled, I was quiet for a moment, mulling over the reality of what they'd done. A week? For a week they'd kept this man tied up, alone in this cell? Smudges marked the area under his steel eyes. The shadow of a beard was beginning to form along his jaw line. A week with no sunlight, apparently no bath. My horror increased. "Why?"

"What would you have us do?" Lewis snapped, finally looking at me. The anger in his gaze was shocking. "We can't let him go. He knows who we are, where we are. We're tired of running, Cam. Tired of hiding. We shouldn't have to."

I looked at the agent again; he was staring daggers as if he blamed me for this entire incident. Why me? I hadn't tied him up. I hadn't even known he was here.

Aaron rested his hand on my shoulder, the touch jarring. "We can't just let him go."

"What does that mean? What will you do with him?" I demanded.

"We have no idea what he knows, that's why we need your help," Aaron said, ignoring my question.

"How," I asked, not sure I really wanted to know.

Aaron cupped my shoulders, stepping in front of me and blocking the man from view. "We need to pull out his thoughts, his memories."

Pull out someone's thoughts? It sounded invasive, wrong. It was one thing to read someone's thoughts that were flowing freely into the universe, but to drag them out? "Okay, so why haven't you?"

Aaron released his hold and stepped back. With a sigh, he rubbed his brow. He looked tired, worried. "S.P.I. places a chip in their officer's heads. A chip that blocks their thoughts from being read by people like us."

"And you want me to remove the chip?" I asked, my voice shrill. Well really, there was a limit to what I would do and I drew the line at surgery.

"No, of course not." Aaron moved around the room, pacing as he rubbed the back of his neck. "If we concentrate hard enough, we can override the chip and pull the info from his mind, but Lewis and I aren't strong enough alone."

Oh God, I didn't need to be a genius to know where this was going. "You need my help."

He nodded.

My stomach twisted in protest. "But I don't know how."

"You do. We've taught you."

I swallowed hard and dared to glance at the man. He was still glaring at me and his gaze sent a shiver of unease over my skin. Those eyes…those eyes promised retribution if he ever managed to free himself. He could easily kill me with his hands. My attention slipped to the ties binding him to the chair, making sure he was secure.

They wanted me to help. What choice did I have? I owed Lewis and Aaron. Besides, this man was responsible for my father's death. This man would kill me if he could. So why did I feel sick at the thought of invading his mind?

Aaron sighed, raking his hands through his hair. "I suppose we could try to use Caroline again."

"No!" She'd had enough, didn't they notice how tired she'd looked? "I'll do it."

Aaron smiled and moved toward the man, edging around him, his gaze unwavering like an animal of prey. Lewis did the same, while I was forced to stay in front. We formed a sort of triangle, three points and the agent was at the center. With my legs trembling, I stood my ground, reminding myself that he was responsible for my father's death. For some reason it didn't make me feel any better. I was far enough away that if he was able to reach out, he wouldn't touch me, but I swear I could feel his hot breath on my face.

He was hunched slightly, like an animal in a cage, his gray eyes piercing me, not wavering, not looking at Lewis or Aaron. He knew I was the weakest link. Heat crawled slowly, torturously, up my neck. He jerked forward. I jumped back. But his bindings held him tight and he merely scooted an inch, his chair scraping against the stone floor.

"Cam, you're all right, he can't escape," Aaron insisted.

Right. Tell that to my heart, which was currently threatening to make a mad leap from my chest and hightail it out of there. I was the one standing directly in front of him and I was the one he seemed intent on coming after. I stepped forward, back to my spot, determined not to flinch under his hard stare. He wasn't much older than me, maybe three years. How had he gotten involved with S.P.I.?

Damn it all, as much as I wanted to hate him, I couldn't. Rationally, I knew he had nothing to do with my father's death; he was too young. But was Lewis right? Would he kill me if he had the chance?

"All right, Cameron," Aaron said. "I want you to relax. Deep breaths in, out, close your eyes. You know the drill."

Being a coward, I was glad to close my eyes so I wouldn't have to look the agent in his eerie steel colored gaze. I tried to relax, I pictured my ocean, breathed in and out, but it was difficult, to say the least. I wasn't sure how many minutes had passed, but I suddenly found myself sitting on my beach, everyone forgotten. Only peace and contentment surrounded me.

You're going to concentrate on the man in front of you, Aaron said, his voice invasive. *Slowly open your eyes, Cameron.*

I didn't want to, but I did. I opened my eyes, but I no longer saw his glare. I only saw that steel gray. A pool of melted metal that I sank into. As I fell, I felt like I was falling through the very universe. Brilliant white stars flashing past me on a cool breeze. I hit something hard, and stopped, suspended between the dark reality of my subconscious.

"You feel it," I vaguely heard Aaron say. "That's the chip that's keeping you out. You have to push against that blockade, Cameron."

I focused more intensely, I couldn't let them down. Aaron and Lewis were counting on me. They'd taken me in, they'd taught me when no one else would.

I didn't question his decision, but reached out and pushed against that wall. It was like I was working on auto pilot; focused only on success. I concentrated as they'd taught me, and a small sense of release whispered through my mind, a slight budge of the wall giving way. Thrilled, I pushed harder. Sweat broke out on my trembling body, but I didn't relent. It didn't take much before the dam burst. I felt as if a river of color was suddenly flooding around me...memories that burst into full bloom.

People swept through my mind in a whirlwind of emotion; laughing, arguing, talking, hugging. I tried to grasp onto them, but they were gone before I had a chance. Christmas trees, presents, birthday cakes, a mother and father beaming down at me. I saw teachers and then college professors, I saw grades, sports…. Then suddenly it switched to men in suits coming to my room, talking about recruiting me…

Everything went so fast I could barely hold onto a single thought. I felt like I was spinning in space, attempting to grasp onto anything that might help. But it was all too quick, too confusing. And then I was looking at a girl…a girl with dark hair and a wide smile and my heart expanded. The girl he loved, I realized.

I'm Maddox, a voice inside my head explained.

Nora, the girl said softly and then in a flash she was gone.

More memories. Nora dancing…Nora slipping her hands through my hair…or Maddox's hair. So many memories…so confusing…And then I heard it…a scream…as if someone was in pain. The sound jerked me from his mind. The memories were gone and I floated in blackness. Suspended for a brief moment in the silence of the universe, those white stars pulsing around me. I couldn't move, couldn't see or feel anything. But I wasn't alone…no, there was a small white light in the distance.

There it was again. A scream of pain.

I dove toward the conscious world, that small beam of light that I knew would send me back into reality. Within moments I slammed into my body. Freezing cold, like I'd been thrown into ice water. Gasping for air. I stumbled back, falling against a warm body. The room spun, the walls wavering in and out of focus. Aaron, frowning with concern, stared down at me, yet there was something else in his eyes…excitement?

"What happened?" I demanded.

Pushing away from Aaron, I focused on Maddox. The man wasn't moving, slouched forward so I couldn't see his face.

"Nothing, everything." Aaron grasped my shoulders and spun me around to face him. Dizzy, I wavered, his beaming face going out of focus for a moment. "Did you get that?" His gaze jumped to Lewis. "The information? My God, with her ability we can break in anywhere."

But Lewis was frowning. "They're coming."

I was barely aware of what they said, barely cared. I felt dizzy, off balance. My stomach was twisting and turning. I glanced over my shoulder. Maddox still hadn't moved. Why wasn't he glaring at me? Why wasn't he trying to curse me out?

"Yes, but we can be ready for them," Aaron was saying.

Unconcerned with my safety, I stepped closer to Maddox and knelt to get a look at his face. For some reason, I needed to see his face. His eyes were closed, his forehead damp and pale. I hesitated a moment, then reached out, nudging him in the shoulder. He didn't move. My heart jumped into my throat. Cupping the sides of his face, rough with whiskers, I lifted his head. Blood trailed from the corner of his mouth. I dropped my hold and jumped back.

"Oh my God."

"What?" Aaron was at my side, his arm around my shoulders.

"He's...he's dead!"

"No. Of course not." Still, if Aaron wasn't concerned why did he leave me and feel the man's neck for a pulse? "He's fine."

Fine? He wasn't fine! Horrified, I stared up at Aaron. He was way too blasé about the fact that Maddox was totally not fine. I threw my hands in the air, unable to stand still. "He's bleeding! From the mouth!"

"It happens, when you break through the chip."

"The scream was his!" I clasped my hands over my mouth, trembling with shock, fear, worry...a jumble of emotions. I'd heard him screaming with pain...a pain I'd caused. Why was no one else upset about this? "No."

My stomach churned, acid rising to my throat. I was going to be sick, vomit all over the floor, but I didn't care. I shook my head and backed up a step. I had to get out of there; I swear I could smell his blood. My lungs shrunk, I couldn't breathe. "I hurt him."

Aaron stepped closer to me, his face full of concern. Concern for me when he should have been worried about Maddox. "Cameron, you have to understand, it's either us or them. I know you feel bad, but do you want to give your life for his?"

I looked at Maddox, so large, yet at the moment so vulnerable. Would he recover? Even though he was my enemy, I prayed he would.

"He's with S.P.I.," Lewis said. "The same branch that's responsible for killing your father." He slammed his hand against his chest. He was angry with me and even though I shouldn't have cared, I did. "My parents."

But he knew as well as I did that Maddox had nothing to do with the death of our parents. "So I have to do this in order to stay here? I have to hurt people?"

Will they throw me out if I don't?

"Of course you don't have to do anything you don't want to." Aaron started toward me. "We'd never throw you out, Cameron."

Damn it! I'd forgotten to close my mind. I didn't want them reading my thoughts, I already felt too vulnerable. I didn't want to hurt people. I didn't want to disappoint Aaron and Lewis. So I did the only thing I could. I pulled open the door and raced up the stairs, leaving them to deal with the mess.

Chapter 15

I pushed open the front door and ran down the steps to the driveway. Darkness called to me, providing a safety and privacy I so needed. My skin crawled with the realization of what I'd done, my heart hammered with the desperate need to escape. The grass, slick with dew, quickly soaked my tennies, chilling my feet. The elements would kill me if I was out all night. I didn't know where I was going and vaguely realized how irrational my escape was, but I didn't care.

Maddox's face kept flashing to mind…that brilliant red blood trailing down the corner of his mouth. I'd taken their word that he still lived, but what if he didn't? What if I'd killed him?

My God, with her ability we can break in anywhere. Aaron's words came rushing back.

Had they used me? Did they not even care how I felt, but only about my abilities? With a cry, I gripped the cold, metal posts of the fence. The need to escape was so overwhelming, I wanted to scream. I jerked on the gates. They didn't budge. No security guards came down from the tower, even though I could see a light and knew they were there.

"Jerks!" I cried.

Just past the road, lay the ocean. Dark and foreboding. Impossible to cross.

Trapped. I was trapped here— on an island I couldn't leave.

"Cameron!" Lewis called.

Furious he'd followed me, I spun around. "Go away, Lewis."

"No," he insisted, pausing a few feet in front of me. His breath came out in cold puffs of air that suspended between us.

I pushed past him and followed the fence line. Maybe it ended somewhere and if it didn't, I'd just keep walking. Like an animal in the zoo, I'd walk in circles, pacing my cage day after day until I went insane.

Lewis rushed after me, I could hear his harsh breathing. "Where are you going?"

"I don't know. I don't care. I want to leave."

"You can't leave, Cam."

Anger and fear hammered through my chest. I spun around to face him. "Why?"

He raked his hands through his hair, obviously frustrated. Well, get in line. "Because…because you'd be in danger."

I released a harsh laugh, and started walking again. "I'm in danger here, in this house, on this island. Didn't you say they were coming, S.P.I.? My God, he found us in town, what makes you think he can't get in here? Maddox did."

"You're safe. Protected. I promise. But out there anything could happen to you." He latched onto my arm, his grip tight. "Cameron, please, you can't leave, I would worry about you."

My heart warmed, even as my mind demanded it not soften. My heart won. Slowly, I turned. "Lewis, I can't do this again. I can't hurt someone like that. Did you see his face? Did you see the blood?"

He gripped both my arms, bringing me closer to his warmth. "I know, but Cam, the man's a criminal."

"You're saying he deserved it?"

"I'm saying he's all right. You don't have to feel guilty." He led me toward a stone bench that rested under one of the few trees in the garden. A tree that had lost all of its leaves and was now a skeletal remain of its former glory. "We had to do it. Don't you get that? There was no alternative."

I sank onto the cold, stone bench. Lewis settled beside me, his body warm and comforting. "Did you try talking to him?"

He smiled, the kind of smile you give a child who believes in the Easter Bunny. "You know we did."

Of course I knew. But I still couldn't help but hope there would be another way out of this mess. What we were doing…what we had done…was wrong. Maddox was a man, a man not much older than me. A man whose memories, his life, had flashed through my mind as if his memories were my own. A man I'd made scream out in pain. A man I might have killed.

Lewis took my hand, his grip strong. "He's a monster, Cam. The moment you underestimate him is the moment you're dead. He'll do whatever it takes to succeed, even if it means killing us. Killing you."

His words should have frightened me. Instead I felt an odd numbing sensation overtake any feelings. "And we'll obviously do the same. So how does that make us any different?"

His face tensed, his grip on my hand tightening, although I didn't think he noticed. "We are only protecting ourselves," he snapped. "They are attacking us."

I was quiet, biting my tongue to keep from snapping back. He was angry at me and I didn't want him angry. He was one of the few allies I had. Besides, I didn't know enough about this situation to win the argument. Why even try? Instead, I stared up at the dark sky, those twinkling stars familiar. The same stars I'd seen my entire life. The same stars I saw when I traveled in my mind. Was I out there, in the universe, when I was mind reading? For some reason it made me feel less alone.

"You won't be safe outside these walls." Lewis rubbed his thumb over my knuckles. "We've known for months they were hunting us and were desperate to protect you."

I pulled my hand away from his. I couldn't think when he touched me. Instead I focused on the moon, bright and full, laughing down at us. "Is that why you found me? You needed my ability?"

He was silent for a moment. "Not the only reason. Aaron thought it was time to teach you to use your powers to your fullest."

My sharp gaze dropped to him. "But only because he suddenly needed me?"

"No." He sighed, raking his hands through his hair. "Your father wanted you involved. He wanted you to have this life. Aaron tried to keep you out as long as possible, but they were going to come for you."

Did I believe him? I didn't dare look into his eyes, for fear he'd read my distrust. I needed time to think, time alone and I didn't want to be influenced by him or his gorgeous smile.

"Give me your hands," he demanded.

I slid him a sidelong glance, but did as he told. "Trust me." He gripped both my hands in his and turned me so I was facing him. Those eyes were so intense that it was impossible to look away.

"Stare into my eyes. Take in my thoughts, my memories."

"No!" I tried to pull back, afraid I'd hurt him as I had Maddox, but his hands only tightened around me.

"I want you to." His gaze was unwavering, his touch reassuring. "I'm going to open my mind. I want you to understand me, Cameron."

I hesitated, feeling like I was invading his privacy, yet at the same time I did want to understand.

"Relax," he whispered.

And I did. With the bitterly cold autumn wind tugging at my hair, whipping it across my face and stinging my skin, I closed my eyes and relaxed as they'd taught me.

"Focus on me," his voice was a soft murmur. "You won't have to dig because I'll be open."

And it was so easy how his thoughts slipped into mine like the warm rays of the sun. I'd gone so long without hearing any thoughts, besides Maddox's, that for a moment I wasn't sure which were mine and which were from Lewis.

I hope she believes me.

I hope she understands why this is so important.

Please, don't leave. I need you here.

The words rushed through my mind, tangling with my own. Thoughts so emotional, so true, that my heart clenched.

"Why," I whispered. "Why do you want me here? So you can use me?"

At first, but now because I think I might be in love with you.

My entire being froze. You couldn't stop your thoughts; you couldn't hesitate and think of the right words, they merely came unbidden. I wanted to open my eyes, I wanted to look at him, to know if his love was true, or if he was playing some mind game Aaron had taught him. But even I knew that a person could speak a lie, but their thoughts would remain true to what they believed.

Lewis might love me. My heart slammed erratically against my ribcage. Did I love him? I'd never been in love. How did I know if I was? But I didn't have time to dwell over my feelings, because seconds later pictures flashed through my mind...memories...his memories.

A tall man appeared before me, smiling. He had dark hair that glimmered in the sun as he leaned over and handed me...no Lewis...a baseball. We were outside, the day was beautiful, the grass cool and soft beneath my bare feet. A woman appeared wearing a pink dress. She had blonde hair and a brilliant smile. She wrapped her arm around her husband's waist and kissed his cheek, then knelt and pulled Lewis into a tight hug. She smelled like vanilla, as if she'd been baking. It was a wonderful scent full of motherly love and happiness.

An odd sensation of warmth and sadness swirled low in my gut. Then the memory changed and I was playing soccer, dribbling the ball down the field. I even felt his euphoria when he scored. Soccer was gone and I was standing behind a tree, a little girl was in front of me. She couldn't have been more than ten. She smiled shyly, her long, dark hair shimmering in the sunlight. She leaned forward, puckered her lips and closed her eyes. His first kiss.

I saw so many things...playing sports, going to the beach, going to school...all these memories flashed quickly through my mind in what seemed like a breathless moment. Then, his thoughts and memories slowed. The colors seemed more intense, the memories more detailed.

I was in a bedroom, the area dark...it was night. I was staring at the ceiling listening to voices argue. The fear tasted bitter in my mouth, but I was too afraid to move. My door creaked opened, and light splashed into the room.

Lewis, Lewis wake up, a woman called out.

I sat up in bed, my heart slamming wildly. I was afraid...or Lewis was afraid.

"What is it?" he asked.

"They're coming, Lewis. They're coming." She pulled me out of bed and started digging through the dresser, tossing clothes across the room. I was trembling, I was so afraid, and it made it hard to dress.

Suddenly, she was back. Lewis's mother grasped my shoulders and shook me gently. Her face was pale, her eyes shimmering. "You need to go."

"What? Where?"

"Aaron will take care of you."

Lewis grasped onto her arm as she tried to let go. "I don't understand. Where are you going?"

"We have to separate, Lewis, it's the best thing for you...for all of us." She tried to pry Lewis's hands away, but he wouldn't let go. "Aaron will take you to your father's brother."

"No, I'm not leaving you."

"You must." She grabbed my hand and pulled me out the door, her other hand carried a suitcase. In the living room, Aaron was there, a little younger, sadder looking Aaron.

"I'll keep you safe," he said, taking Lewis's hand.

And then he was pulling me...pulling Lewis toward the door. Tears stung my eyes, trailing down my cheeks. My tears, or Lewis's, I wasn't sure. Just as I reached the door, Lewis's mom grabbed me. She pulled me into one last hug, her soft cries gut-wrenching. Then we stepped out into the darkness and the memory faded.

"It was the last time I saw them," Lewis whispered, breaking into my thoughts.

I blinked from my trance, feeling the bite of the night wind once more. My cheeks were wet, my head hurt slightly, a soft pounding. Too many memories in too short of a time. I felt heavy, sad with Lewis's depressing memories. My hands tightened in his grip. I wished I could see his face better in the dark. I wanted to pull him close, hug him and offer comfort in some way.

"I couldn't even go to their funerals because my uncle was afraid something would happen to me," he whispered.

"Lewis, I'm so sorry."

He gave me a sad, half smile and looked out over the dark lawn. "I know. When I was with my uncle..." He shook his head looking distant, as if recalling a memory he'd rather not. "It was like when you were with your grandmother. Constantly running. Constant secrecy."

I released one of his hands and swiped at my damp cheeks. "How'd they die?"

He looked down, nudging the toe of his tennies into the grass. "They had met with your father and a few others the night before. They were going to bond together, and demand they be released of their duties with S.P.I. Someone betrayed them. We have no idea who. Our parents were…murdered."

I closed my eyes and rested my elbows on my knees. My father had been murdered. I covered my face with my hands as my stomach twisted with fear. My father had been murdered, gunned down like some bad movie.

"How old were you?" I asked him, my voice muffled through my fingers.

"Seven," he whispered. "Aaron took me to my uncle's. When he died, Aaron came for me. I owe him everything."

Seven, so young, not much older than I'd been when Mom abandoned me, yet….something was off, something not quite connecting, something that tapped at the edges of my mind. I jerked upright. "I'm only…a year younger than you."

He nodded, frowning.

"My dad was killed when your parents were killed."

"Right…"

He still wasn't following, but I was. Oh God, I felt sick. Angry, horrified. "My dad…I was told my dad died when I was a baby."

Realization dawned, his gaze glimmering with the truth. He looked away, but not before I saw the guilt in his eyes. "He thought you'd be better off without him."

"You knew?"

He didn't answer, but he didn't need to.

"All that time…." Tears blurred my vision. "All that time I thought he was dead. All that time I was living with my grandma, he was still alive?"

Lewis swallowed and nodded slowly, still not looking at me.

A warm tear slipped down my cheek. "When did you know? About me?"

"I heard him talking to my parents one night. I heard him talk about you, how much he missed you. He wondered if what he'd done was right." He was silent for a moment. "I'm so sorry, Cam."

I sniffed, my nose stinging. "Not your fault. It's just that…I could have had time with him."

"Or you could have been killed too," he whispered.

He didn't wait for my permission, but wrapped his arm around me and pulled me close. I sank into his warm body and closed my eyes. I couldn't help myself. He was the only one here and he…he thought he loved me. I wrapped my arms around his waist and pressed my face to his shoulder, breathing deep his scent. He smelled so good, like soap and warmth.

"Stay with me Cameron." *Don't leave me.*

He hadn't closed his thoughts. Did he realize? Had he left himself open on purpose? I tilted my head back and looked up into his face. So gorgeous, so kind. Maybe he was right. Maybe we had to hurt Maddox for our own good. Maybe it would be stupid not to fight back.

I want to kiss her.

I smiled. "So kiss me."

He stiffened, surprised that I had read his thoughts, or surprised that I would be so bold? I didn't care, all I cared about was Lewis…kissing me. I gripped the front of his shirt, the cotton soft and warm from his body, and tugged him closer. I didn't want to think anymore of depressing memories.

When he leaned down, I lifted my face eagerly. He pressed his lips to mine and my entire body burst to life. His hand slipped into my hair, cupping my head and deepening the kiss. And I let him. Even though thoughts of Maddox nagged at me, I let Lewis kiss me because I didn't want to think anymore. I only wanted to feel.

His tongue darted out, slipping across my lips. A shiver raced over my skin. I felt so completely and utterly warm, warmer than I'd ever been. I didn't want it to end, never wanted that kiss to end.

I realized, with a start, that I might be a little in love with Lewis as well. But how could I love someone I wasn't sure I fully trusted?

Chapter 16

For two days I managed not to think about my father, Maddox or death in general. For two days I managed to live in a state of romantic bliss, focusing only on Lewis, thoughts of his smile and his kiss. But once my eyes closed for the night and my mind slipped into dreamland, I could no longer pretend.

So it wasn't with surprise that I found myself staring at my clock at one a.m. while the house slept silent and still. I wondered if Caroline was okay. I wondered if Maddox was well, if he was cold down there in that basement, if they were giving him enough to eat. And then I felt guilty for caring and thoughts slipped to my father. Had he died quickly or had he suffered?

And then my mind returned to Lewis, as it usually did. As thrilled as I was that he cared for me, I couldn't help but dwell on the fact that in the beginning, Lewis had come to my school to use me. He'd flirted with me, he'd pretended he cared, when in reality he'd had ulterior motives. How did I know he wasn't doing the same now?

With a groan of frustration, I rolled onto my stomach and pressed my face into my pillow as if that could stop my thoughts from spinning. Grandma had always made me hot chocolate when I couldn't sleep. Funny how now that I was free of her dictatorship, Grandma didn't seem so bad. I'd been here for two weeks and she still hadn't called. As much as I hated the thought of contacting her, I knew I needed to know she was okay. Perhaps, deep down, I was hoping she'd offer some sage advice.

The wind howled outside, autumn in full force. The eerie sound ate at my nerves. It sounded so much like someone crying that I had to resist the urge to go looking. Unable to sleep, I pushed aside my cover and slipped out of my warm cocoon. But as I made my way out of my bedroom and into the long, dark hall, anxiety overcame my need for freedom. No matter how much I wanted it to be, this mansion would never be home.

Wearing sweats and a t-shirt, I felt under dressed as I moved through the many rooms on the first floor…empty room after empty room. No personal objects. No toys, no video games, not even a family photo. The house was silent and watchful. Not welcoming, not home. I felt like I was doing something wrong by being out of my room unescorted. Like I was invading someone's privacy.

My foot hit the marble tile of the foyer entry and I immediately thought of the basement below and of course Maddox. Could he hear my footsteps? Or was he dead because of me? My stomach clenched at the thought. Sure, Lewis had said he was fine and of course Lewis never lied. I scoffed at my naivety. Truth was, I wouldn't rest until I saw Maddox for myself. But how would I? The man was behind a steel, locked door.

Why I cared, I hadn't the slightest. Lewis was right, because of this man, my father was dead. Well, technically not this man, as Maddox wasn't much older than me. But considering he worked for S.P.I., weren't their actions indicative of what he could do as well? If only I hadn't seen him as a person… seen his life…his parents…his girlfriend…everything. To me he was as human as Lewis. Not a monster.

Walking into the kitchen was like traveling into the future. The room was large, the tiled floor cold through my socks. Just about everything was stainless steel, making the room feel sterile and chilly. The space was clean, but high tech and impersonal. I couldn't help but think of our table back home; that stupid, little table where I'd had just about every meal of my life, the table that my Grandma insisted came from England. For some odd, inexplicable reason, my chest felt tight and my nose burned from the sudden sting of tears. Crying over a damn table, no less. Believe me, I knew it was ridiculous.

In that brief moment I wanted to do nothing more than return home to Grandma. But my rational brain caught up to my irrational emotions. Could I do it? Could I truly go back to Grandma and leave Lewis? Could I truly go back to my old life in which I'd had to hide my identity? I rested my hand on the smooth, polished surface of the stainless steel table. No dents, no scars, no life. Instead of family meals, I could see a person doing an autopsy.

But no. Because of the whole Maddox thing I was merely feeling a bit down. I seriously couldn't miss my old life, could I? Sniffing, I pulled open a cupboard, looking for hot chocolate. There were energy bars and fruit, nothing fun. Who the heck didn't have hot chocolate in Maine? I closed the door with a frustrated sigh.

"What are you looking for?" Olivia's voice reached out from the dark.

I shouldn't have been surprised, the girl liked to shock me. Still, my heart lurched and I spun around, searching through the dim light for her shadow. She was hunkering over the counter at the end of the room, drinking something. Probably blood.

"Looking for hot chocolate," I admitted.

She sipped, a loud slurping sound that wasn't exactly attractive. "Don't have any."

I crossed my arms over my chest, partly from anger, partly because I was cold. I couldn't even get a damn cup of hot cocoa. "What are you drinking?"

"Green tea."

We were silent for one long moment as I debated whether or not I wanted to lower my standards to green tea. Definitely a no. I wasn't in the mood for something that was good for me.

"Good night," I muttered and turned to leave. I was so not going to hang around and try to make conversation with Miss Dour Teen U.S.A. She could seriously be the poster child for teenage depression and I didn't need anything else to worry about.

"You saw him?"

I froze. "Who?"

When she didn't respond, I turned. I could barely see her face, and of course I couldn't read her thoughts. Surely she wasn't talking about Maddox.

"That man, the S.P.I. agent," she said.

Shocked, it took a moment for me to answer. "Maybe," I mumbled, wondering if she was tricking me into admitting something I wasn't supposed to speak about. I wouldn't put it past her.

She straightened, her body stiff, as if somehow I'd annoyed her. "Oh please, like it's some big secret, like I can't know."

I flushed. That's exactly what I'd been thinking, but I wasn't going to admit it to her. Did she know? Could she tell me anything? "I didn't mean...just forget it." Having had enough, I started toward the door again, only to pause, realizing she might actually know more than me. "Is...is he okay?"

"Who?"

I turned toward her. Was she intentionally being obtuse? "Maddox, the man downstairs. Is he okay?" I felt like I was in freaking *Alice in Wonderland* and having a chat with the Mad Hatter.

She shrugged and dumped her tea into the sink. "Wanna check?"

Trepidation fought with excitement, a tingling thrill that coursed through my body. "What? How?"

"Uh, you go into the room." Sarcasm dripped from her tone and I could just imagine the look she was giving me. She was such an obnoxious brat. Unfortunately if I wanted to sleep, I didn't have a choice but to go along with her. That didn't mean I trusted her. Was she setting me up for a fall? I'd deal with the consequences later; I had to know if Maddox was alive.

"You have the code?" I tried not to sound eager.

She shrugged, making her way toward me. "Sure." I read the arrogance in her voice, as if she was saying, *don't you?* She paused near the window, the moonlight highlighting her round face. "Well? Do you want to go see him or not?"

She was daring me. In most instances I would have walked out the door and ignored her taunt. The problem was, I needed to know how Maddox was doing. "Will we get in trouble?"

"If we get caught."

I had to trust her if I wanted to see Maddox. But trusting Olivia was impossible. Hell, trusting anyone in this house was becoming rather like jumping off a twenty story building in hopes that you'd suddenly grow wings; not a good idea. Still, my curiosity got the better of me. I could peek, just look in the door, make sure I hadn't killed the agent and then maybe I'd be able to sleep tonight.

"Okay, let's go," I rushed the words, worried I'd change my mind.

She didn't hesitate, the bad ass that she was, and started down the hall. I followed more cautiously, my wide gaze darting from shadow to shadow, waiting for the moment we'd be caught. And let's face it, this was like a horror movie, so we would be caught. When she pulled open that basement door, I was finally able to breathe with some normalcy.

At the keypad, I watched as she typed the numbers. "Ten," she glanced over my shoulder. "Twenty-five and thirty-six."

Olivia was being helpful, way too helpful. Still, I committed the numbers to memory. I wasn't about to ask her for help if I decided to come down here again. Not that I would come down here again…

"Better block your thoughts, just in case. We never know what they're truly capable of."

Shoot, I hadn't been blocking my thoughts? Heat shot to my face as I frantically tried to remember what she'd overhead, and at the same time I tried to put up that wall. The door popped open. The dim light bulb glowed harshly from the ceiling, providing the agent with no darkness to sleep. Maddox lay on his cot, facing the door. He looked huge on that tiny bed. So large, that for a moment I froze in fear.

His eyes were open as if he'd been waiting for me, and that glare was still in place. I swore he could drill a hole through my skull just by staring. I swallowed hard, my attention jumping to the handcuffs wrapped around his wrists and attached to an iron bar on the wall. To say I was relieved would be an understatement.

Olivia stepped closer to me. "I figure you have about five minutes before Aaron realizes we're down here. If you're caught, you better make sure you don't rat me out." With that said, she stepped back into the hall. I could hear the thump, thump, thump of her feet as she raced up the steps. She might have let me in, but she sure as hell wasn't going to watch my back. Not that I blamed her for hightailing it out of there. I was about ready to run myself.

"I…I wanted to make sure you were okay," I managed to get out.

He didn't respond even though the gag was gone.

"I didn't mean to hurt you."

Slowly, he sat upright, the cot creaking a protest. I had to resist the urge to step back and slam that door shut. I could return to bed, pretend like I'd never seen him. So why wasn't I leaving? Why weren't my feet moving?

Because there was something about his eyes that held me captive. He was big with broad shoulders and dark hair. That scruff along his jaw was turning into a beard which made him look older than what he was. Dark and mysterious…dangerous. I suppose I would have thought he was gorgeous if I wasn't so afraid he was going to murder me.

I took a big step backwards. "Well then, guess I'll…go."

I waited for him to protest, to beg me to help him. He didn't say anything, merely sat there glaring at me. In fact, he didn't think anything. I paused, realizing his silence was more important than I'd realized. "I can't read your thoughts," I blurted.

He swallowed hard, his throat working. "They taught us to block them with meditation." His voice was deep, but rich, like honey. "The chip in my brain was for backup."

I was so surprised by the sound of his voice that the importance of his response was lost on me for the moment. I shook my head, trying to regain control. "And…can you read my thoughts?"

He didn't respond, just glowered at me. Worried we were running out of time, I glanced back. The basement was dark, the house still silent. I met his gaze. "Please, I need to know."

"I can't read your thoughts," he snapped. "Only your kind can."

"My kind?" I released a harsh laugh. "You say that like we're freaks or…inhuman."

He shrugged, smirking.

I had the feeling he was trying to hurt me. It worked. I guess he hadn't forgiven me for breaking into his mind. Well, screw him. "You know what, I'm not the enemy here."

He laughed and jerked on the handcuffs, his muscles bunching under the white dress shirt. "Oh really? You're not the one who broke into my thoughts? How'd I bust my brain open then?"

I ignored his harsh words and the guilt. It wasn't my fault; he deserved what he got. At least, that's what I tried to tell myself. "I had help, if you remember."

He surged to his feet, tall, intimidating. He might have only been a few years older, but he was twice my size. I refused to move back any more than I already had.

"You think they were helping?" He laughed, a deep chuckle that seemed to vibrate through my very body. "You were doing the work, Sweetheart."

Flabbergasted, I wasn't sure how to respond. "I wasn't... they needed my extra ability so they..."

He started laughing again, great big laughs that would surely wake someone up.

"Shhh!" I hissed.

He merely rolled his shoulders as if to ease the ache. "You were doing the work, believe me. It was all coming from you."

I crossed my arms over my chest, my body trembling. "You're lying." So why did I suddenly feel sick? No, Lewis would have told me. I hadn't been the only person responsible for making Maddox bleed. "I don't believe you."

He shrugged, looking completely unconcerned. "I don't really give a crap. What I care about is the fact that I've had a damn headache ever since you broke into my thoughts, so thanks for that."

I shook my head, feeling cold, close to panicking. "We...I....had to. You'll kill us."

He lifted a dark brow and settled on the edge of the cot. The bed creaked and groaned under his weight. Even sitting he seemed huge. "Kill? What the hell kind of nonsense has he been feeding you?"

I frowned, confused when I shouldn't be. He was trying to twist the facts. But I knew the truth and the truth was he was partially responsible for the death of my father. "Your little group killed my father."

He was silent for a moment, but I could read nothing in his hard gaze. "Is that so?"

I didn't respond. What was the point? He'd never admit the truth. "I have to go." I started toward the door again, intent on leaving. I wouldn't listen to anymore of his lies. I wouldn't let him sway me, even for a minute.

"Ask them about George Miller."

I froze, my heart slamming wildly in my chest. "What do you mean?"

"You think the shooting in the café was a coincidence? Or the murder? You don't think it odd that the man shows up in your small town? No one knows him. You don't think it weird that he starts dating one of your best friends and because of him, you finally start using your abilities?"

My blood had run cold, fear giving way to anger. "What I find weird," I spun around to face him, "Is that you know the details of my life."

He just smirked. Was he playing with my mind? No way George was a fraud, or planted by Aaron merely to get me to use my powers. No. It was too sick to even think about. I turned and started for the door. He might not tell me about George, the psycho murderer, but Lewis would.

"Wait," he demanded.

There was something to his voice, an anxiousness that made me pause.

"I want to show you something."

As my Grandma used to say, too curious for my own good, I glanced over my shoulder.

He reached for his sleeve and rolled the dirty material, the handcuff rattling with the movement. His forearm was just as muscled as the rest of him. But his muscles were suddenly the least of my worries. He flipped his arm over and I saw it…there on the underside of his forearm…a tattoo of an animal…a bird with a lion's body.

Unwillingly, I stepped closer. It was oddly familiar….so familiar, yet I couldn't place it. "What is it?"

"The Griffin. A symbol of what we stand for."

For some reason I was finding it hard to breathe. I couldn't look away from that tattoo. A picture that clawed at my memory, begging me to understand. "Why does it seem familiar?"

"Because your father had one just like it."

I jerked my gaze up to him. He was completely serious. "No, he…" But even as I thought the words, a memory flashed to mind, a memory I'd always assumed was some fantastical dream. Dad had taken me to the ocean, intent on teaching me to swim. We were in Florida, some ancient stone fort nearby. I think I was four, although not positive. He'd told me not to be afraid, that he'd keep me safe, he'd always keep me safe. Was it real? Had he truly visited me?

Tears burned my eyes, I shook my head. "S.P.I. betrayed him—"

"No, we didn't." His hard gaze flashed with anger and something that looked suspiciously like compassion. Dare I believe him? But if he was telling the truth, what did this mean?

"I don't believe you."

He held his arms as wide as the handcuffs would allow. "Why would I lie to you? I have no reason."

"You have every reason," Aaron spoke sharply from behind me. "Get away from him, Cameron."

Maddox's gaze turned to steel. Before I could even blink, the agent surged from the cot, latched onto my arm and jerked me back, directly into his hard chest. A muscled forearm wrapped around my throat with enough pressure that it brought tears to my eyes.

"Leave her alone," Aaron said softly, as if he was in total control.

Maddox chuckled, his breath warm on the top of my head. "You know I could so easily kill her."

"And then what?" Aaron asked, holding his arms wide, a look of bewildered amusement on his face. "I'll kill you? What's the point?"

"At least you won't have her ability to add your little collection."

Even through the pain and confusion, his words bothered me. Add to his collection? As if we were priceless dolls. Maddox's arm tightened. Air couldn't get down my throat. I squeezed my eyes closed as blackness taunted.

"She's just a girl!" Aaron snapped.

"And I was only eighteen the first time you and your little friends captured me."

They knew each other? I barely had time to consider that comment before Maddox's arm tightened, crushing my throat. Light faded, the world spun.

"So what?" Aaron hissed. "You're going to kill her? Then do it." His tone was stern. He was totally serious. I was going to die, here in this dungeon. I'd been worried I'd killed Maddox, instead he'd kill me. Lewis had been right.

Then, just as suddenly as he'd grabbed me, Maddox relaxed his hold. My body quivered as glorious air seeped into my lungs. Maddox shoved me away. Off balance and practically unconscious, I stumbled. Aaron was there, reaching for me, but I didn't want him to touch me. I didn't want anyone to touch me. I evaded his grasp and spun around, falling back against the wall.

"Cameron," Aaron called to me.

I shook my head. I had to get away. Away from them. Away from this dungeon. Not looking at either man, I turned and raced through the door. Aaron would have let Maddox kill me. Maddox wasn't on my side. I couldn't trust anyone. I stumbled up the steps, clinging to the railing for balance. I'd been so stupid to think I could deal with this, that I could submerge myself into this lifestyle.

"Cameron?"

Lewis was there at the top of the stairs. Olivia had told him, or maybe he'd read my thoughts. It didn't matter, all that mattered was he was there. I didn't pause, but slammed into his hard body.

He caught me, holding me tight against his bare chest. Vaguely I was aware that he wore only cargo shorts, apparently having come from bed. He smelled warm, and wonderful and comforting.

"What's going on?" he demanded.

"Nothing," I sniffed, cursing the tears that were forming in my eyes. I didn't want him to see me cry, but I didn't want to leave him either. "Everything." The numbness in my body was fading fast and my throat ached.

I felt his body stiffen right before he cupped my shoulders and stepped back. Instead of compassion, he looked furious. "Damn it, you went and visited that agent, didn't you?"

Shock gave way to fury. Immediately I threw up my mind wall. "Don't read my thoughts!"

His face flushed. "I can't help it!"

There was only a foot between us, but suddenly it felt like miles. I pushed him aside and rushed into my room, slamming the door shut. I needed someone to comfort me, not condemn me.

Lewis had apparently never heard of privacy and opened my door, barging in. "Why, Cam? Why would you go down there? Why would you put yourself in danger?"

I stomped my foot. "Because I have a heart! I couldn't sleep until I knew he was okay." But we both knew what I was implying…it was there, hanging in the charged air between us. I hadn't trusted Lewis to tell me the truth about Maddox's well-being.

His jaw clenched. "You have a lot of compassion for the man who killed our parents."

I flushed, feeling guilty as hell and at the same time angry that Lewis would say something so insensitive. "He didn't have anything to do with their deaths, he's too young."

He shook his head, pacing across my room. "You know what I mean."

As much as I wanted to love Lewis, there was a part of me that realized he was a tiny bit delusional. I would never be foremost in his mind and heart because his vendetta would always be first.

"How do we even know it's the truth?" I asked softly, trying a different tactic.

He froze and looked at me like we were five and I'd just told him Santa Clause wasn't real. "What do you mean?"

I paused for a moment, wondering if I dared to go on. Why not, I'd already pissed him off. Aaron was probably angry at me too. What did I have to lose? "I mean, who saw it? How do we know it happened?"

His face flushed with anger. "Aaron saw it! He saw the destruction! What was left after they attacked!"

What was left. My stomach revolted at the image. I pressed my hand to my gut and settled on the edge of my bed. I'd pushed him too far. Perhaps so far that we'd never recover.

Lewis snorted, obviously disgusted with me, and moved toward the door. "This isn't some game, Cam. This isn't some high school drama bullshit. This is real and you need to pick sides."

"Or what?" I whispered, feeling bitterly cold, and not really sure if I wanted the answer.

He paused at the door, but didn't look back. "Or maybe…you should leave."

Chapter 17

I should have let it go. At the least, I should have been angry with Lewis and avoiding him. Instead, at 3 a.m. after tossing and turning, I found myself standing outside Lewis's bedroom door. I lifted my fist to knock, only to hesitate. I'd never truly had a boyfriend, therefore never gotten into an argument. I felt unsure about how to proceed.

Before I could make a decision, the door opened and Lewis stood there. His eyes were intense, drilling. He wore only shorts, no shirt, and his hair was mussed. Although he wasn't a body builder, he was cut; his muscles obvious.

I knew, standing there, that I had forgotten to cover my thoughts and I knew he heard me thinking about how gorgeous he was. But instead of putting up my wall, in some spiteful way, I found myself leaving it down, wanting to be honest, wanting to force him to be honest with me.

The house and hall were quiet as we stood there, not saying a word to each other. But we didn't need to say much. I could tell by the stiffness of his body he was still angry with me. I was confused. I was hurt. I was a little afraid and I wanted him to know…to understand. I also wanted him to hold me because he looked good, really, really good and in this mansion, in this world, he was the only person I could turn to. Damn it all, I wanted him to pull me close; I wanted him to hold me. And he knew these thoughts and still he didn't reach out, merely looked away. It broke my heart.

"Do you really want me to leave?" I hadn't meant to say the words, to sound so pathetic and weak…the sort of girl I hated. But here I was, practically begging him with my sad puppy-dog face to say that he was still, possibly, in love with me. Frankly, I hated myself for it.

He sighed and rubbed his hand over his face as if he was tired. Tired of me? Tired of my questions? Or tired of the situation?

He reached out, latching onto my arm and pulled me into the room. Safely inside he closed the door. I fell back against the wall and he stepped toward me, pressing his body to mine, the side of his face to mine.

For a moment he just held me there. Our bodies intimately close, his warm breath tickling my ear. I wrapped my arms around his waist and soaked in his essence; felt the thump of his heart against mine. God, I didn't want it to end. After a few moments, he stepped back, leaving me alone and cold. I curled my hands against my thighs, resisting the urge to latch onto him. He didn't look at me, but stared at some point across the room.

"Well?" I finally demanded. "You didn't answer my question. Do you want me to leave?"

He raked his hands through his hair and paced toward the large, Queen bed. "Of course not. I want you here, but I want you on my side."

"It's not about sides," I insisted. "It's about right and wrong."

He spun around to face me. "Right and wrong?"

He was getting angry. I was just as frustrated, realizing he was too emotional to have a simple conversation. This isn't what I'd wanted to accomplish by coming here. "How can you not understand?"

He threw his arms in the air. "Understand what? That if that man was released he'd report immediately to his supervisors and we'd end up captured or worse, dead like our parents?"

My blood went cold at his words. "You don't know that."

"I do, I've dealt with people like him before."

Stunned, I found myself stuttering. "You...you mean to say you've captured others and tortured them?"

He stood near his window, framed by the dark blue curtains that matched his eyes. "How else do you suggest we get information?"

I felt sick. He hadn't denied it. I had this slow, horrible feeling I didn't know anything. "You're torturing him! You saw his life, you saw the man he was and is. He has parents, a sister, a girlfriend, two nieces. He played soccer. He went to college—"

He slammed his hand against the wall. His anger frightened me more than I wanted to admit. "Stop! Damn it, Cameron, I'm protecting you. How do you not understand that?"

Sure, maybe my heart should have fluttered romantically at his words, but it didn't. I wanted to shake sense into him. I felt like I was talking to a brick wall. "And if he dies because of what we've done?"

Determined steps brought him closer to me, his face set in stern lines of seriousness and intent. "He's not going to die."

"If he does?"

He paused directly in front of me, his lips parted as if to argue. With a frustrated groan, he latched onto my upper arms and pulled me into his chest. He was so warm, so lovely and his scent so wonderful that for a moment I just sank into him.

"What does it matter?" he whispered.

I froze, horrified. Surely he didn't mean he didn't care if Maddox died. "You don't mean that."

He was silent for a moment. "We'd be safer with him gone."

I shook my head, staring up at him, knowing I would ruin everything with my next words. But I couldn't help myself and I couldn't think with him touching me. I shoved my hands against his shoulders, pushing him out of the way. "How can you say that?"

He latched onto my arm, his grasp desperate. "You'll walk out? Run away because it's gotten complicated?"

I wanted to ignore my feelings, to pull Lewis close and forget everything that had happened. Instead, I tugged my arm away from him. "No, because what you're doing is wrong, Lewis."

"You know nothing—"

"What about George?"

He shook his head, looking confused.

"Did you send George to my town on purpose?"

"Do you even hear yourself? Do you realize what you're saying? That's insane, Cameron! How can you think that?"

"I don't know what to think anymore!" I cried out. "Before you there was hardly any crime in our town. And Maddox said—"

He laughed, a harsh laugh. "And here we go again. You'll believe a murderer over me."

I didn't respond, I wasn't sure how to. He grew silent and there was something there behind his eyes, a sadness that tore at my heart. He knew, before I'd realized, what I was going to do.

"You want to leave," he said softly.

Hot tears burned my eyes. "I can't stay here, Lewis, not knowing what you're doing. I can't be a part of that."

"And what about us?" his voice caught.

For one long moment, I couldn't respond knowing if I answered him, it would be over; any relationship we had. But the truth just flowed from my mouth, unheeded. "How can there be an us? We don't believe in the same things. You think it's perfectly fine to torture a man, to imprison him like he's an animal."

He shook his head, obviously disappointed in me. My throat closed with tears and emotion.

"And you think it's perfectly fine to release a person who will kill you without flinching," he stated.

"You don't know that."

He laughed and looked away. "Then try. Leave, Cameron. Put yourself out there where anything can happen. Test that theory, but just remember I won't be around to save you."

His words annoyed and hurt me, at the same time they gave me strength. "I don't need you to save me. I never did."

Having the last word, I pushed past him and burst into the hall. Even though my heart was hammering with the need to escape, I refused to run. I didn't even flinch when I heard his door slam shut. I couldn't turn back now. If I returned to Lewis, I'd give in and beg him to forgive me. I couldn't, because I knew deep down I was right. Sometimes being right sucked.

Halfway to my bedroom, my emotions got the better of me. I paused in the middle of the hall as tears stung my eyes and blurred my vision. I had to leave this place. I knew that now. I no longer felt safe. I no longer felt like I belonged. But go where? Back to Grandma?

Suddenly, I missed her. Missed our small kitchen, and the eggs and pancakes she forced me to eat every morning. I missed the fact that on week nights we'd watch reality T.V. and argue about who would win that rose. I missed my small bed that creaked every time I rolled over and the floorboards that were so cold I had to wear two pair of socks.

I had to leave. I had to leave Lewis.

I fell back against the hallway wall, my legs weak. Oh God, I had to leave Lewis. The sob that had been stuck in my throat for the past five minutes came out in a strangled sob.

"Psst," someone whispered.

Startled, I managed to contain myself. Olivia peeked out of an open door a few feet down the hall. She waved me toward her. I stood there for a long moment, wondering what to do. What sage wisdom did she have tonight? I really didn't have the energy to deal with her.

"I'm tired, I want to go to bed." I turned toward my door, intent on ignoring her.

"I have to show you something."

Damn if I didn't pause and glance back. She was pulling at her hair in that way that made me want to cringe. I wanted to refuse, to leave her standing there, but when I looked in her eyes and saw the desperation, I found myself making my way toward her.

I'd never been in her bedroom and I admit I felt weird, like I shouldn't be there. We weren't exactly B.F.F.'s. The room was purple, the curtains white lace. A lamp glowed on a bedside table, offering a warmth to the area. It was completely girly, yet almost too young, like for a five year old. There was even a set of porcelain dolls on the bed. It was kind of creepy, but then I expected nothing less than to be creeped out by her.

"What is it?" I asked, eager to leave.

She hesitated, and drawing that lock of hair between her lips, she nibbled on it like corn on the cob. Just when I was about to leave, her eyes went wide like an animal cornered. She was scared. Whatever she was about to tell me, she shouldn't.

I swallowed hard. "Olivia, what is it?"

She spun around, and rushed to her bedside table. The drawer creaked as she pulled it open. This wasn't the dour and blunt Olivia I'd come to know. This was a little girl, afraid of her own shadow. There was a soft rustling, as she searched through the drawer, her movements jerky and frantic. Curious and more than a little nervous, I stepped closer.

She turned, clutching a silver frame to her flat chest. "Here." She shoved the picture at me. With no choice, I took it. A man, woman and a little girl with dark hair, stared back at me. A happy family, as photos often portray. Even though the child couldn't have been older than five, I could tell she was Olivia.

I looked up at her. "Your parents?"

She nodded and snatched the picture from my hands. Of course there were a million questions I wanted to ask her, but before I could even open my mouth, she shoved the frame back into the drawer, hidden from prying eyes. When she faced me again, she looked odd, her eyes shining, her face flushed...almost excited or nervous, like there was something more she needed to share, something she shouldn't.

"What happened to your parents?" I asked, warily. Were they, too, destroyed in the great epic battle? "Did...did they die when my father and Lewis's parents died?"

She didn't respond, merely took her hair between her lips. For one long moment, I stared at her while she stared at the floor. Something had happened, and I wasn't leaving until she got the courage to tell me the truth. I was tired of the secrets, the lies.

I stepped closer to her, anger propelling me forward. "Damn it, Olivia, I need—"

"I want to show you something," she whispered, looking up at me with anxious eyes. "Will you come with me?"

I hesitated. The last time I'd gone with Olivia, Aaron had found me in Maddox's room. And look how well that had worked out.

"He won't find us," she said, her gaze solemn.

Startled, I was silent for a moment. She'd read my mind when I'd had my wall up.

"Come on." She raced past me and was in the hall before I'd even decided to follow. With a sigh, I knew I had no alternative. I rushed after her just in time to see her disappear around a corner. "Olivia!" I whispered furiously, trying to follow her dark shadow down a narrow back set of stairs. "How can you read my mind when I had the wall up?"

"I've always been able to," she whispered back. "No one can block their thoughts from me."

I caught up with her on the first floor. "I don't understand."

"What's there to understand?" Olivia cracked open a door I'd never been through, peeked inside, and finding the area empty she darted down a hall.

I made sure no one was there, and followed after her. I had no idea where we were as I'd never been to this part of the house before. Just ahead I could see her, a dark shadow, pull open another door and dart down another set of stairs. We were headed into the basement, although at the opposite end of where Maddox was being held.

I paused for one moment, my heart hammering madly. Did I want to start this all over again? Hell, yes. I rushed down those narrow steps, delving into the darkness.

"I don't understand." I reached out, pressing my hands to the stone walls on each side for balance. Olivia paused at the bottom, a dark shadow waiting for me. "If you can read anyone's thoughts, why didn't they use you to read Maddox?"

"Because he has something different blocking his thoughts, something man-made." She continued down a narrow hall, pausing outside a thick, steel door. Not completely like Maddox's cell. This door had a window. I stood on tiptoe and peeked through the glass, but whatever was on the other side was concealed with darkness.

"Move." Olivia nudged me aside with a pointy elbow and then punched in a code at yet another keypad. Vaguely I was aware that whatever was in there must have been important. There was a click as the door unlocked. Such a soft sound, yet my pulse hammered madly. Quietly, she pushed the door wide.

"Where are we?" I whispered. Narrow windows lined the tops of the walls, too high to see out of, but allowing moonlight to filter into a long, large room.

But Olivia didn't answer and for one moment, we just stood there. Maybe she was waiting for my eyes to adjust, maybe she wasn't sure how to explain, or maybe she regretted her actions. Whatever her deal, it was too late. Shadows morphed into objects. Objects became small beds lined along the perimeter of the room. And little forms huddled on the beds were obviously children. Small children under blankets, children fast asleep. The soft sound of deep, even breathing was the only noise in the dorm…or orphanage…whatever it was.

Olivia started forward and so I followed, my shoes thumping eerily against the linoleum. "Who are they?" I demanded in a harsh whisper.

"Children with powers," Olivia whispered back. "Children like us."

Caroline. I froze. I could have sworn for one brief moment my heart stopped beating. Shock held me immobile. Children like us. I didn't know what I'd been expecting, but it hadn't been this. There were at least twenty kids in this room, Olivia and I not included.

My little tour guide continued down the aisle. I hurried after her, frantic to understand. "Olivia, explain!"

"That girl there." She pointed to the first bed on the right like a flight attendant pointing out exits. "She can cause people to feel pain. Real, horrible, physical pain."

My stomach clenched.

"And that boy," She pointed toward the left, indicating a small bundle of a child who couldn't be more than six. "He can make you think you see things that aren't really there."

She pointed toward Caroline, who slept soundly curled into a tight ball, her long blonde hair glimmering under the light of the moon. "She—"

"Okay," I whispered furiously and latched onto her arm, forcing her to pause in the middle of the room. "Enough. I get it." But I didn't get it. I didn't understand anything and frankly I was tired of being the stupid one in class. How could these children be here without me knowing? Shouldn't I have heard yelling? Laughter? Something! But all I'd heard was crying. I pressed my hands to my stomach, the room fading, the world fading.

Crying. All those times I'd heard that eerie sound at night, those times Aaron had brushed off my questions by saying it was merely the wind. Crying. Frightened, little children kept under lock and key.

"He kept them quiet. He didn't want you to know right away. He was afraid you'd think it was weird." Olivia took that strand of hair between her lips and watched me as she chewed, waiting for my response.

He thought it would be weird? It was beyond weird. It was creepy. I tried to calm my racing heart. "How did they get here? Did their parents die? Were their parents murdered?"

"No," she said, shaking her head.

"Then how?" I swiped my damp hands on my sweats. "Did their parents send them here to learn how to use their powers? Is this like a school of some sort?"

She shook her head again.

Frustrated, I resisted the urge to yell at her. "Olivia," I snapped, my voice harsh. I glanced around, to make sure they still slept. None of them stirred; they were like little statues. "How did they get here?"

She lowered the lock of hair from her mouth, her large dark eyes looking directly at me. "He took them."

Chapter 18

I was trembling when I made my way back to my room. An icy chill had settled deep within my bones and I couldn't seem to get warm. Olivia was nuts, right? Surely Aaron hadn't taken innocent children from their beds. Stolen them from their families. Olivia had made it up, just as she'd made up other things. I jerked open my top dresser drawer and pushed aside my socks and underwear.

Where had I left my cell phone?

Maybe I should ask Lewis about the children. No, I should demand the truth, not ask. But would he tell me? Frustrated, I grabbed my purse off the nightstand and emptied the contents onto my bed. Chapstick, wallet, gum. No phone. .

I paused, in the middle of the room, and took a deep breath in, out, like Aaron had taught me. Thoughts of the man made me sick. I wrapped my arms around my belly and sank onto the edge of the bed. I didn't want to be in a place where I didn't know who was good and who was bad. I wanted to be home. So maybe I wasn't going to buy her a mug with World's Best Grandma anytime soon, but at least at home I'd never felt so confused, so scared.

Grandma might have been wrong in keeping the truth from me, but I knew without a doubt she had my best interest at heart. With Aaron, even with Lewis, I had a feeling they'd give me up in an instant if it would help the mission. They were determined and no one would stop them or get in their way, certainly not me.

I had to call Grandma and hopefully she would answer. She could pick me up at the ferry dock on the mainland. Somehow I'd leave here, whether I snuck out, which I'd prefer as the coward in me couldn't face Lewis and Aaron, or if I had to, demand that they take me to the harbor.

I was going home.

I pulled open my bedroom door and made my way into the hall. It was almost dawn. Grandma would still be sleeping but hopefully she'd answer. When I moved by Lewis's room, I made sure my mental wall was up. I forced myself not to pause, not even to think about him. I'd die if he heard my thoughts and woke up. I couldn't face him, not now. If I saw him, I might not have the courage to leave.

The house was still and dark and silent. No crying this morning. I couldn't help but think of those children downstairs, locked away like animals. Did their parents miss them? Were they afraid? Some were so young. And I thought about myself, when I was five and I'd been dropped off at Grandma's, a person I hadn't even met until that day. How afraid I'd been. How terrified. It wasn't right; these children were here without their families. Yet, what could I do?

The kitchen was empty. No Olivia having her late night snack. I reached for the phone, slid down the wall, sitting on the floor, my back against the cold wall. With trembling fingers I dialed Grandma's number.

Nothing happened. No dialing tone, no beep, nothing.

I hung up and tried again.

Nothing.

A floor board creaked. My heart slammed against my ribcage. Fear fought with panic. Gripping the phone to my chest, I fell to my knees and crawled behind the island counter in the middle of the kitchen. Crouching low, I leaned against the counter and held my breath.

Soft footsteps thudded through the room…closer….closer.

"Cameron?"

Aaron's voice jolted through me. I surged to my feet and bit back my scream. He stood against the island, his arms folded over his chest. How long had he been there? I couldn't read his face in the darkness and didn't know if he was angry.

"I…I missed my Grandma and wanted to call her." True enough.

"Why?" He moved around the island counter, coming closer to me. I had to resist the urge to dart behind the barrier. "She's done nothing for you."

The moonlight coming in through the windows hit his face. He'd changed from sweats and t-shirt and was wearing gray slacks and a button up black shirt, his hair combed neatly into place as if nothing had happened last night. As if he was up this early every morning, dressed, ready to take on the world, ready to steal more children.

"I wouldn't say nothing." I certainly saw the irony in the fact that I was suddenly defending Grandma. "She's kept me safe all this time. Besides, she's family. My only family."

He rested perfectly manicured hands on the countertop. "We're your family, Cameron."

More irony. How I'd pathetically dreamt of Aaron being my dad and now...now I didn't even want him as a friend.

I felt the slightest push inside my head. So slight that before I wouldn't have noticed it. My insides froze. He was trying to read my mind. Testing the barrier to see if I'd put up that wall. I forced my lips to lift, my face to remain passive.

"I know you're my family," I lied. "But..." I shrugged with a nonchalance I sure as heck didn't feel. "I've lived with her most of my life. It's normal to miss her, isn't it?"

I waited for his answer, waited to see if he'd buy my logic, prayed he would.

He smiled and still I wasn't sure if I should be nervous or relieved. "I understand."

Relieved. Definitely relieved. "But, umm, anyway, the phone doesn't seem to be working." I replaced the phone, hoping he didn't notice the way my hand trembled. "And I can't find my cell."

"Hmm," he glanced briefly at the phone, then back to me. "Well, the winds must have done damage somewhere on the island. Besides, it's late and you've been busy tonight." He smiled. It seemed genuine. I didn't buy his friendliness in the least. "I know about your visit to the dorm. Olivia told me."

That didn't make sense. Why would Olivia tell him when it would make her guilty? Unless she'd twisted the facts. "Sorry," I muttered, watching him closely. "I thought I'd seen a little girl when I'd first arrived."

He placed his arm around my shoulders, his golden hair silver in the moonlight. My entire body went cold. As he led me out of the kitchen, I had to resist the urge to shrug him off. "I try to help as many children as I can. It's impossible to turn them away when they have nowhere to go."

I nodded, all the while wondering if he was lying. Or was Olivia the liar? Someone wasn't telling the truth. I didn't question him further; it would only make me look suspicious. My goal at the moment was to get as far away from him as possible.

We strolled into the main foyer. He'd turned on the lights and it added a soft glow to the area. "I'm sure," he continued, giving my shoulders a little squeeze, "your grandmother would appreciate you waiting until the sun rises to call her."

I forced myself to smile. "Yeah, sure."

"And of course if you don't find your cell, we'll get you another one."

Of course he would. Why didn't I buy that in the least? We paused at the bottom of the steps. "Okay, thanks."

He was smiling, but it didn't reach his eyes. "Good night, Cameron."

I could feel his gaze burning into my back as I made my way up the stairs. I didn't dare look over my shoulder, but kept my gaze straight ahead, even as my heart hammered madly in my chest.

In the hall, I didn't bother to look at Lewis' door. I was too hurt. Only ten more steps… ten more steps to relative safety. I pushed open my door and closed it tightly behind me.

"Cameron?" a soft voice whispered through the darkness.

I jerked my head toward the bed. A small shape was huddled on the mattress, her knees tucked to her chest, that white nightgown glowing. "Caroline?"

She sniffed, like she'd been crying.

My nerves lurched. "What is it? What's wrong?"

"Can I… can I sleep with you?"

My heart melted. Thank God it was dark, I didn't want her to see the tears. "Yeah, sure." I tried to keep my voice light, calm, but truth was I needed the comfort of another person as much as she did.

"Move over." I shoved her playfully and pulled back the cover. How many times had I wished for a sibling to share secrets with? But at the moment I wished she was anywhere but here. She didn't deserve this. I didn't deserve this.

I lay down and she cuddled next to me. I threw my mental wall up. She wouldn't know what I was really feeling. I wouldn't frighten her even more. Biting my lower lip, I refused to let my tears fall.

"I miss my mom," she whispered.

I squeezed my eyes shut, the tears I'd been trying to keep at bay raced down my cheeks. "I know." I didn't say anymore. I didn't need to. She understood how I felt. I understood her.

As I rolled onto my back I realized there were three things I knew for sure. One, I could no longer trust Aaron. Two, I wasn't any safer here than I'd been at home. Three, I knew, without a doubt, I had to escape as soon as I could.

****

"What are you doing?"

I didn't bother to look up from my suitcase; I knew Lewis's voice well by now. I'd woken this morning to find Caroline gone and perhaps it would be easier this way. I didn't want her to see me leave. After all, I couldn't exactly take her with me, could I?

Lewis was angry, and a little surprised. The sun was up, had been for a few hours and my outlook had changed. With the brilliant rays of the sun, I felt stronger, more sure of what I had to do. But I still feared that if I actually looked Lewis in the eyes, I'd completely fold. "I'm packing."

"For what?"

"Aren't you the one who said I should leave?" Finally, I looked up at him.

The light coming in from the windows highlighted his brown hair, making it shimmer. He was paler than normal, dark circles under his blue eyes. He'd slept about as well as I had. My gaze dropped to his lips. For a moment my heart lurched, remembering the few kisses we'd shared. But there would be no more. I forced myself to look away.

"Cameron," his voice was soft. "I didn't mean it."

I refused to answer, but continued to shove some sweaters into the suitcase that lay open on the floor. I still hadn't found my cell and was beginning to worry. How would I get a hold of Grandma once I'd reached the mainland? I had only ten bucks.

"Stop," he insisted, dropping beside me. He latched onto my wrists and held my arms tight, forcing me to pause. Only a foot separated the space between us. I couldn't move as I stared into those brilliant blue eyes. His face was tense, his lower lip quivering. And for one brief moment my heart expanded, warming with an emotion I didn't dare explore. "I don't want you to leave."

"Why?" I asked, dropping my gaze to his neck, staring at the pulse that beat furiously fast. "Because you can't use my powers if I leave?"

"No." He released my hands and pulled my packed clothing from the suitcase, tossing it to the bed with frantic movements. "Because I…" He paused, swallowing hard. "I don't want you to go."

I felt the stinging sensation of tears. How I wanted to be with him. The thought of leaving Lewis left me aching and cold. And he wanted me. I could see that now. Not because of my powers, but because he actually cared.

"Come with me," I whispered, more like pleaded.

"What do you mean?"

He knew what I was asking. "When I leave, come home with me." I grabbed his hands. His fingers were cold. "You can live with me and Grandma. Or, you're eighteen, you can get an apartment."

He pulled away. "I can't."

I wasn't surprised, but it still hurt. "Why?"

"Because…" He stood and paced to the windows. With every step further away from me, my heart broke a little more. He would come up with any excuse not to leave. "Because we have a job to do."

It was just as I'd thought. Lewis would always pick his supposed mission over me. "What job?" I snapped, surging to my feet and feeling dizzy with anger, pain, and lack of sleep.

He spun around to face me. "Protect us! People like us, people like you."

"Protect us from what? Because so far the only threat I've seen is some pathetic guy chained up in the basement."

"And do you have any idea what that pathetic guy would be capable of doing if he were released?" His hands fisted at his sides, his anger palpable. "My God, how can you not understand? They killed your father! They killed my parents!"

My heart ached. Literally ached when I looked at his beautiful face full of frustration and pain. When I'd first met Lewis I'd envied his freedom, but he was no freer than I was. Less so, maybe. "And so what, you'll kidnap little children and force them to do your bidding like some pathetic evil villain in a cartoon movie?"

He stiffened, as if I'd slapped him. "What are you talking about?"

I threw my arms wide, pointing toward the door. "I know, Lewis. I know about the kids. I know they all have special powers. I know Aaron took them from their parents in order to use them."

He looked away. "You don't know anything."

If I was wrong, why was he avoiding eye contact? "Did he take you from your uncle without the man's consent? Is that what happened?"

He pressed his palm to his heart, his face growing tense with emotion. "He saved me. My uncle had no clue what my mother and father could do. He hadn't a clue what I was capable of. I was a freak to him. When Aaron arrived, I was more than willing to go."

It didn't make sense. There had to be more to the story than he was letting on. "And your uncle just let you go?"

He didn't respond, but he didn't need to. I knew the answer. Olivia had been right all along. Aaron and Lewis didn't care about me. Aaron had taken Lewis and Lewis seemed to think it was fine. His silence was further proof that our morals didn't mesh.

"What did Aaron do to him?"

Lewis shrugged, his eyes growing hard. "It was for his own good."

I stepped closer to the guy I still loved. "What did he do?" I demanded, my anger and fear mounting.

He was silent for one long moment, as if weighing whether to admit the truth to me or not. "He erased his memory."

"Oh my God." I collapsed onto the edge of my bed. I felt sick. Afraid. Confused. "And that's what he's done to these children, isn't it? To their parents?"

Lewis stood his ground, didn't dare step any closer. It was as if a wall had been suddenly built between us. He knew I wouldn't understand. "He had to. They weren't safe with their parents."

Tears burned my eyes. I was sad because I knew Lewis didn't understand, perhaps he never would. "He stole these children and erased any memory from their parent's minds that they'd ever existed?"

Lewis didn't respond, but he didn't need to. How could he not see what he did was wrong?

I swiped angrily at the tears seeping from my eyes. Lewis might not ever understand my position, but he sure as hell could explain the facts. "How did he do it?"

Lewis shrugged, strolling across the room. To anyone else his walk would seem at ease, but I knew his steps were too controlled. "Everyone has their own special ability, unique to them. His is the ability to erase memories."

Just as I'd thought, he'd erased any memory of these children. "And yours? What is your ability?"

He paused for a moment, his square jaw clenched as he weighed his next words carefully. "As you know, I...I can move objects, small objects." But there was more, I could tell he was holding something back.

"What else Lewis?" I demanded.

His jaw clenched, those sharp eyes coming to rest on me. "I can influence people's emotions."

For one moment I was confused as my mind turned his words over and over, attempting to make sense. Emotions. All the feelings I'd had for Lewis came rushing back in a wave of nausea. The instant affection. The silly jealousy. "Did you...to me..."

He was silent, but I read the truth in his beautiful blue eyes.

Panic clawed its way up into my throat. My heart slammed wildly against my chest. I wanted to hit him. I wanted to grab him by the shirt and demand he take the words back. "Lewis, did you make me think I was in love with you?"

He closed his eyes and rubbed his temples. "Cameron..."

"Tell me!" I demanded, standing.

He opened his eyes and looked directly at me. "Only at first."

"Oh my God." I moved across the room, the furthest away from him I could get. I felt trapped, an animal in a cage. Nowhere to go. So much for our love being true and pure.

"I'm not now, Cameron." Lewis came toward me. "Only those first couple days. You thought I was the murderer, I needed you to like me, to trust me."

He paused in front of me, his gaze pleading. He started to reach for me, but apparently realized it was too soon and dropped his arms to his side. "Please, believe me. I haven't influenced you in weeks. What you feel…what I feel…it's real."

At that moment the only feeling I had was hate. Pure hatred because he'd made me doubt my love for him. It all made sense now…. why I'd had barely any misgivings about leaving town with a boy I'd just met. Grandma had been right, something had been off. I leaned back against the wall, my hands fisted.

"It's how you got me to go with you. I should have known, I did know…something wasn't normal. That pull you had over me."

"Cameron," he said, reaching out for me.

"What is my ability? Why does Aaron want me here?"

"He's always wanted you here, partly because he feels responsible for you. You're like a daughter to him."

I snorted in disgust.

"It's true."

"Why am I here?" I demanded again.

He sighed and raked back his hair. "You have more power than any of us, Cameron." He paced in front of me, as if he couldn't stand still, as if he wasn't sure what to do. "Your ability to break into people's thoughts is amazing."

"Olivia can read thoughts."

"Only from normal people, like us. But that chip in that man's head stopped her cold. You busted through it like it was nothing. We're not even sure what you're capable of. It's why it's so important for you to practice, to learn. I think you'd be amazed at what you could accomplish."

"You mean what I could accomplish for you and your little secret club."

He glared at me, obviously frustrated. "We're only trying to protect—"

"Bull!" I tilted my chin high, staring directly into his angry eyes. Lewis wouldn't frighten me. I was sick of being afraid. "I'm going home."

He didn't respond, remaining stubbornly silent. I wanted to scream, to stomp my foot like a child. I needed to have my wits about me, but I couldn't think when he was so close, his scent so warm and wonderful. And in the back of my mind I realized that this could very well be the last time we spoke. But my emotions and anger wouldn't let me care.

"I'm going home, even if I have to walk or swim."

He raked his hair back, his hand trembling. "Don't be ridiculous."

I pushed him aside and grabbed the pink sweater Grandma had gotten me last year for Christmas. My hands shook as I tossed the clothing back into my suitcase. "Where's my cell phone? Aaron took it, didn't he?"

"Think long and hard about what you're doing Cameron."

I froze, looking up at Lewis. "Are you threatening me?"

He looked oddly sad. "No, only warning you."

I ignored the tingling fear working its way up my spine. "Save your warning. I don't need you. I don't need anyone. I'm leaving."

He strolled to the door, his steps slow, controlled. At the hall he paused and looked back, a sympathetic gleam in his eyes. "I'm sorry, Cameron, but there's only one way you're leaving, and that's if you let Aaron erase your memories."

Chapter 19

Only an hour until sunrise. Only an hour and I would be at the docks and on that first ferry across the harbor and to the mainland. Only an hour and my life would be on its way back to normalcy. I hoped.

I had no idea how I'd get home from the harbor, but I didn't care. One step at a time. I had to keep my mind centered. Still, I was shaking as I made my way to my bedroom door. I didn't dare take my suitcase, but had stuffed anything of importance into my backpack, leaving behind the rest.

I kept my mental wall up, not daring to let my thoughts seep from my mind and alert others to my presence. But concentrating was hard under the circumstances. Unwillingly my gaze went to Lewis' bedroom door. The urge to try one more time to talk him into reason overwhelmed me. I forced my feet to keep walking, tore my gaze from that door and rushed, as quietly as possible, down the dark hall, following the path Olivia had taken the other night. I'd seen that exit near the children's ward and hoped it was the best way out. If I'd gotten my directions right, it would lead to the back of the house and the beach. I'd follow the shore to town.

Heading down the first set of steps, I pressed my hands to the narrow walls to keep my balance in the darkness. Lewis had disappointed me in so many ways. I thought we understood each other. I thought we believed in the same things. We should have, after all we'd had similar childhoods, similar pasts.

In reality we were completely different people. But it didn't matter. I still loved him and each step further away from Lewis, broke my heart a little more.

I turned left, walked ten feet down a dark tunnel only to realize I should have turned right. A cold sweat broke out between my shoulder blades. I didn't have time for mistakes. One mistake could mean the difference between me leaving with my memory intact and me leaving with no recollection of what my life had been.

I had a plan; sneak into town right at the moment when the first boat was leaving. Jump on the ferry and be gone. I couldn't think further than that, and I couldn't think about the plan going wrong. Any mistakes would be my downfall. I turned right and made my way toward the door where the children lay sleeping.

The closer I got, the more my stomach churned, threatening to bring up the chicken and rice that had been brought to my room by a nameless servant. At the door, I froze. I could see them sleeping through the small window, those tiny bundles of power. How could I leave them here? But what could I do? It would be pretty hard to go incognito with twenty small children at my side. As much as it pained me to leave them behind, I knew, for my own sake, I had to.

Turning away from the children's dorm, I focused on the door that would lead outside. Metal, bullet proof, impenetrable, no doubt. A bolt locked the door in place. To the normal person the door would seem secure, but I couldn't help but wonder where the rest of it was. Shouldn't there be an alarm? A camera? But the hall was surprisingly empty.

I slid back the deadbolt and stepped outside into the crisp morning air. Easy enough. Everything was going exactly as planned. And that worried me. It was all too simple. And then I saw the fence and realized life was one big joke. That tall fence continued from the front of the house and apparently wrapped around the back. A fence much too tall to climb.

A cold wind swept from the ocean, stinging my face. Across the harbor, lights from the mainland twinkled and glowed, calling me home. Already the seagulls could be heard, crying their good mornings. It was the right time to leave, but how could I when that huge iron fence rose up from the earth surrounding the yard? I hadn't had much of a plan when I'd decided to leave. I was hoping God or Fate would smile down on me.

"Hello?" I whispered, looking toward the gray sky. "Could use some help about now."

Shockingly, God didn't respond.

"Fate it is."

I moved along the fortress Aaron had built, my hands scratching against the rough brick. To think I'd believed this place a stunning, magical home when I'd first arrived. I knew better now. It was nothing more than an elegant prison. At the corner of the estate, where the bricks met in a sharp angle, I paused. Still too dark to see much of anything, but I could just make out that ocean shimmering under a crescent moon.

"Where are you going?"

The soft, sudden voice sent my heart leaping into my throat. I spun around. "Caroline?" She wore jeans and a sweatshirt, but no coat. I glanced sharply around, looking for someone who might claim her. There was no movement in the darkness beyond.

"Are you…did you come from the children's dorm?"

She nodded, her bangs whispering across her eyes with the movement.

"You should go back. It's cold. If they find you missing they'll worry." And come looking, which wouldn't be good for me.

"Are you leaving?" she asked, her lower lip quivering. My heart clenched at the thought of lying to her. I had no choice! I couldn't take her with me.

"No, of course not," I said, stumbling over the words. "Now go back to bed, okay?" I shooed her with my hands, but she just stood there, staring at me like a dog after a treat. "Listen kid, you have to go, please."

"You look like my sister."

I hadn't realized she had a sister, but that was good. It meant she had someone here with her. "Yeah?" Damn, if my voice didn't catch. "Well, she probably misses you, so go back to your room so you can see her, okay?"

"She's not there."

Crap. This just kept getting better and better. "Did they take you from your family, Caroline? Did they make you leave your sister?"

She nodded, her large eyes shimmering now. She was going to cry and then I'd cry and we'd be caught.

"I miss her, but I can't talk about her because they won't let me."

The anger I felt toward Aaron rushed through my body in a heated wave. For one insane moment I wanted to tear through the door and demand they return the children. Instead, I knelt before Caroline, my knees hitting the hard dirt with a thud that jarred my body. "Did your parents know? Did they understand that you were being taken away? Or did…Aaron do something to make them forget?"

She shrugged, looking confused. "I don't know."

"It's okay." I grasped her narrow shoulders. "Do you know when they took you? A year ago? Two? "

Her brows drew together, her lips puckering. "It was winter and cold. I didn't get to open my Christmas presents."

No Christmas presents? Now that was just plain wrong. "Do you remember where you lived Caroline? What town?"

She frowned. "Ohio, I think."

Ohio? Ohio might as well have been another country at the moment. I hadn't realized these abductions took place across states. I stood. I knew what I had to do and even as I thought the words, Caroline said, "Take me home?"

How could I refuse? What was one kid anyway? Surely we could sneak onto the boat together. They'd think we were siblings. In fact, it might work better this way. And if her parents didn't remember her, Grandma would let her live with us.

"Okay, come on." I took her hand, her tiny fingers chilled. We needed to make it to town fast; she wouldn't last long in this cold weather. It was a ridiculous plan. I knew that, but I had no choice.

"Where will we go?"

Already with the questions? It wouldn't take long before she'd realize I hadn't a clue what I was doing. "I'm not sure." I slipped one of the straps of my backpack from my shoulder, intent on finding a sweater that would fit Caroline. She needed something to block the wind.

She latched onto my sleeve and tugged. "This way."

I didn't miss the fact that she was pulling me back toward the house and the way we'd just come.

"No," I said. "We need to leave now." What had the kid forgotten? A stuffed bear or some other ridiculous object that didn't matter at the moment? Didn't she understand how important it was that we escaped ASAP?

"Caroline, we can't go back."

"Please," she whispered. "I know where we can get out."

My knees almost buckled in relief. "Are you sure?"

She nodded. What choice did I have? Follow a kid or stumble around the yard on my own until I was caught? We followed the outside wall of the southern end of the house, heading toward the back. The entire way, that damn fence followed, mocking us. The sky was turning to gray, dawn breaking. My anxiety flared.

"Caroline, are you sure—"

"There." She pointed to a dark impression in the earth that ran underneath the fence. "A secret tunnel."

I darted the small distance and hunched down. It was a drainage pipe that led underneath to the shore. Definitely small enough for Caroline to fit through, maybe small enough for me. When I lowered myself to my belly, I could see the gray light at the end of the dark tunnel, beckoning freedom. There was also a thin layer of water along the bottom of the metal pipe. I didn't have time to think about what could be living and growing in that water.

My top priority was the diameter of that tunnel. If I got stuck, or if there were rats or spiders...no, it didn't matter. I had to try. Stepping back a few feet, I slipped my backpack from my shoulders and tossed it over the fence. Fortunately it sailed over the top and landed with a thud in the sand on the other side.

"I'll go first," I muttered.

Caroline nodded her agreement, her little round face full of trust. For a moment panic took hold. My God, this little kid trusted me to get her out of here. I should have forced her to return but it was too late now. My conscience wouldn't let me leave her behind.

I lowered myself into that small gully, then lay flat on the cold ground, frost biting into my sensitive palms. The dirt was hard as I inched my way into the metal tunnel. Small rocks bit through my jeans and jacket, scraping my legs and stomach.

I reached the tunnel, didn't pause, but flattened myself to the ground. The thin layer of ice that had formed over the water cracked. Bitterly cold, it soaked my clothing, chilling my flesh. I bit my lower lip, dug my elbows into the ground and surged forward on my forearms into the pipe. I just fit, my shoulders scraping against the metal sides. This was my only chance. Caroline was counting on me. I couldn't let Aaron erase my memory.

The moment my torso was inside that tunnel, a tinkling of panic threatened to overwhelm me. What if my hips got stuck? I ignored the shouts of warning coursing through my mind. I told myself the tunnel would remain the same size all the way through, that if I fit now, I'd fit ten feet in; I wouldn't get stuck halfway and drown when the tide came.

Thankfully, it was too cold and damp for spiders and rats. One small blessing. My harsh breath echoed against my metal coffin. No rats, no spiders, but the ground could collapse, my panicked brain taunted. I could get stuck.

I shook my head, clearing my thoughts. No, I was almost there. If I could straighten my arms, untuck them from my body, I'd be able to touch the cold air ahead.

"Almost there, Caroline," I said, forcing my voice to sound jovial. I pushed my elbows under my body and inched forward, slower than a snail. The ridges along the pipe hurt, digging into my muscles. "Almost…"

"Cameron!" Caroline screamed.

A firm grip grasped each of my ankles. I froze. Suddenly, I was jerked backwards. My elbows hit each ridge of the metal pipe, thump, thump, thump.

"No!" I screamed, digging my fingers into the ridges and trying to cling as if my life depended on it. My nails bent painfully upward and with a yelp, I let go. "Caroline!" I called out, as if the child could help.

My shoulders scraped against the sides of the pipe and suddenly I was pulled outside, the cold, clean air swooshing into my lungs.

A tall man loomed above me, an ugly scowl on his round face. One of the guards. I wasted no time and lifted my hips, shoving my feet into his gut. He grunted, stumbling back. I flipped over and scrambled to my feet. Without looking back I surged forward, into the gray dawn.

I could hear someone running after me, the thump of footsteps, heavy breathing. I didn't dare look back. It didn't matter how fast I ran, I had nowhere to go. I sensed him right before a body tackled me to the ground. With a cry, I stumbled forward. My knees hit the dirt. I twisted as I fell to my back. Lewis fell on top of me, his hard body pinning me to the frosted grass.

"Lewis," I whispered his name, but he heard all the same. I felt betrayed, hurt in a way I couldn't stand. That same body that had offered me comfort before, was now a foreign object keeping me imprisoned in this hell.

"Lewis," my voice caught, my fingers curling into his sweatshirt. His face was hard, but his eyes…dare I believe that his eyes were softening as he stared down at me? "Don't do this. Please let me—"

"You don't understand," he whispered, confusing me.

"What the hell do you think you're doing, Cameron?" Aaron suddenly appeared behind Lewis. Aaron never lost his cool, but now, as he stared daggers down at me, I was seeing the man for who he truly was, and he was irate. "Not only are you endangering your life, but the life of a child."

Lewis stood. I jumped to my feet, stumbling back. Four guards stood behind Aaron, waiting to do his bidding. Deborah, the gorgeous Indian woman, held Caroline's hand, doing nothing to calm the little girl who was crying. No hugs, no whispered words to tell her everything was going to be alright. Caroline was terrified and cold and that really pissed me off. It was one thing to scare me, but a little girl?

"We have alarms on the doors for protection," Aaron said. He wore dress pants and a button up shirt, as if he'd been awake for some time. Like a father, dressed for work. "Did you really think you could just leave without someone knowing?"

I had hoped, but decided to keep that to myself. I crossed my arms over my chest, attempting to keep my body from trembling. It was no use. Between the wet clothes, cold air and the fear working its way through my gut, I was an anxious mess.

"I'm leaving," I snapped, daring them to disagree.

Aaron frowned. "There is a front door you could use, you know."

Was he being sarcastic? "You'd let me leave?"

"Of course I would. I'm not a prison keeper." He started to turn.

"Could have fooled me," I grumbled under my breath.

Aaron jerked his head toward me. I resisted the urge to step back, realizing I might have gone too far. For one long moment he just stood there glaring at me. Not one person said a word, everyone stood still…as if waiting to see what would happen next.

Finally, he looked at Deborah. "Take Caroline back to the dorm."

"Come along," Deborah snapped like a general giving orders.

Caroline looked at me, her eyes pleading, as if she expected I could do something to save her. She didn't realize I was as trapped as she was. I didn't believe for a moment that Aaron was going to let me leave. Just like that, Caroline was gone, forced back into her prison and I realized I'd failed her and that hurt more than anything else.

"Lewis, escort Ms. Winters to her room." Aaron started toward the house, having no further use for me.

"You said I could leave," I reminded Lewis and the guards.

Lewis stepped forward. I stepped back.

"And you will," he said. "But you're soaking wet. I won't let you leave like this. Although you seem to think I am, I'm not a monster. You'll take the ferry home."

I brushed past Lewis and raced after Aaron. "And what about Caroline?"

Aaron didn't bother to glance back. "Caroline is a child and I am her guardian. I have the papers. You have no say in how I raise her."

"She wants to go home! She misses her family. It's not right, stealing kids from their parents!"

He paused near the back door, his gaze cold. "Caroline's parents were going to put her in a mental institution."

I stiffened. It wasn't true. He was lying, I was sure of it. Yet, what if he wasn't…"I don't believe you."

"You are an immature child who knows nothing about what is truly out there. I've done all I can to protect you, yet you still resist. You will not endanger the others here. Tomorrow you will leave and you will be forced to live with the repercussions."

He pulled open the very door where I'd made my escape only moments before, and disappeared inside. I couldn't seem to move, even though the cold air was freezing my wet clothes and my body was trembling, I couldn't move.

Doubt crept through me. Why was it that every time I talked to Aaron, I was left feeling unsure? I knew I was right, but I couldn't help but question my own sanity when he seemed so rational. Was it true? Had he done these children a favor by taking them in? Lewis paused next to me.

"So, you weren't going to say goodbye?" His voice was hard, angry.

"I didn't think I had a choice," I whispered, unable to meet his gaze.

He didn't respond but pulled open the door and moved inside. I dared to glance back at the small army of guards who were behind me. Yeah, I was outnumbered and out muscled, to say the least.

I stepped into Aaron's home and hurried after Lewis. "Lewis, I—"

He paused at the bottom of the steps, his back to me. His shoulders were tense, his entire body trembling. "I can't stop you, can I?" He looked back at me, his gaze piercing. "I've tried to protect you, but you just don't get it." He turned and started up the steps once more, as if done with me altogether.

"No, you don't get it." I rushed up the stairs, knowing this could be my last chance to make him understand. "These children deserve to be with their parents." We paused on the main floor. "You should know that better than anyone."

He latched onto my arm, his grip painful. "No matter how we explain the facts, you twist them and turn them. I have nothing more to say to you, Cameron. Go to your room." He pulled me up the steps to the second floor, going so fast, I tripped beside him. At my bedroom door, I jerked away from his hold. It was over. Anything we had, any emotions we'd shared, they were over.

"Don't try to escape again," he said. "You can wait until tomorrow to leave. And you sure as hell better not try to take any of the kids with you. You'll only endanger them as well."

Somehow the tables had been turned. I felt horrible, as if I was the one making mistakes, as if I was the one in the wrong. Maybe I was. "And just like that, huh?" I whispered. "I can leave tomorrow?"

He took a step back, his gaze pinned to me. "Tomorrow, you can leave," Lewis said, his voice hard. His gaze no longer held any emotion. "You'll go home."

I lifted my chin defiantly, not willing to let him see how his indifference hurt. "I don't buy it."

He took another step back. "You're right. Nothing comes without consequence. We must protect the good of the Mind Readers. In the evening, Aaron will come for you. Your memory of this place, of me…all of it…will be gone. You'll finally get what you want."

Chapter 20

The sun wavered on the edge of the horizon, hovering there for eternity, taunting me as if knowing that once it slipped below, my life would change forever. Afternoon was fading fast into evening. With evening, they would arrive.

Lewis' face flashed to mind. *Aaron will come for you. Your memory of this place, of me...all of it...will be gone. You'll finally get what you want.*

But he knew I didn't want this. Who would want their brain turned into mush? I pressed my fingers to the window, my breath fogging the cold glass. I couldn't rest. I couldn't eat. I couldn't do anything but wait for the thump of Aaron's footsteps in the hallway outside my bedroom door.

I glanced over my shoulder at the clock on my bedside table. The minutes flashed; brilliant red numbers that glared at me. For three hours I'd barely moved. For three hours I'd stared at that clock until I thought my retinas would burn. I thought about my dad and wondered if he had known his best friend was a psycho. I wondered about Caroline, if she was still crying. If she had gotten into trouble because of me. But mostly I wondered about Lewis, and if he really cared.

Aaron would arrive any moment now. I knew that. It was almost as if I could sense him coming closer. Frustrated tears burned my eyes. I swiped angrily at my wet cheeks. The waiting was unbearable.

He'd posted a guard at my bedroom door. I glanced outside. The big, burly man who had ripped me from that tunnel stood below my window. Aaron wasn't leaving anything to chance.

Lewis wouldn't help me. Grandma had no clue where to find me. I was alone in this mess.

How much of my memory would they take? Everything I knew about Lewis, every experience we'd ever shared. As much as I resented him, the thought of forgetting Lewis completely killed me. This island, this home…all gone. The children…Caroline…gone. What if Aaron screwed up and erased more? What if I became some vegetable with no thoughts, no life?

It wasn't right. He had no right to do this to me. He had no right to do this to anyone.

As angry as I was at Aaron I was even more so at my supposed boyfriend. How could Lewis let this happen? Some girls complained because their boyfriends didn't pay them enough attention, or buy them gifts. But let's face it, Lewis could pretty much hands down win *Worst Boyfriend Of The Year.*

I spun around, anger propelling me forward, pacing back and forth, stuck in this stupid room. Should I even try to fight him? Or were my chances of winning just too pathetic? He had his henchmen to hold me down. I'd never really have a chance. My legs suddenly weak, I sank onto the edge of the bed. Would it hurt as I'd hurt Maddox? Would I bleed? I suppose I deserved it after what I'd done. Maybe this was what they meant by karma.

A soft murmur of voices interrupted the quiet. I surged from the bed and stumbled back until my shoulder blades hit the wall. My time had come. I patted my jean pocket, searching for the feel of the Swiss Army Knife that had belonged to Dad. It might be a sad weapon and they'd probably find it on me, but for now it was the only protection I had.

Someone knocked, which made me laugh, a strangled manic laugh. I found their use of manners and privacy ridiculous considering the circumstance. I didn't bother to respond, but turned toward the windows, offering whoever it was my back. Could I lie? Pretend I'd changed my mind and wanted to be one of them again?

The door opened. My heart leapt into my throat. I didn't turn to look; I could see Lewis's reflection in the windows. He hesitated in the doorway and I wished I could see him better. Why I cared what he was thinking, I wasn't sure, but I wanted to read his mind.

Did he regret doing this to me? Or was his need to see S.P.I. destroyed so great that he'd sacrifice our relationship so easily?

"We have to go…now," his voice was strong, sure as if he didn't care at all what was about to happen.

My stomach churned and bile raced up my throat. I refused to puke in front of him.

"We need to hurry," he said, his voice softer this time. "It will take only a few moments, you'll rest and then we'll escort you home tomorrow."

"Will it hurt?" I cursed my voice for catching.

He was quiet for a long, telling moment. "A little."

I cringed, despite trying not to. "A *little* like we only hurt Maddox a *little*?" I turned, facing him.

He wore jeans and a fitted t-shirt that hugged his broad shoulders. Gorgeous…always gorgeous. But he was pale and there were dark circles under his blue eyes, indicating he hadn't slept. Well, good. It served him right.

"It's the only way," he whispered. "I thought this was what you wanted."

At one time he'd cared about me, cared if I hurt, if I was injured. "I want…" No, I wouldn't say it. There was no point, but I couldn't stop the words from tumbling through my head. I wanted things back to the way they were. Just me and Lewis. But I'd die before I'd say the words aloud.

"Sir," one of the guards muttered, "we need to hurry."

So while Lewis stood there staring at me with those fathomless eyes, I tilted my chin arrogantly high and snapped out, "Let's get this over with."

I wouldn't look at him. I wouldn't beg him to help. If he wanted me to forget about him, I would. As I moved by him, he reached out, his fingers warm on my wrist. The moment he touched me, tears burned my eyes. I couldn't control myself around him.

"Cameron," he whispered. He jerked me to him and I didn't protest. I sank into his body as he hugged me and I hugged him back, afraid to let go. "I'll miss you." His words tore at my heart. He cupped the sides of my face and pressed his lips to mine, a hard kiss. And I knew it would be our last.

Tears slipped down my cheeks. I tried to memorize everything about him…the way he smelled, the way his lips felt against mine. I clung desperately to those memories even as I knew that within moments they could be gone, erased from my mind forever.

He tore his mouth from mine and backed up, his gaze intense, his breathing harsh.

"Lewis." I raised my hand. I wanted to beg him to go with me, beg him not to let this happen.

He turned away. My hand dropped to my side, my heart crumbling to the pit of my belly. I wouldn't plead. No, not again. He'd picked this stupid mission over me plenty of times. I would not beg him again.

"Let's go," one of the guards demanded.

Lewis moved into the hall, not bothering to look back to see if I followed. He knew I had no choice. I barely noticed the length of the hall. The stairs seemed too steep and high for my trembling body. Each step down sent my heart racing faster, so fast I thought I'd faint. Closer to Aaron's study…closer to the end. I felt like I was headed toward my hanging.

It would hurt, even Lewis had admitted that much. I wasn't a coward, but I certainly didn't like pain. As I made my way toward Aaron's office door, my body felt numb, the situation unreal. It was as if my mind couldn't take the truth and my body was shutting down. We paused and I was vaguely aware of Lewis knocking. I tried not to think about what would happen, tried not to think about the pain, tried not to think about the fact that no longer would I know there were others like me. Instead, I focused on the fact that tomorrow I'd be in my narrow bed, in my small room at Grandma's.

The door opened and Aaron appeared dressed as immaculately as always in black slacks and a blue button up shirt. I was so disgusted by the sight of him that for a moment I didn't notice the frantic look in his gaze. But as he scowled down at me, I realized there was something more to his gaze, something that looked oddly like worry.

"It's too late," he snapped. "Take her to the dorm, now."

"They're already here?" Lewis demanded. "What happened?"

No *why* or *Okie Dokie*, not even a *Yes Sir*, but a *what's happened*. Which made me realize that taking me to the dorm had not been the original plan. Aaron slid me a suspicious glance, then looked back at Lewis. "They've breached the fence."

"Shit," Lewis whispered.

"They who?" I asked.

Aaron turned, heading back into his office. "Get her downstairs, we're under lock down."

Lewis grabbed my arm and dragged me down the hall. "Lewis, what the hell's going on?"

I could feel his body trembling as I tripped beside him. Was he trembling from fear or anger…I wasn't sure. "All those S.P.I. agents you've been defending have breached our security. They're coming. Better pray they don't get into the mansion."

My fear turned bitterly cold as panic flooded my body. I was barely aware as we stumbled down the steps to the basement. Having a piece of your memory erased didn't seem so bad compared to being murdered. Would they kill us? Imprison us?

So focused on my fear, I was surprised to suddenly find us standing in front of the Children's Ward. Lewis punched in a code and the door slid open. The children were sitting on their beds, but awake, a sea of round, chubby faces staring at me.

"You'll all stay in here, understand?" Lewis asked, pushing me inside. Everything was moving too quickly, my mind couldn't grasp the situation. But I was well aware that Lewis was leaving me, abandoning me, here.

He was at the door when I finally found my voice. "Lewis! Where are you going? You can't leave me here!"

He didn't bother to turn around. "It's the safest place for you."

He slammed the door in my face. My stomach dropped. I grasped onto the cold, metal handle and pulled. It didn't budge. Trapped. I spun around. The children were sitting there, watching me with patient acceptance. I found Caroline almost immediately, a golden beacon of hope. She was two beds down, her face showing no emotion.

"It's fine. We'll be okay," I said softly to myself, or to the children, I wasn't sure who.

No one responded to my pathetic attempt at a pep talk. But then again at least they didn't look afraid. Why didn't they look afraid? Maybe this happened often, maybe they didn't care. "I'm saying we're safe here."

Still no response.

"We know," Caroline finally said.

"Oh, so this has happened before?"

She nodded. I shook my head, disgusted. What a wonderful way for a child to live. I couldn't leave them here. I had to find a way to take them with me. As soon as the thought entered, I realized how ridiculous it was. Right, it was going to be hard enough to slip out unnoticed, how would I escape with twenty kids?

There was nothing I could do for these children at the moment. Instead, I focused on doing something proactive...like pacing. I walked up and down the aisle between the beds, my mind spinning. Lewis could be hurt, even killed. And I hated myself for caring about him, and wondered if this was his powers of mental and emotion persuasion at work once more. And what about Maddox? Would he escape? Or would they, seeing him as a threat, get rid of him altogether?

Footsteps thundered above, making the ceiling vibrate. The children gasped as one, finally reacting like normal human beings. They scampered from their little beds, huddling together against the far wall.

"It's okay," I insisted, although I knew it was far from okay. If those footsteps were from S.P.I., that meant they'd invaded the house. The million dollar question was were S.P.I. good or bad? What if they could help and escort me to my Grandma's? What if they killed us all? It didn't matter, I had to try.

"Does anyone know the code on the door?"

Caroline parted from the group, her long nightgown brushing against the floor. "Promise you'll come back for me?"

I didn't have to think twice. "Yes."

Tears shimmered in her trusting eyes. "Twenty-eight, thirteen, five."

A door from the back of the room burst open, nearly scaring me to death. Deborah rushed through, her usually beautiful face a bit wild with panic. So maybe being attacked wasn't common, or the attack was worse than in the past.

"Come, children. To the back, just as we've practiced."

Caroline glanced over her shoulder, a tear trailing down her pale cheek. "You promised." Then she turned and raced after the other kids. Obedient little children, too afraid to argue. But I knew an opportunity when I saw one.

"You too." Deborah waved me over, her face set stern as if she was in no mood to argue. "Don't worry." She said the words as an afterthought, as if she wasn't used to comforting others.

I nodded, pretending I was as gullible as the kids she was currently escorting through the back door, leading them only God knew where. I took a few steps forward, following slowly. Deborah wasn't worried about me; she had more important matters at the moment. It would be the perfect time, perhaps the only time, to escape. I waited until Deborah disappeared into the back room.

Frantic, I spun around and sprinted to the door. "Numbers," I muttered, my hand hovering in front of the keypad. "What had Caroline said?"

Twenty-eight, thirteen, five. The numbers rushed through my head and afraid they'd disappear just as quickly, I punched in the code. The lock clicked, the door popped open. I stumbled back, my heart slamming wildly in my chest. If I ran into anyone...if Lewis and Aaron found out...if S.P.I. really was the threat Aaron proclaimed...

"You can't leave!" Deborah's voice snapped, the tone edged with fear.

I glanced over my shoulder. She was rushing toward me. I stepped back, through the door and into the hall. "I have to. Don't follow, you'll only endanger yourself and the children."

Her face was furious. "You can't!"

"Sorry, but I can." I moved into the hall and pushed the door shut, hearing it click in place. I couldn't leave through the exit where I'd escaped last time. I needed to somehow make it out the front, where I'd be closer to those gates. I bolted down the dark corridor, swerving around storage boxes and old furniture.

Deborah wouldn't dare come after me and put not only herself, but the kids in danger. Would she? Sure enough, when I glanced back, she was peering at me through the small window on the door. Relief was swift and sweet. One down...

If S.P.I. agents had entered the house and were looking for Maddox, they'd eventually end up down here. I paused, resting against a cinder block wall, trying to hear noise above, but it was impossible with blood rushing to my ears and the harsh pant of my breath. Every crack and pop startled me. Every shadow was a threat.

"The west end is secure. I'll check on the children," someone said, his voice echoing down the hall.

Not S.P.I. but just as bad. One of Aaron's henchmen. I dove behind a pile of boxes, scrunching up as small as I could. The cinderblock wall was rough and cold against the side of my face but I didn't dare move to try and ease the discomfort. The floor vibrated, heavy footsteps coming closer...closer...

When they checked on the kids, they'd know I'd escaped. Would they bother to search for me? I could only hope they'd be too busy with S.P.I.

Two hulking forms rushed by, the beams from their flashlights highlighting dark corners of the corridor, the light bouncing against the walls. I squeezed back and held my breath.

Their bodies faded into the darkness, the hall growing silent once more. I finally released the air I held. Who the hell was I kidding? I had no idea how to escape. I had the ridiculous thought that if I just stayed here, hidden behind these boxes, everything would be okay.

Even if I managed to make it outside, that sewage drain had most likely been covered. How would I make it through the gates? I pressed the heels of my palms over my eyes. I wouldn't make it out of here alive, but there was one man who might be able to help. The very same man who could keep S.P.I. from killing me on sight. Could I trust him? Did I have a choice? Before I was able to think about the ramifications of my decision, I surged to my feet and bolted down the long corridor, hoping it would lead to the opposite end of the house. Maddox was my only chance. He was a secret agent, if anyone could escape, it was him.

I didn't miss the three empty chairs as I raced by. Aaron had placed guards outside Maddox's door. Guards who had left their stations probably to fight S.P.I. But they would be back soon, I was sure of that. What I wasn't sure of was whether to be relieved or scared to death when I saw Maddox's steel door.

I froze, there in front of the door. For a moment, as panic overwhelmed me, I forgot the code Olivia had given me. Deep breath in, deep breath out. Calming my nerves I practiced my meditation in the middle of the hall, in the middle of a war. How ironic that the practices Aaron had taught might help me escape. The code came back to me and I quickly punched in the numbers. The door popped open. Most likely Aaron had some sort of alarm on the door, which is how he'd found me the first time I'd come here alone. I'd have only seconds. I pushed the door wider and rushed inside the small room.

Maddox, wearing the same clothing he'd been wearing since the day he'd arrived, was tied to that chair again. He lifted his head, that familiar glare oddly comforting. His face was pale, dried blood caked to the corner of his mouth. Had they tried to break into his thoughts again, or was the blood from someone's fist?

Disgusted with the entire situation, I started cautiously toward him. "Listen to me, we don't have long. I need your help, and I'll…help you."

"Ah, so they've broken through the gates?" Maddox grinned. "Maybe I don't need your help."

"And maybe Aaron will stop them, or kill you." I paused far enough away so he couldn't touch me if he broke through those bonds. "I release you and you help me and the children escape." My words were blunt, with little explanation. I hoped he'd understand because we didn't have time to chit-chat.

He quirked a dark brow. "The children?"

I swallowed hard, wondering how much he knew. "There are others. Younger Mind Readers."

He looked me up and down slowly, as if judging my worth. "How do you know I won't kill you when I'm free?"

My heart skipped a beat, but I refused to let the fear show on my face. "Because I don't believe you're that bad."

He was still smiling when he responded, "Fine." He'd agreed quickly enough…too quickly.

My suspicion was immediate. "Swear on you girlfriend's life."

He narrowed his eyes, his anger almost palpable. "Go to hell, Sweetheart."

I didn't let him frighten me, I didn't have time. "I mean it."

He was silent for one long moment, mulling over his possibilities. He knew as well as I that he was limited in choices.

"Hurry," I urged, glancing out the door. "We need to hurry!"

"Fine, I agree. Don't really have a choice, do I?"

"Well, that's heartening," I muttered, edging closer.

I didn't trust him in the least, but I didn't have a choice either. I dropped to my knees and pulled out my pocket knife. With trembling hands, I sawed at the rope around his ankles. The twine popped apart and Maddox flexed his feet, grimacing. I moved to his back and sawed at the rope holding his wrists. Although I was in a hurry, I couldn't help but notice his skin was red and raw. His hands free, I shoved the knife back into my pocket. He pulled his arms in front of him, rolling his hands around and around as if to get the blood pumping.

I knew his muscles hurt from lack of use, but we didn't have time for him to do yoga. "Let's go." I didn't wait for him, but rushed into the hall, hoping he'd follow. "There's an exit I used yesterday, just down here."

I turned to see him stumbling after me. His hands were braced against the hallway wall, his face pale and sweaty. He didn't exactly look good. I hadn't thought about the fact that his muscles would be weak. God, I hoped he could make it; there was no possible way I could carry him out of here. I paused, waiting for him to stumble toward me. When he was close enough to touch, I slipped my arm around his waist. He stiffened, obviously surprised or disgusted by my touch. I didn't have time to be offended.

"We have to hurry," I insisted. "The door isn't far."

I focused on the end of that hall, trying to ignore the warmth of his body and the way it made me feel safe, for some odd reason. Instead, I focused on a plan. If we could make it outside, the battle would be half won. But Maddox was heavy and I worried I'd made a mistake and he would be more of a hindrance than a help. Too late to go back now and I couldn't leave him behind.

Sweat broke out on my forehead. "We're almost there," I managed. Was it my imagination or was he getting heavier?

He didn't respond.

I dared to take my focus off Maddox and instead listened for shouting or movement above. But I couldn't hear a damn thing. We turned the corner and there was the door. My heart leapt with relief. I didn't know how we'd get through the fence, but at the moment, it didn't matter. Shifting my arm away from Maddox, he leaned against the wall and I reached for the door handle.

"Stop," Aaron's voice was a hard command that offered no room for disobedience.

Maddox's arm shot out, wrapping around my waist. Suddenly I was slammed against his chest, my Swiss Army Knife at my throat. He flipped open the blade and pressed it to my skin, the metal cold and sharp. I didn't dare move, barely breathed.

"Come any closer and she's dead," Maddox said.

He wasn't leaning anymore, he wasn't trembling. Obviously his entire weakened state had been an act. I wasn't sure if I should be scared or pissed that he'd lied. And to top it off, he'd somehow stolen my knife.

"You jerk," I hissed.

His arm around my waist tightened. "Trust me." He spoke so softly, that I wasn't sure if I'd truly heard the words, or if it had been wishful thinking. "We're walking out of here," he said, his voice loud and sure. "Or she dies."

"So do it," Aaron said as he came strolling from the shadows, into the flickering light that shone from above. There were two silent guards behind him, big burly men who made Maddox look small. "Kill her. It will keep me from having to erase her memory. She's no use to me anymore."

"Bullshit," Maddox growled. "You think I don't know why you want her alive?"

I resisted the urge to tell Maddox it was true. Aaron didn't want me. He probably didn't care if I died. Maddox seemed so confident in his beliefs, that against my better judgment, I bit back my comment. But I couldn't stop the tingle of warning from racing over my skin. I had a bad feeling this was all too easy.

Maddox didn't release his hold. In fact, he took a step back, toward the door, dragging me with him. "You're letting us go."

Aaron clasped his hands behind his back, his face passive, thoughtful. "Yes, perhaps I might have let you go. But unfortunately the men behind you with the pistols pointed directly at your head…well, they, I'm afraid, won't be so accommodating."

I could tell by the hardness of his gaze that he wasn't lying. I managed to turn my head just enough to glance behind us. Sure enough, there were two of Aaron's guards with guns pointed at Maddox's gorgeous head. Surprise, surprise.

"Well, this sucks," I whispered.

Maddox loosened his hold. "You can say that again."

Chapter 21

I'd always had mixed feelings about my ability to read minds. For the most part, I thought of my ability as a blessing. I wouldn't have had the friends I'd had. I wouldn't have had the grades I'd had. I wouldn't have had the life I'd had.

But as we stood under gunpoint, I could unequivocally say I wished I was normal.

Rough hands grasped my upper arms and shoved me against the wall, the brick scratching the side of my face. I bit my lower lip to keep from crying out and watched as they did the same to Maddox. My pathetic little Swiss Army Knife lay useless on the cement floor. A guard grabbed my hands and jerked my arms behind my back. Before I could protest, something was wrapped tightly around my wrists, pinning my arms together.

"Upstairs, now," Aaron demanded, his hard tone leaving no room for argument.

The guard grabbed my left arm and jerked me up the steps. My heart plummeted. Maddox might be some sort of secret agent, but unless he was Harry Freaking Potter, there was no way he could get us out of this situation. At the top of the steps we were met by two more guards, only adding to my despair.

I dared to glance back at Maddox, as if he could help. But I realized, even in my panicked state, that it was too dangerous. The men behind him still had their pistols trained to his head. I'd never seen a gun in real life. One false step and it could misfire. Any one of us could be dead in a matter of moments. Maddox wouldn't take that chance, not for me, a person he barely knew. And so I turned toward Aaron, the only person who could help at the moment.

"You don't have to do this," I said, feeling I had to say something. "Just let us go and you could probably negotiate something with S.P.I."

Aaron chuckled, a harsh sound that annoyed the heck out of me. "S.P.I. has been taken care of. You don't need to worry about my welfare."

Taken care of. I assumed he didn't mean he'd given them a hearty meal and seen them off to bed. My feet hit the marble tile on the first floor and my fear flared to life. Dear God, this was not happening. I had not been caught yet again.

"They'll be back, you know," Maddox had to chime in from behind me, his voice arrogantly sure.

Why couldn't he just shut up? I started to turn in order to tell him so, when Lewis appeared at the end of the hall like some sort of wonderful nightmare. I froze. I didn't even move when I felt Maddox's hard body run into my back, shifting me off balance.

Although Lewis' face was passive, there was something in his eyes that made me think he was surprised to see me and maybe...could it be? No, it couldn't. Lewis did not look disappointed.

Aaron latched onto my arm, jerking me forward and back into reality. "I told you, Cameron, you don't have to worry about your safety here. It's outside these walls you have to fear."

Lewis started toward me, his steps unwavering, sure. I didn't want to see him, I didn't want to feel him near, I sure as hell didn't want him to touch me for if he did, I might start crying. Yet, here he was, reaching out and latching onto my arm like I was a kid playing hooky and he was forcing me back to school.

He was a stranger to me now, his touch no longer warm and comforting. His gaze was brittle; his eyes held no compassion. Where had the guy gone who I'd fallen in love with? The man who'd wanted to protect me no matter what? He'd thrown me over for his mission. In a few minutes he'd see me tortured, my memory of him erased and all without batting an eyelash. It was obvious he felt nothing for me now. He'd hardened his heart. It was over, done.

The situation overwhelmed me and I stumbled. Lewis caught me, pulling me close to keep me upright. As much as I didn't want his touch, my legs didn't seem strong enough to hold me any longer. The rest of the group walked by, Maddox sliding me a knowing look, as if he realized my heart belonged to the enemy and wasn't sure how much he could trust me.

I didn't know why Lewis and I didn't follow. Maybe he had some compassion left after all and was giving me time to compose myself. Hell, I should've just started blubbering like a baby and hoped it made him feel guilty. I was well on my way to sobbing anyway.

I dared to look up at him through my blurry gaze. Did he feel anything for me? Anything at all? "He'll erase my mind now?"

Lewis swallowed hard and nodded. "Don't cry," he whispered. Then, shockingly, he cupped the sides of my face and brushed the tears away with his thumbs. And it hurt even more, knowing that he cared, but not enough.

I jerked backward. "Don't touch me."

He closed his eyes, as if my words caused him pain. Well, too damn bad. "I'm sorry, Lewis. I'm sorry I couldn't be the person you wanted me to be. I'm sorry I couldn't believe what you believe." And I was sorry, but obviously not enough or I wouldn't be willing to go through this ordeal in order to be free of them. I knew it and he knew it.

"Don't," he whispered. "Don't apologize."

For one long moment we just stared at each other. And I wanted to hate him, and I wanted to walk away, but I couldn't, knowing this would probably be the last time we would be alone. "I don't want to forget you."

He was silent for one long moment, but his eyes, Lord, his eyes showed his emotions. "Deep down, you won't forget. I know it."

He stepped closer and slid his finger under my chin, tilting my head back. I saw the longing there, in his gaze, a longing that tore at my heart. When he lowered his head and pressed his lips to mine in a soft, gentle kiss—our last kiss—I didn't push him away, I didn't slap him like I should have. The other's had disappeared into Aaron's study. We were alone. For this brief moment I could pretend everything was normal.

All too soon Lewis pulled back and I forced myself to let him go. But mostly, I forced myself not to beg him to help me. I would be brave.

"I have to believe you won't forget," he said.

And I wanted to believe as well, but I didn't have such grandiose hopes. And I couldn't, in good conscience, even pretend that I believed all would be well.

"Lewis," Aaron called out, his voice sounding oddly compassionate. But no, it must have been wishful thinking. Aaron was nothing but a monster. A monster who was ending our last moment together.

I didn't bother to look at the man who would steal my memories. Instead, I kept my gaze pinned to Lewis, even as he stepped away from me, his face shifting once more into that hard, emotionless man I didn't know. It was over. Our moment gone. Lewis gripped my arm, his attention forward as he marched me to Aaron's study.

With its warm colors, the room was just as comfortable as I remembered. Leather chairs next to a large desk. Book shelves and a large fireplace. And I remembered my first night here—the dreams that I thought were being fulfilled—and I felt like such an idiot for believing.

Everything in this room was the same, except for the large wooden chair in the middle of the floor. A chair much like the chair Maddox had been tied to. Even though there was nothing particularly scary about that chair, it had me sweating.

"Pay attention," Aaron said, his gaze pinned to Maddox. "Because you'll be next."

Maddox didn't look concerned as two guards pushed him into the sofa, and then trained their guns at his head. The man merely growled low in his throat. I wished I could be as defiant. Instead, I was shaking as I was pushed gently into the chair.

"Tie her up," Aaron demanded.

"No!" I shot from the chair, desperately seeking Lewis.

Strong hands gripped my upper arms, drawing me to a stop. Lewis averted his gaze, his face flushed red. Lewis, the man who supposedly loved me, didn't protest as two guards roughly jerked me back into the chair. He didn't protest when I cried out, twisting and turning in a lame attempt to break their hold. And he sure as hell didn't protest as one guard held my arms while the other tied my legs to the chair.

"No!" I screamed, throwing a fit Emily would have been proud of. "You get off tying up a helpless girl?"

The two goons didn't reply, merely backed up a space, transferring their attention to Maddox, who had gone slightly pale, perhaps remembering his own time locked away and realizing he would be next. I met his gaze, hoping...heck, I didn't know what I was hoping. He was as helpless as I was.

"Sorry, Sweetheart," he said softly and I knew he was apologizing for not being able to help. I wouldn't cry in front of them.

"It's for your own protection," Aaron said. "I need you to keep as still as possible."

I narrowed my eyes into a glare. Vaguely, I was aware of the door opening, of Deborah stepping inside with a small case in hand, but I had eyes only for Aaron. I seethed hatred and hoped he felt it. I wouldn't let him know that nausea churned in my stomach, bile rising in my throat.

"Is this what my father would have wanted?" I asked.

Was it my imagination or did he actually flinch?

Hope swelled within me, tempting and sweet. I'd found a weakness. I shifted, the binding around my wrists burning the skin. "My father trusted you—"

"Your father would have wanted me to do what was best for everyone."

His words hurt to the core, worse than Aaron, or even Lewis' betrayal. He was implying that my father would have given me up if it was for the good of the whole. I couldn't believe that; I wouldn't. They could do what they wanted with me, but they would not take away the belief that my father had been a good man. I closed my eyes and lowered my head. In the struggle, my hair had fallen from its ponytail and hung in a protective curtain around my face. I wouldn't look at Aaron. I couldn't, or I'd get sick all over him. And I refused to look at Lewis.

"Do it then," I whispered.

There was a moment's silence as if I'd stunned them all. With a wave of Aaron's hand, the entire world shifted back into focus, everything oddly brilliant. Deborah swept forward walking like she was on a runway, that small metal case dangling from her manicured fingertips. Aaron scooted a chair closer, sitting directly in front of me, the spicy scent of his cologne adding to my unease.

"I'm sorry. I'm not going to enjoy this, Cameron. It's necessary." As I looked into his blue eyes, so close that I could see the black flecks around the irises, I almost believed he was sincere in his apology. Or maybe it was Lewis, standing across the room and making me think I was calm, but an odd sense of ease swept through my body as if I was no longer there, but watching a play.

"Try to relax. Open your mind and it will be less painful."

Painful. The word brought me back into cold reality. I jerked forward, my wrists and ankles pulling at my bindings; it was an automatic response. Instinct forced me to try to escape. But the bindings just rubbed against my wrists, burning my skin. I was pathetic. I was trapped.

Oh God, I couldn't prevent it from happening.

"Deborah." Aaron nodded.

Confused, I glanced at the beautiful woman as she stopped beside me. She tapped a needle like some crazy scientist out to do an experiment on a rat. A needle. A needle.

"Relax," Aaron said softly, leaning forward so that I could only focus on him. He was staring hard at me, peering into my eyes, attempting to delve into my brain. Vaguely I was aware of the slight sting of a needle piercing my arm, but I couldn't seem to look away from Aaron, mesmerized by the odd glow of his eyes. I felt the slightest nudge on my mind and I knew it was Aaron invading but I couldn't seem to care. Someone, or something, was holding me captive.

Fight back. The words whispered through my mind, a message from God, or the universe, I wasn't sure. It could have been a message from the fairies for all I cared, but the words were enough to make me regain control of my mind...if only a little.

My body hardened and my attention refocused. I remembered why they'd brought me here in the first place, because according to them, I was the most powerful Mind Reader they'd met. A glimmer of hope had me reeling.

Fight back.

The words came again. Lewis? No, surely it wasn't Lewis. I was imagining his voice because I so badly wanted it to be him. I didn't spend time thinking about the ramifications. Instead, I let instinct take over. I closed my eyes, and I waited…waited for him to attack.

I felt that gentle nudge again, like someone had pressed their finger into my brain, testing its ripeness like a piece of fruit. I forced myself to think of Lewis, the hurt of his betrayal so Aaron wouldn't know the direction of my true thoughts. A prickle of pins tapped against my skull like a thousand needles in a pincushion. He'd broken in easily enough. I cringed, gritting my teeth, forcing myself not to react…not yet…

"Relax," Aaron murmured.

Screw you.

I threw the thought out right before I slammed up my mental wall. I vaguely heard Aaron's gasp of surprise, but I didn't dwell on it. No, I knew he'd come back full force. I dared to open my eyes. Our gazes locked, our minds at war. As I'd done with Maddox, I fell immediately, swimming in the sea of his gaze. I was in his mind before he'd even realized I had turned on him. I didn't have time to gloat.

Full colored memories suddenly flashed through my mind.

"Aaron, we do not speak while adults are speaking." A beautiful woman was glaring down a long table at me. Aaron's mother. I felt immediate shame and embarrassment as the other adults watched on. I'd only wanted to prove my intelligence but had been reprimanded.

Another memory came to mind. *"I don't want to go to England!"* I screamed, or Aaron screamed. He was ten, being sent to boarding school.

And then the memories came more quickly…*girls, sports, classes.* So quickly, so many memories, that I had a hard time truly seeing them. Vaguely, I heard someone shouting, the voice odd, as if coming from outside my mind. Lewis, I realized with a start. I started to slip, my walls crumbling.

Suddenly my father flashed before my mind. "It's not right, Aaron," he said, his face flushed furious.

"The vaccine isn't working!" Deborah called out, her voice mingling with the memories so I wasn't sure if she was real or not. I ignored the woman and slammed that wall back up, reaching out to Aaron's mind and grasping onto the memory of my dad.

My father paced back and forth in Aaron's study. *"What you're doing isn't right and I want no part…"*

The memory shifted. A woman twirling in a white sundress, her back to me. She stopped, her laughter somehow familiar.

Slowly, she turned.

My mother…

Bam!

A thousand fists seemed to hit my body. I gasped, my head jerking back at the impact. My eyes opened, my body straining against my bonds. The sudden light from the lamp above entered my pupils and momentarily blinded me. The pain faded slowly, torturously, tearing the air from my lungs and leaving me gasping. I noticed Lewis first…pale, trembling as he stood only feet from me, closer, but still not close enough to help. The entire room had grown still and I would've thought nothing had happened, but for their faces…surprised faces full of shock and some worry. They knew I'd done something.

My gaze jerked toward Aaron who was still sitting across from me, but now he was glaring at me with a mixture of anger and awe. Sweat dripped down the sides of his handsome face; his nostrils flared as he gasped for air. I'd done that to him, broken into his private thoughts. I had a feeling it hadn't happened to him often and I couldn't prevent the sick sense of accomplishment from coursing through me. I wanted to laugh. I wanted to gloat, even knowing that more pain would arrive and I'd most likely come out the loser.

His lips lifted into a snarl, those blue eyes flashing as cold as ice. "I said you were good, but I didn't say you were better than me." Before I could even blink, sharp pain sliced through my brain. I screamed out, arching my back, jerking against my bindings like a worm on a hook.

"I told you it would go better if you relaxed. I gave you a chance," Aaron's voice managed to weave its way through my pain.

Frantically, I tried to imagine those steel walls. But the images slipped away as quickly as they came. Gone, like ghostly memories and I was left standing in darkness, the pain roaring through my body like fire. The pain increased, twisting, slicing through my mind like a corkscrew. The only thing connecting me to reality was the awareness of my hot tears slipping down my cheeks.

"Enough," I heard someone demand, the strength in his voice giving me hope, hope that this would all end…the pain…the suffering…

Then I heard no more and my hope faded as quickly as it had come. Memories slipped through my mind, floating by me like movies on a theater screen. My memories.

Me, crying as my mom dropped me off at Grandma's.

Sleepless nights, too scared to close my eyes in an unfamiliar home.

The police coming to our home in Michigan because the neighbors thought something was off with me and they'd heard the rumors.

All these memories flashed quickly through my mind like Aaron had my brain on fast-forward. Suddenly, I was standing at Lakeside and everything slowed. The colors became pristine. I felt the cold autumn wind, smelled the scent of salt water, heard the horrified shouts from the students around me.

My heart slammed wildly against my chest. I was there, in that moment, reliving Savannah's death. Slowly, I turned and there was Lewis standing in the parking lot. The first time I'd seen him. Lakeside disappeared just as quickly as it had come.

Lewis, at the front of the class, looking at me.

Lewis, walking with me down the hall as he hinted that he could read minds.

Lewis. Lewis. Lewis.

And I knew Aaron had reached the memories he needed. The memories he would steal. The memories that warmed my heart at night. The memories that made me want to be here, alive, now.

"No!" I screamed, jerking against my bindings. But even though I could have sworn my eyes were wide open, I saw no one in the room, only my memories. "No, please!" He would take my memories. He would take Lewis from me forever. "Please, Lewis!"

But no one came and my memories kept shifting, slipping past me without my consent.

Lewis and me on the ferry coming over to the island.

Me looking out my bedroom window and seeing Caroline below.

Me being pulled from that drainage pipe.

And then it stopped. Just as suddenly as the memories had come, they stopped. Everything went black.

I didn't know where I was. I didn't understand. I couldn't feel my body. For one long moment I merely stared into that darkness, floating, waiting...too afraid and confused to move. I was only a conscious mind in some dark reality. At the edges of that darkness, was a thrumming pain threatening to flare to life.

"Please!" I cried out, my voice hollow, echoing in the empty space that had somehow become my world.

Was I dead?

"Enough!" A deep voice growled, shaking the very air around me.

I didn't know if he was talking to me and I didn't care. It was an unfamiliar voice, but I grasped onto it anyway, my lifeline, my way out of this nothingness. Suddenly, I felt heavy, as if I was sinking...sinking into something thick, like quicksand. Warmth flooded my body, starting at my toes and seeping upward, and with the warmth the ache in my head flared to life. Vaguely I became aware of something wet trailing from my nostrils to my lips and into my mouth. The metallic taste of blood swept over my tongue. I grimaced, my stomach revolting.

"Open your eyes. Come on, Sweetheart."

I didn't want to open my eyes. I wanted to sink back into that darkness, sink away from the pain thumping against the side of my head. Warm palms cupped my cheeks, anchoring me to reality. The man was persistent. Slowly, I lifted my lashes. A face wavered before me, a masculine face of hard planes and all I could think about was how he'd look so much better without that dark beard over his cheeks and chin.

Worried gray eyes studied me. "You'll be all right," the man insisted.

But I didn't care. My mind was spinning, my stomach clenched into a tight knot so I thought I'd be sick. Too weak to speak, I closed my eyes again. I was vaguely aware of someone pulling at my arms, then my legs. With nothing to hold me up, I slouched into a hard form. Apparently my bones had disappeared. Muscled arms slipped under my legs and around my back, pulling me close to a warm body.

"Cam, Cam, please, dear God, please look at me." It was a different voice calling to me. A male voice that sent my heart racing for some odd reason.

I wanted to look at the speaker. I wanted to look at whoever was calling to me. If it was the last thing I did, I knew I needed to look at him. Slowly, I lifted my eyes. A concerned blue gaze stared down at me. Someone familiar; this man slightly younger than the one holding me. Someone I should know, but couldn't place.

"Please Cameron, please talk to me."

But I couldn't talk because blood was seeping down my throat, and the taste was making me nauseous. My stomach twisted. I felt cold, bitterly cold. Voices came in and out of focus. Faces appeared hovering over me, shadows that came and went like the sun. Was I dreaming? Maybe dying. Yes, probably dying.

"Take her," someone said. "Take her to her grandmother. Hurry."

I was moving, floating, those muscled arms still around me; warm, and comforting. A heart beat strong and sure against the side of my arm. Someone was carrying me, someone human. No Angel of Death. I tilted my head back and stared into the man's gray gaze.

"Don't worry," he said as he carried me through a door and into a hall. "Let go, Cameron. Just let go."

And so I did.

I closed my eyes and let the world fade to nothing.

Chapter 22

Six Months Later

The woman sitting at the table across from me was thinking about having an affair with her scuba instructor.

She was imagining his dark skin glistening under the warm sun, his muscles flexing as he wrapped his arms around her waist and lowered his mouth to hers. Or maybe, she thought, she'd have an affair with the guy who cleaned her pool. Her husband was heading back to the U.S. for business and would never know.

I wanted to tell her it wouldn't work, that in those desperate housewife shows, they always suspected the pool guy. Instead, I hid my grin by lowering my head and swiping down the counter where I'd been serving fruity drinks, hotdogs and meat pies since eleven this morning.

I wished she'd keep her R-rated thoughts to herself. I really didn't want to imagine her, her Scuba instructor, or the pool guy naked. But I guess she couldn't help it. The thoughts seeped from her mind like the warm breeze currently drifting in from the Caribbean Sea.

Their hopes, their dreams, their nightmares...

What they thought about, *I* thought about.

Sometimes it really sucked to be able to read minds.

With a sigh I focused on the ocean not thirty feet from me. The soft roar of the waves was always calming. Sure, our little café wasn't exactly five star, but you couldn't beat the view. Pink and orange rays from the setting sun pierced the late afternoon clouds, trailing pastel fingers across the waves. The telltale fins of dolphins crested the water's surface, always thrilling me like a kid on Christmas morning. And you couldn't beat the uniform, shorts and a tank top.

It was hard to believe that almost seven months ago I was freezing in Maine, forced to wake up every morning at six and trudge to a school where I had to pretend to be normal. No more hiding. No more pretending. This…this was freedom. And I wasn't going to waste another moment.

"Closing time."

I pressed stop on the CD player, putting an end to Bob Marley, for today at least. The evening was cool and promising. I hopped over the counter, my bare feet sinking into the sand. Why wear shoes when you lived on the beach?

"Anyone need a drink for the ride home?"

The natives eating meat pies shook their heads, their thoughts on sleep. With a wave, they stood from their wooden benches, taking their pies with them, and made their way toward their bikes. They were regulars who often stopped on their way home from work.

But Mrs. Miller, the woman who was thinking of seducing the hired help, still sat at her small table, looking lost and forlorn, almost like some cartoon orphan child. She was lonely. She didn't want to go home to an empty house, even if her house was a mansion. I felt bad for her, but not bad enough to stick around and listen to her sob story.

Besides, today was my birthday. Today I was eighteen. No way in heck I was working any longer then I had to. Funny how a year could make such a difference in a person's life. Gazing out at the water, I pulled my dark hair from the ponytail I'd secured this morning, massaging my scalp. Only a short time ago my need to please would have had me walking over to Mrs. Miller and asking her if she was okay. Not now. Nope, when you faced death things changed, big time.

"It's so quiet here," the woman drawled in her southern accent.

I nodded noncommittally, not daring to look her in the eyes. I wasn't going to be sucked in by the puppy-dog gaze. Instead, I welcomed the breeze ruffling my hair, and focused on the swaying palm trees. Of course it was quiet. It was paradise. A paradise I'd craved after being in a hospital for over a month. And don't bother asking what was wrong with me, they never did figure it out, the doctor saying some nonsense about how sometimes people slipped into comas for no reason.

Whatever. It didn't matter because I wasn't going to waste any more time hiding, or trying to please others. That month of illness had been a blessing. Grandma had apparently been thinking the same thing. The moment I'd regained consciousness, she had packed our bags, sold the house in Maine and we'd ended up here. I sure as heck wasn't going to complain.

I paused, listening to the sad cry of a gull. Still…there were times when I felt like I'd missed something…something important. The doctors claimed a coma would do that to a person, make them feel lost. But there were also times when I'd catch my grandma watching me with this odd combination of sadness and worry in her hazel gaze, as if she knew something I didn't.

"Guess I should head home," Mrs. Miller said in that sugary drawl.

She stood, slapped a huge straw hat on her bleached blonde hair and sauntered toward her small, red convertible. She wasn't our typical customer, but she'd stopped by once and liked the place because we seemed to know *exactly* what she wanted even before she said a word. Yep, to her, we were the perfect little servants.

I gave her a wave as she drove away, then swiped down the small benches and tables that seated our customers. Our restaurant, if you could call it that, boasted three tables and a small bar, all outside seating. Still, it was ours, Grandma and me, and we had plans to expand eventually…when we weren't busy sunbathing, snorkeling and collecting shells.

"All done?" Grandma asked, strolling out of the small abode where she'd been cooking. She hung her white apron on the hook outside the door. It was hot work, but we could always take a break and dip into the ocean for a quick swim. Really, my job couldn't get any better. I was even second guessing college. Why leave paradise?

"Yep." I picked up the few pieces of trash that littered the white sand, stuffing them into the trash bag Grandma had grabbed.

I'd been living with her since I was five and my mind-reading ability had surfaced. Mom pretty much thought I was a freak and shoved me into Grandma's capable arms, the one person who understood. Another freak. Yep, Grandma, too, could read minds which made it hard for me to sneak out after curfew. Even though we had that ability in common, it didn't mean we got along. Until my illness, we'd rarely had a civil conversation.

"I'm heading home now," she said.

Home was a two bedroom cottage across the street that hung heavy with white Jasmine, a fragrant flower I could smell through my bedroom window at night.

"Okay, I'm almost done."

She paused at the road, her short dark hair wavering on the cool breeze. "Whose pink moped?"

I shrugged and made my way toward her. It was a cute Vespa, a soft pink in color with a white helmet dangling from the handlebar. I'd been admiring it earlier and even now couldn't resist running my fingers over the white seat.

"Not sure. It's been here awhile though. Was here when I got in this morning." I frowned, glancing at the beach where palm trees swayed on the breeze. The ocean might look peaceful, but underneath the surface was a world of danger to unsuspecting victims. "Should we be concerned?"

It had been known to happen that tourists would go snorkeling and be taken out by the current, never to be seen again.

Grandma grinned, a mischievous sparkle in her eyes. She wasn't like most grandmas and looked younger than she was. We spent many mornings hiking the island, exploring waterfalls and bays. "Nah. I think I know the owner."

Confused, I watched her warily. I couldn't read her thoughts, I'd never been able to no matter how hard I tried. While thoughts from others flowed freely into the universe, Grandma's remained firmly encased in her brain.

Until a few months ago, Grandma had been able to read mine, much to my ever growing annoyance. But since my illness Grandma had taught me things I'd always wanted to know, like how to block my thoughts from being read by others like us. Not that I knew anyone else who could read minds. Still, it was a handy trick to have and made me feel as if freedom was within my grasp, instead of some far off dream.

"Who's the owner?" I asked.

She tossed something toward me. Instinctively I caught the small, shiny object. A key, cool against the palm of my hand. I glanced up at her, shocked. She couldn't mean…

She grinned. "Happy birthday. The moped is all yours."

My mouth dropped open. "Are you serious? But we can't afford it!"

She waved her hand through the air, dismissing my comment. "Don't you worry about that."

I threw my arms around her neck. Before my illness, we'd barely touched. I hugged her often now and much to my delight, she hugged me back. We'd both changed since moving here, and both for the better.

After a few seconds, she pulled away, looking like her gruff self once more, but she couldn't fool me. "Finish cleaning, then go for a ride, I know you want to. But don't be out too late." She strolled across the road to our small cottage, her gait easy and carefree.

I tossed the trash in the brown dumpster that sat alongside the dirt road, eager to test out my Vespa. On the island a scooter was pretty much like having a car. I'd be able to see the entire place on my own. Meet up with friends, go on dates. And I wanted to date so badly it hurt. I was eighteen years old, for God's sake. It was time to fall in love…to truly be kissed. My gaze strayed to two tourists who strolled the beach hand in hand. Sure, I'd had boyfriends, but no one had made my hormones flare to life. No one had made me want to sneak out of the house and make out on sandy beaches. Slowly, I started back toward the bar.

My heart gave a painful squeeze. For one brief moment I forgot my Vespa, forgot my illness as I stood suspended in some odd reality where something important lay just out of reach and if only I could touch it, I'd know....

The couple shifted and there, further down the beach, I noticed a man walking my way. An odd tingle of awareness pulled me back to earth. Alone, but he didn't seem lonely. No, he was too tall, too gorgeous, and his stroll too confident to be lonely. I tilted my head, leaning against the bar, feeling confused.

There was something about the way he walked...the way his dark hair glimmered under the light of the setting sun...the way, I swore even though I couldn't see his eyes through his sunglasses, he stared at me.

Perhaps I was dreaming. Or maybe this island truly was magical and had sent me the boyfriend I wanted. I grinned at the thought.

There was nothing unusual in the cargo shorts and t-shirt he wore. Not even in the way his body moved fluidly, all muscle. He was gorgeous, simply put. And I'd seen a lot of hot guys on the island, natives and tourists. But something about his man gave me pause; something that made my smile fall and my heart beat a little faster. Something I couldn't explain. He didn't follow the coastline, but headed toward me. So close I could see the scruff along his chin and cheeks. I shifted, placing the counter between us.

"Sorry," I said, as he started toward the café. "We're closed. I can get you a drink to go if you want." Much to my horror, my voice came out a little breathless and telling. Lord, I desperately needed a date.

This close, I realized he was taller than what I'd expected. He settled on a bar stool near me, the lightest hint of spicy cologne permeating the air. He had a black backpack slung over one shoulder and I wondered what was in that bag. His presence was overwhelming and I had to resist the urge to take a step back. The breeze ruffled his dark hair, but it did little to soften his look. Who the heck was he?

"Hello, Cameron."

I drew back, startled. For a moment, I merely looked at him, too shocked to respond. He knew my name, but I didn't know him. At least, I didn't think I knew him. Yet, I couldn't deny that there was something familiar in the way he smiled at me.

Warning bells clamored in my head. A hundred memories of Grandma telling me to keep quiet about my abilities came rushing back. Had I slipped and told someone something I shouldn't have? Is that why he was here? I rested my hand on my thigh, feeling the weight of my Swiss Army Knife in my pocket. It might be a pathetic weapon, but it made me feel better all the same.

"How do you know my name?" I demanded.

He held out his hand, a strong, tanned hand with long fingers. "We've met before, Sweetheart. Although you won't remember."

I didn't dare touch him, afraid if I did, something would change, although what, I wasn't sure. A shiver of awareness caressed my skin, a warning that something wasn't quite right. I glanced around the beach, taking comfort in the fact that the couple was still nearby, cuddling close enough that if I screamed they'd hear me.

"Sorry, but we've never met. And I'm headed home." I stepped away from the bar, backing up a couple feet.

"I have something to tell you."

My heart hammered madly as indecision gripped me. Instinct told me to run, to dart across that road to safety. Except, something held me back. Something inexplicable. Something that said I needed to know, *must* know, what he was going to tell me.

"What?" I asked, in no mood for guessing games.

He lifted his hand to his face and slowly removed his sunglasses. Piercing gray eyes met mine. A gaze so relentless, I felt it all the way to my soul. "My name is Maddox. Your father sent me."

I laughed, a harsh sound of disbelief. "That's impossible, because if you really knew me, *Maddox,* you'd know that my father is dead."

"He's not." Maddox stood, towering over me. "Your father is alive and well, and he's sent me here to protect you." He slipped his sunglasses back into place, hiding those steel eyes behind mirrored lenses. "Whether you believe me or not, Sweetheart, I'm pretty much the only thing standing between you and death."

The End

The Mind Readers Series:

The Mind Readers, book 1

The Mind Thieves, book 2: Available now!

The Mind Games, book 3: Available now!

About Lori Brighton

Lori has a degree in Anthropology and worked as a museum curator. Deciding the people in her imagination were slightly more exciting than the dead things in a museum basement, she set out to become an author. Lori writes Romance for adults, as well as Young Adult books for teens and adults.

To find out more about Lori visit her at: www.LoriBrighton.com

Made in the USA
Lexington, KY
18 April 2014